About the author

Hector Hugh Munro was born in Burma in 1870 where his father was an Inspector-General of the Burma police. His mother died in 1872 and he was raised by two severe maiden aunts in England. His education began at Bedford Grammar School and was completed by his father who took him travelling all over Europe. He joined the Burma police but resigned after one year's service due to ill-health and embarked upon a literary career. He wrote political sketches for the *Westminster Gazette* and was foreign correspondent for the *Morning Post*. His first collection of short stories, *Reginald*, was brought out in 1904, followed by *Reginald in Russia* (1910), *The Chronicles of Clovis* (1911), and *Beasts and Superbeasts* (1914). He also wrote three plays and two novels, *The Unbearable Bassington* (1912) and the pro-war fantasy, *When William Came* (1914). He enlisted as a private in 1914 and died in 1916 while serving as a sergeant in France. There were two further posthumous collections of stories *The Toys of Peace* (1919) and *The Square Egg* (1924).

The Unrest-Cure

AND OTHER BEASTLY TALES

PRION HUMOUR CLASSICS

* for copyright reasons these titles are not available in the USA or Canada in the Prion edition.

The Unrest-Cure

AND OTHER BEASTLY TALES

SAKI
(H H Munro)

with a new introduction by
WILL SELF

PRION

This collection published in 2000 by
Prion Books Limited,
Imperial Works,
Perren Street,
London NW5 3ED

Introduction copyright © Will Self 2000
Edited and selected by Andrew Goodfellow © Prion Books 2000

ISBN 1-85375-370-X

Jacket design by Keenan
Jacket image © Hulton Getty Picture Collection
Printed and bound in Great Britain
by Creative Print & Design, Wales

Contents

INTRODUCTION

by WILL SELF

It's not often that you can say of a writer's works that they saved your life; although it's often claimed – usually by the least transformable people you know – that such-and-such a book 'changed' their life. But saved? Never. It conjures up distinctly unsavoury images of biblical timpani, Koranic kinkiness, or other weird workings of the Word. To even claim that a book has changed your life – excepting in the sense that it occupied a few of your hours, taught you a few more comparisons and facts – is verging on the preposterous. I've always maintained that important texts are like important lovers: to have a handful of significant ones in a long lifetime is fortunate; to claim a plethora – nauseating. And what's more, the capacity to entertain new life-changing texts, like new, life-changing loves, declines with age and inflexibility.

Nevertheless, Saki's stories did save my life. I picked up a cheap but reliable edition, one afternoon a few years ago at the Strand Bookstore in New York. The Strand, which offers its customers eight miles of secondhand books, was itself a poultice on the running psychic sore which was my mind, but the Saki was a panacea. I was facing a twenty-two city promotional tour to coincide with the Stateside publication of one of my books. Not, you might venture, a deathly predicament in and of itself – but how wrong you are. If the enemies of promise are the bottle and pram in the hall, they gang up and become murderous when the writer goes out on the road. There are many many bottles (albeit usually miniatures) to be encountered; there are the opportunities to sire multiple baby buggy-loads of uncalled-for off-spring; and there is the evacuation of the soul implied by very short-letting identical modern hotel room after hotel room. The writer A N Wilson has said that a North American book tour was the only time in his adult life when he has been driven to hysterical weeping.

Set against the terrifying rootlessness of the book tour I was able to rediscover the triumphantly rooted character of Saki's stories. Set beside the polyglot babel of American language I was soothed anew by the secure authenticity of Saki's prose voice. And, acting with an acerbic alacrity which reminded me of acid biting into metal, I was able to wince pleasurably as again and again Saki's distinctively English capacity for irony ran amok, pitted itself against the hamburger banalities which enfolded me. Yes, Saki's stories saved my life.

I've heard it said that these stories should only be consumed in small doses. That to read more than one or two at a sitting can induce a kind of literary indigestion; or worse, the aesthetic equivalent of that tasteless sensation which occurs when you launch yourself into a cocktail niblet binge. The first five, ten, or even fifteen cheese footballs may bounce happily down the gullet; but by the time you hit forty all is a salty goo of E additives. Saki's stories, to paraphrase Wilde, are not so much the epitaphs as the death notices of emotions. They're not simply short – they're very short. On length alone they would have to be classed as vignettes and *feuilletons* rather than stories proper. But what a teeming world Saki manages to encompass within such brevity. Arresting metaphor follows terse description; banjaxed aphorism succeeds extravagant idea. The whole is a glittering fractal of the part.

Into the notionally tedious settings of country house parties, gentlemen's clubs and all the long twilights of Victorian imperialism, Saki intrudes a very pagan unease, an irrational attack, a most un-English quality of the sleek and the *soigné*. It is as if Damien Hirst had arrived at Blandings Castle and pickled Lord Emsworth's prize pig in formaldehyde. And, I may add, that even when the stories have foreign settings and foreign characters, Saki's abroad is just that – a place in which the Englishman can promenade, in search of what is distinctive about his own sensibility, far more than another country.

Should the stories be imbibed in tiny sips? Perhaps, but to do so is to attempt the most fragmentary of geological surveys. For, each Saki story is a kind of core sample of his own, inimitable, alternative reality. The curious witticisms which lie, like parings, about his prose, are the twists of curly swarf which the serious business of drilling produces. While any given core sample of Planet Saki can be examined at leisure – and was there ever another writer with a greater gift for the telling micro-detail, the nuance of a nuance? – it's immeasurably more satisfying to read on, to gather further core samples, to begin to build up a comprehensive, three dimensional awareness of these ironic tectonics.

So, by all means read the stories seriatim, but with this important proviso: be aware of the privilege that you're being granted, and don't gobble. The very manner in which most of the stories begin, often breaking into situations or conversations that have clearly already been obtaining for some time, gives the reader the distinct impression that he is privy to the doings of others, and thus privileged with the information. As the Baroness says in 'The Story of St Vespaluus', "tell me a story just true enough to be interesting and not true enough to be tiresome." This is the *obiter dictum* of Planet Saki and perhaps it should be that of our own world as well.

The facts of Hugh Hector Munro's life are well known. Born in 1870 in Burma, he was the son of the Inspector General of the Burma Police. His mother died soon after his birth, and Munro, together with an older brother and sister, was sent back to England and placed in the care of two maiden aunts who lived near Barnstable in North Devon. This is what became the essential topography of Planet Saki, a lush tessellation of farmland, lapping against the wild uplands of Exmoor. In Saki's realm the countryside is secure at one moment – hostile the next.

Aunt Tom and Aunt Augusta were, by all accounts, envenomed to such an extent that throughout Munro's childhood each had her fangs sunk securely in the neck of the other. Governesses came and went, but being a sickly child, he had to put up with thirteen years of their loveless privations. He escaped into books and the realm of the imagination. Initially, like so many imaginative children, a prolific cartoonist, Munro soon became a precocious reader, favouring history and natural history. Many commentators have remarked on the importance of the aunts as the bogeywomen of Saki's fictional world; their meanness, stupidity, conventionality and sheer lovelessness are the animating characteristics of the succession of upholstered gentlewomen who come and go in the stories, talking a lot – saying very little.

Eventually, at the age of fifteen, Munro finally escaped to Bedford Grammar School. Two years later his father retired from the Burma Police and returned to England. The following six years saw the Munro family together but still peculiarly rootless. There were many tours around Europe, and they spent much of the year at Davos, a small town in the Rhaetian Alps of Eastern Switzerland, favoured as a destination by convalescents. The peripatetic life, the relentless leisure, the cultural sophistication and linguistic facility Munro acquired during these years, were all elements he incorporated into his dangerously witty protagonists, Reginald, Clovis and Cosmus.

At twenty-three Munro followed the family tradition and entered the Burma Police. He lasted only a year before cumulative bouts of malaria nearly finished him off. He returned to Devon for two years of rest and recuperation, resuming late Victorian lack-of-business as usual. In 1896 he finally arrived in London to begin a proper career as a writer. Initially he produced *The Rise of the Russian Empire*, a history of the emergent nation up until the seventeenth century. Heavy on the Grand Guignol and laced with humour, the work was not regarded as serious history. Next he turned his attention to satirical sketches of parliament, collaborating with a cartoonist, Francis Gould. They portrayed parliamentarians as characters from Lewis Carroll's classic, and the results were collected as a book *The Westminster Alice*, which sold very well.

By 1902 Munro had established a reputation as a political commentator and joined the *Morning Post* as a correspondent. The paper sent him out to the Balkans to cover the war there. This set the pattern for the professional life Munro led up until the First World War. On the one hand he was a correspondent for newspapers, travelling extensively in Poland, Russia and France; on the other he was a short story writer contributing to the magazines of the day. The first book of Reginald stories was published in 1904, and the second in 1910.

For the last few years before the war Munro was firmly settled in London, where by all accounts he led a routine life, almost verging on the dull. He eschewed the literary coteries of the day, keeping to an uncelebrated circle of friends and acquaintances. He lived in rooms in Fitzrovia, belonged to an undistinguished club, played bridge and went away for the weekend to the house parties which were the lifeblood of upper middle-class Edwardian social existence. It would appear that he kept his true energies for his writing. In 1911 *The Chronicles of Clovis* appeared; in 1912 a novel *The Unbearable Bassington*. Another novel *When William Came* was published in 1913; and in 1914, his last book to be published during his lifetime *Beasts and Superbeasts*.

When the war came Munro refused a commission, and despite his advanced age, forty-four, enlisted in the ranks. He was sent to France in 1915 and promoted to lance-sergeant. In November 1916 he joined an attack formation, and while resting in a shallow shell crater was shot through the head, another human animal pole-axed in the Flanders abattoir. The story is – although it sounds apocryphal – that the instant before he was shot he cried "put that bloody cigarette out!".

So, the outline of a life is there, but of the inner life we know very little. Much of the direct reporting of Munro's character we owe to his sister, who published her own biography. It's from the sister that we learn of the cloistered childhood, the chivalry-obsessed adolescence, the dryly respectable adulthood, and the blood sacrifice on the altar of nationalism. Do we believe in it as it stands? No, not at all. I think that the sister's biography is revisionism pure and simple, and nothing gives the lie to it more securely than the fact that she refused access to her brother's papers after his death and eventually burnt them. All subsequent biographers, given the paucity of firsthand accounts of the man, have had to labour under her own wishful thinking.

No, the Munro who peeps out at us from behind the cultivated disinterest of Saki's sexually null – but emphatically male – protagonists, is a gay man who came of age during the white heat of the Wilde scandal, and was forced to affect the strongest possible of protective colorations. There's no doubt in my mind that he was sexually active but highly circumspect – as he would have to be.

The frontispiece quote from Euripides which Saki used for 'The Remoulding of Groby Lington' is "A man is known by the company he keeps"; and the story itself can be read as an allegory of a man's fear of 'sexual deviance' being discovered. One theory of the origin of Munro's *nom de plume* (advanced by his sister), is that he took it from the name of the cup bearer in the *Rubaiyat of Omar Khayyam*; another is that the pet ape owned by the eponymous hero of 'The Remoulding of Groby Lington', which Saki describes as superficially gentle yet capable of extreme arousal, was intended to be a saki; a silent, long-tailed monkey from South America. If the latter is the case, then what better and more circumspect way of indicating the author's own unutterable allegiance? If the former is the case, well, in terms of gay iconography the Rubaiyat is almost *de trop*.

But anyway, I don't wish to trawl either the work or the life for evidence of Munro's sexual predilections – I think they're obvious and scream forth. To take one strand of the stories alone – Saki's savagely unsentimental way with children. This has always been crudely interpreted as a cathartic expression of the treatment he himself received from the hated Aunts, but doesn't this ignore the sheer glee with which Saki records the loss of Erik in 'The Quest', and the subsequent cynicism of his proxy retrieval? And what of the gypsy child despatched by Esmé in the story of the same name? Is there not perhaps the authentically misanthropic voice of the man who knows paternity will never be for him, speaking through these pages?

There's no need to search for effete men and stentorian women in the Saki's stories – because that's what they're mostly about. There's no requirement for a skilled exegesis to untangle the threads of dandyism, orna-mentation, erudition and affection – because that's what his prose weaves together. But I have no interest in proposing Munro himself as a martyred gay icon, I wish to celebrate Saki the writer as an iconic gay. Given a few tweaks and twists on the contrast and colour knobs, and from the protective coloration of Saki's stories would come prancing the screaming queens of Ronald Firbank's fictional jungle of the id.

Anyway, there's no need to worry about any of this, gentle reader, simply turn the page and get on with the work at hand. Delight in Saki's capacity to render the sensate in terms of the insensate, as he compares the soul to a drawing room, or comments on the pain threshold of toast. Titter nervously as he avers that the oyster is more beautiful than any religion. And gasp with delight as your expectations are not so much reversed as sent into free fall. Saki had the skill of a Kafka when it came to the realistically deadpan presentation of the fantastical, and it is this as much as anything which makes these stories astonishing. To have the opportunity of reading Saki's stores for the first time – well, I envy you. To have the leisure to reread them you must, like me, be in need of a little life saving. I hope you catch the ring.

Reginald on Besetting Sins

There was once (said Reginald) a woman who told the truth. Not all at once, of course, but the habit grew upon her gradually, like lichen on an apparently healthy tree. She had no children—otherwise it might have been different. It began with little things, for no particular reason except that her life was a rather empty one, and it is so easy to slip into the habit of telling the truth in little matters. And then it became difficult to draw the line at more important things, until at last she took to telling the truth about her age; she said she was forty-two and five months—by that time, you see, she was veracious even to months. It may have been pleasing to the angels, but her elder sister was not gratified. On the Woman's birthday, instead of the opera-tickets which she had hoped for, her sister gave her a view of Jerusalem from the Mount of Olives, which is not quite the same thing. The revenge of an elder sister may be long in coming, but, like a South-Eastern express, it arrives in its own good time.

The friends of the Woman tried to dissuade her from over-indulgence in the practice, but she said she was wedded to the truth; whereupon it was remarked that it was scarcely logical to be so much together in public. (No really provident woman lunches regularly with her husband if she wishes to burst upon him as a revelation at dinner. He must have time to forget; an afternoon is not enough.) And after a while her friends began to thin out in patches. Her passion for the truth was not compatible with a large visiting-list. For instance, she told Miriam Klopstock *exactly* how she looked at the Ilexes' ball. Certainly Miriam had asked for her candid opinion, but the Woman prayed in church every Sunday for peace in our time, and it was not consistent.

It was unfortunate, every one agreed, that she had no family; with a child or two in the house, there is an unconscious check upon too free an indulgence in the truth. Children are given us to discourage our better emotions. That is why the stage, with all its efforts, can never be as artificial as life; even in an Ibsen drama one must reveal to the audience things that one would suppress before the children or servants.

Fate may have ordained the truth-telling from the commencement and should justly bear some of the blame; but in having no children the Woman was guilty, at least, of contributory negligence.

Little by little she felt she was becoming a slave to what had once been merely an idle propensity; and one day she knew. Every woman tells ninety per cent of the truth to her dressmaker; the other ten per cent is the irreducible minimum of deception beyond which no self-respecting client trespasses. Madame Draga's establishment was a meeting-ground for naked truths and overdressed fictions, and it was here, the Woman felt, that she might make a final effort to recall the artless mendacity of past days. Madame herself was in an inspiring mood, with the air of a sphinx who knew all things and preferred to forget most of them. As a War Minister she might have been celebrated, but she was content to be merely rich.

"If I take it in here, and—Miss Howard, one moment, if you please—and there, and round like this—so —I really think you will find it quite easy."

The Woman hesitated; it seemed to require such a small effort to simply acquiesce in Madame's views. But habit had become too strong. "I'm afraid," she faltered, "it's just the least little bit in the world too—"

And by that least little bit she measured the deeps and eternities of her thraldom to fact. Madame was not best pleased at being contradicted on a professional matter, and when Madame lost her temper you usually found it afterwards in the bill.

And at last the dreadful thing came, as the Woman had foreseen all along that it must; it was one of those paltry little truths with which she harried her waking hours. On a raw Wednesday morning, in a few ill-chosen words, she told the cook that she drank. She remembered the scene afterwards as vividly as though it had been painted in her mind by Abbey. The cook was a good cook, as cooks go; and as cooks go she went.

Miriam Klopstock came to lunch the next day. Women and elephants never forget an injury.

Reginald's Drama

Reginald closed his eyes with the elaborate weariness of one who has rather nice eyelashes and thinks it useless to conceal the fact.

"One of these days," he said, "I shall write a really great drama. No one will understand the drift of it, but every one will go back to their homes with a vague feeling of dissatisfaction with their lives and surroundings. Then they will put up new wall-papers and forget."

"But how about those that have oak panelling all over the house?" said the Other.

"They can always put down new stair-carpets," pursued Reginald, "and, anyhow, I'm not responsible for the audience having a happy ending. The play would be quite sufficient strain on one's energies. I should get a bishop to say it was immoral and beautiful—no dramatist has thought of that before, and every one would come to condemn the bishop, and they would stay on out of sheer nervousness. After all, it requires a great deal of moral courage to leave in a marked manner in the middle of the second act, when your carriage isn't ordered till twelve. And it would commence with wolves worrying something on a lonely waste—you wouldn't see them, of course; but you would hear them snarling and scrunching, and I should arrange to have a wolfy fragrance suggested across the footlights. It would look so well on the programmes, 'Wolves in the first act, by Jamrach.' And old Lady Whortleberry, who never misses a first night, would scream. She's always been nervous since she lost her first husband. He died quite abruptly while watching a county cricket match; two and a half inches of rain had fallen for seven runs, and it was supposed that the excitement killed him. Anyhow, it gave her quite a shock; it was the first husband she'd lost, you know, and now she always screams if anything thrilling happens too soon after dinner. And after the audience had heard the Whortleberry scream the thing would be fairly launched."

"And the plot?"

"The plot," said Reginald, "would be one of those little everyday tragedies that one sees going on all round one. In my mind's eye there is the case of the Mudge-Jervises, which in an unpretentious way has quite an Enoch Arden intensity underlying it. They'd only been married some eighteen months or so, and circumstances had prevented their seeing much of each other. With him there was always a foursome or something that had to be played and replayed in different parts of the country, and she went in for slumming quite as seriously as if it was a sport. With her, I suppose, it was. She belonged to the Guild of the Poor Dear Souls, and they hold the record for having nearly reformed a washerwoman. No one has ever really reformed a washerwoman, and that is why the competition is so keen. You can rescue charwomen by fifties with a little tea and personal magnetism, but with washerwomen it's

5

different; wages are too high. This particular laundress, who came from Bermondsey or some such place, was really rather a hopeful venture, and they thought at last that she might be safely put in the window as a specimen of successful work. So they had her paraded at a drawing-room "At Home" at Agatha Camelford's; it was sheer bad luck that some liqueur chocolates had been turned loose by mistake among the refreshments— really liqueur chocolates, with very little chocolate. And of course the old soul found them out, and cornered the entire stock. It was like finding a whelk-stall in a desert, as she afterwards partially expressed herself. When the liqueurs began to take effect, she started to give them imitations of farmyard animals as they know them in Bermondsey. She began with a dancing bear, and you know Agatha doesn't approve of dancing, except at Buckingham Palace under proper supervision. And then she got up on the piano and gave them an organ monkey; I gather she went in for realism rather than a Maeterlickian treatment of the subject. Finally, she fell into the piano and said she was a parrot in a cage, and for an impromptu performance I believe she was very word-perfect; no one had heard anything like it, except Baroness Boobelstein who has attended sittings of the Austrian Reichsrath. Agatha is trying the Rest-cure at Buxton."

"But the tragedy?"

"Oh, the Mudge-Jervises. Well, they were getting along quite happily, and their married life was one continuous exchange of picture-postcards; and then one day they were thrown together on some neutral ground where foursomes and washerwomen overlapped, and discovered that they were hopelessly divided on the Fiscal Question. They have thought it best to separate, and she is to have the custody of the Persian kittens for nine months in the year—they go back to him for the winter, when she is abroad. There you have the material for a tragedy drawn straight from life—and the piece could be called 'The Price They Paid for Empire.' And of course one would have to work in studies of the struggle of hereditary tendency against environment and all that sort of thing. The woman's father could have been an Envoy to some of the smaller German Courts; that's where she'd get her passion for visiting the poor, in spite of the most careful upbringing. *C'est le premier pa qui compte*, as the cuckoo said when it swallowed its foster-parent. That, I think, is quite clever."

"And the wolves?"

"Oh, the wolves would be a sort of elusive undercurrent in the background that would never be satisfactorily explained. After all, life teems with things that have no earthly reason. And whenever the characters could think of nothing brilliant to say about marriage or the War Office, they could open a window and listen to the howling of the wolves. But that would be very seldom."

Reginald's Christmas Revel

They say (said Reginald) that there's nothing sadder than victory except defeat. If you've ever stayed with dull people during what is alleged to be the festive season, you can probably revise that saying. I shall never forget putting in a Christmas at the Babwolds'. Mrs. Babwold is some relation of my father's—a sort of to-be-left-till-called-for cousin—and that was considered sufficient reason for my having to accept her invitation at about the sixth time of asking; though why the sins of the father should be visited by the children—you won't find any notepaper in that drawer; that's where I keep old menus and first-night programmes.

Mrs. Babwold wears a rather solemn personality, and has never been known to smile, even when saying disagreeable things to her friends or making out the Stores list. She takes her pleasures sadly. A state elephant at a Durbar gives one a very similar impression. Her husband gardens in all weathers. When a man goes out in the pouring rain to brush caterpillars off rose trees, I generally imagine his life indoors leaves something to be desired; anyway, it must be very unsettling for the caterpillars.

Of course there were other people there. There was a Major Somebody who had shot things in Lapland, or somewhere of that sort; I forget what they were, but it wasn't for want of reminding. We had them cold with every meal almost, and he was continually giving us details of what they measured from tip to tip, as though he thought we were going to make them warm under-things for the winter. I used to listen to him with a rapt attention that I thought rather suited me, and then one day I quite modestly gave the dimensions of an okapi I had shot in the Lincolnshire fens. The Major turned a beautiful Tyrian scarlet (I remember thinking at the time that I should like my bathroom hung in that colour), and I think that at that moment he almost found it in his heart to dislike me. Mrs. Babwold put on a first-aid-to-the-injured expression, and asked him why he didn't publish a book of his sporting reminis-cences; it would be *so* interesting. She didn't remember till afterwards that he had given her two fat volumes on the subject, with his portrait and autograph as a frontispiece and an appendix on the habits of the Arctic mussel.

It was in the evening that we cast aside the cares and distractions of the day and really lived. Cards were thought to be too frivolous and empty a way of passing the time, so most of them played what they called a book game. You went out into the hall—to get an inspiration, I suppose—then you came in again with a muffler tied round your neck and looked silly, and the others were supposed to guess that you were *Wee MacGreegor*. I held out against the inanity as long as I decently could, but at last, in a lapse of good-nature, I consented to masquerade as a book, only I warned them that it would take some time to carry out. They waited for the best part of forty minutes while I went and played wineglass skittles with the page-boy in the pantry; you play it with a champagne cork, you know, and the one who knocks down the most glasses without breaking them wins. I won, with four unbroken out of seven; I think William suffered from over-anxiousness. They were rather mad in the drawing-room at my not having come back, and they weren't a bit pacified when I told them afterwards that I was *At the end of the passage*.

"I never did like Kipling," was Mrs. Babwold's comment, when the situation dawned upon her. "I couldn't see anything clever in *Earthworms out of Tuscany*—or is that by Darwin?"

Of course these games are very educational, but, personally, I prefer bridge.

On Christmas evening we were supposed to be specially festive in the Old English fashion. The hall was horribly draughty, but it seemed to be the proper place to revel in, and it was decorated with Japanese fans and Chinese lanterns, which gave it a very Old English effect. A young lady with a confidential voice favoured us with a long recitation about a little girl who died or did something equally hackneyed, and then the Major gave us a graphic account of a struggle he had with a wounded bear. I privately wished that the bears would win sometimes on these occasions; at least they wouldn't go vapouring about it afterwards. Before we had time to recover our spirits, we were indulged with some thought-reading by a young man whom one knew instinctively had a good mother and an indifferent tailor—the sort of young man who talks unflaggingly through the thickest soup, and smooths his hair dubiously as though he thought it might hit back. The thought-reading was rather a success; he announced that the hostess was thinking about poetry, and she admitted that her mind was dwelling on one of Austin's odes. Which was near enough. I fancy she had been really wondering whether a scrag-end of mutton and some cold plum-pudding would do for the kitchen dinner next day. As a crowning dissipation, they all sat down to play progressive halma, with milk-chocolate for prizes. I've been carefully brought up, and I don't like to play games of skill for milk-chocolate, so I invented a headache and retired from the scene. I had been preceded a few minutes earlier by Miss Langshan-Smith, a rather formidable lady, who always got up at some uncomfortable hour in the morning, and gave you the impression that she had been in communication with most of the European Governments before breakfast. There was a paper pinned on her door with a signed request that she might be called particularly early on the morrow. Such an opportunity does not come twice in a lifetime. I covered up everything except the signature with another notice, to the effect that before these words should meet the eye she would have ended a misspent life, was sorry for the trouble she was giving, and would like a military funeral. A few minutes later I violently exploded an air-filled paper bag on the landing, and gave a stage moan that could have been heard in the cellars. Then I pursued my original intention and went to bed. The noise those people made in forcing open the good lady's door was positively indecorous; she resisted gallantly, but I believe they searched her for bullets for about a quarter of an hour, as if she had been a historic battlefield.

I hate travelling on Boxing Day, but one must occasionally do things that one dislikes.

The Innocence of Reginald

Reginald slid a carnation of the newest shade into the buttonhole of his latest lounge coat, and surveyed the result with approval. "I am just in the mood," he observed, "to have my portrait painted by some one with an unmistakable future. So comforting to go down to posterity as 'Youth with a Pink Carnation' in catalogue-company with 'Child with Bunch of Primroses', and all that crowd."

"Youth," said the Other, "should suggest innocence."

"But never act on the suggestion. I don't believe the two ever really go together. People talk vaguely about the innocence of a little child, but they take mighty good care not to let it out of their sight for twenty minutes. The watched pot never boils over. I knew a boy once who really was innocent; his parents were in Society, but they never gave him a moment's anxiety from his infancy. He believed in company prospectuses, and in the purity of elections, and in women marrying for love, and even in a system for winning at roulette. He never quite lost his faith in it, but he dropped more money than his employers could afford to lose. When last I heard of him, he was believing in his innocence; the jury weren't. All the same, I really am innocent just now of something every one accuses me of having done, and so far as I can see, their accusations will remain unfounded."

"Rather an unexpected attitude for you."

"I love people who do unexpected things. Didn't you always adore the man who slew a lion in a pit on a snowy day? But about this unfortunate innocence. Well, quite long ago, when I'd been quarrelling with more people than usual, you among the number—it must have been in November, I never quarrel with you too near Christmas—I had an idea that I'd like to write a book. It was to be a book of personal reminiscences, and was to leave out nothing."

"Reginald!"

"Exactly what the Duchess said when I mentioned it to her. I was provoking and said nothing, and the next thing, of course, was that every one heard that I'd written the book and got it in the press. After that, I might have been a goldfish in a glass bowl for all the privacy I got. People attacked me about it in the most unexpected places, and implored or commanded me to leave out things that I'd forgotten had ever happened. I sat behind Miriam Klopstock one night in the dress-circle at His Majesty's, and she began at once about the incident of the Chow dog in the bathroom, which she insisted must be struck out. We had to argue it in a disjointed fashion, because some of the people wanted to listen to the play, and Miriam takes nines in voices. They had to stop her playing in the 'Macaws' Hockey Club because you could hear what she thought when her shins got mixed up in a scrimmage for half a mile on a still day. They are called the Macaws because of their blue-and-yellow costumes, but I understand there was nothing yellow about Miriam's language. I agreed to make one alteration, as I pretended I had got it a Spitz instead of a Chow, but beyond that I was firm. She megaphoned back two minutes later, 'You promised you would never mention it; don't you ever keep a promise?' When people had stopped glaring in our direction, I replied that I'd as soon think of keeping white mice. I saw her tearing little bits out of her programme for a minute or two, and then she leaned back and snorted, 'You're not the boy I took you for,' as though she were an eagle arriving at Olympus with the wrong Ganymede. That was her last audible remark, but she went on tearing up her programme and scattering the pieces around her, till one of her neighbours asked with immense dignity whether she should send for a wastepaper-basket. I didn't stay for the last act.

"Then there is Mrs.—oh, I never can remember her name; she lives in a street that the cabmen have never heard of, and is at home on Wednesdays. She frightened me horribly once at a private view by saying mysteriously, 'I oughtn't to be here, you know; this is one of my days.' I thought she meant that she was subject to periodical outbreaks and was expecting an attack at any moment So embarrassing if she had suddenly taken it into her head that she was Cesare Borgia or St. Elizabeth of Hungary. That sort of thing would make one unpleasantly conspicuous even at a private view. However, she merely meant to say that it was Wednesday, which at the moment was incontrovertible. Well, she's on quite a different tack to the Klopstock. She doesn't visit anywhere very extensively, and, of course, she's awfully keen for me to drag in an incident that occurred at one of the Beauwhistle garden-parties, when she says she accidentally hit the shins of a Serene Somebody or other with a croquet mallet and that he swore at her in German. As a matter of fact, he went on discoursing on the Gordon-Bennett affair in French. (I never can remember if it's a new submarine or a divorce. Of course, how stupid of me!) To be disagreeably exact, I fancy she missed him by about two inches—over-anxiousness, probably—but she likes to think she hit him. I've felt that way with a partridge which I always imagine keeps on flying strong, out of false pride, till it's the other side of the hedge. She said she could tell me everything she was wearing on the occasion. I said I didn't want my book to read like a laundry list, but she explained that she didn't mean those sort of things.

"And there's the Chilworth boy, who can be charming as long as he's content to be stupid and wear what he's told to; but he gets the idea now and then that he'd like to be epigrammatic, and the result is like watching a rook trying to build a nest in a gale. Since he got wind of the book, he's been persecuting me to work in something of his about the Russians and the Yalu Peril, and is quite sulky because I won't do it.

"Altogether, I think it would be rather a brilliant inspiration if you were to suggest a fortnight in Paris."

The Reticence of Lady Anne

Egbert came into the large, dimly lit drawing-room with the air of a man who is not certain whether he is entering a dovecote or a bomb factory, and is prepared for either eventuality. The little domestic quarrel over the luncheon-table had not been fought to a definite finish, and the question was how far Lady Anne was in a mood to renew or forgo hostilities. Her pose in the armchair by the tea-table was rather elaborately rigid; in the gloom of a December afternoon Egbert's pince-nez did not materially help him to discern the expression of her face.

By way of breaking whatever ice might be floating on the surface he made a remark about a dim religious light. He or Lady Anne were accustomed to make that remark between 4.30 and 6 on winter and late autumn evenings; it was a part of their married life. There was no recognised rejoinder to it, and Lady Anne made none.

Don Tarquinio lay astretch on the Persian rug, basking in the firelight with superb indifference to the possible ill-humour of Lady Anne. His pedigree was as flawlessly Persian as the rug, and his ruff was coming into the glory of its second winter. The page-boy, who had Renaissance tendencies, had christened him Don Tarquinio. Left to themselves, Egbert and Lady Anne would unfailingly have called him Fluff, but they were not obstinate.

Egbert poured himself out some tea. As the silence gave no sign of breaking on Lady Anne's initiative, he braced himself for another Yermak effort.

"My remark at lunch had a purely academic application," he announced; "you seem to put an unnecessarily personal significance into it."

Lady Anne maintained her defensive barrier of silence. The bullfinch lazily filled in the interval with an air from *Iphigénie en Tauride*. Egbert recognised it immediately, because it was the only air the bullfinch whistled, and he had come to them with the reputation for whistling it. Both Egbert and Lady Anne would have preferred something from *The Yeomen of the Guard*, which was their favourite opera. In matters artistic they had a similarity of taste. They leaned towards the honest and explicit in art, a picture, for instance, that told its own story, with generous assistance from its title. A riderless warhorse with harness in obvious disarray, staggering into a courtyard full of pale swooning women, and marginally noted "Bad News", suggested to their minds a distinct interpretation of some military catastrophe. They could see what it was meant to convey, and explain it to friends of duller intelligence.

The silence continued. As a rule Lady Anne's displeasure became articulate and markedly voluble after four minutes of introductory muteness. Egbert seized the milk-jug and poured some of its contents into Don Tarquinio's saucer; as the saucer was already full to the brim an unsightly overflow was the result.

Don Tarquinio looked on with a surprised interest that evanesced into elaborate unconsciousness when he was appealed to by Egbert to come and drink up some of the spilt matter. Don Tarquinio was prepared to play many rôles in life, but a vacuum carpet-cleaner was not one of them.

"Don't you think we're being rather foolish?" said Egbert cheerfully.

If Lady Anne thought so she didn't say so.

"I dare say the fault has been partly on my side," continued Egbert, with evaporating cheerfulness. "After all, I'm only human, you know. You seem to forget that I'm only human."

He insisted on the point, as if there had been unfounded suggestions that he was built on Satyr lines, with goat continuations where the human left off.

The bullfinch recommenced its air from *Iphigénie en Tauride*. Egbert began to feel depressed. Lady Anne was not drinking her tea. Perhaps she was feeling unwell. But when Lady Anne felt unwell she was not wont to be reticent on the subject. "No one knows what I suffer from indigestion" was one of her favourite statements; but the lack of knowledge can only have been caused by defective listening; the amount of information available on the subject would have supplied material for a monograph.

Evidently Lady Anne was not feeling unwell.

Egbert began to think he was being unreasonably dealt with; naturally he began to make concessions.

"I dare say," he observed, taking as central a position on the hearth-rug as Don Tarquinio could be persuaded to concede him, "I may have been to blame. I am willing, if I can thereby restore things to a happier standpoint, to undertake to lead a better life."

He wondered vaguely how it would be possible. Temptations came to him, in middle age, tentatively and without insistence, like a neglected butcher-boy who asks for a Christmas box in February for no more hopeful reason than that he didn't get one in December. He had no more idea of succumbing to them than he had of purchasing the fish-knives and fur boas that ladies are impelled to sacrifice through the medium of advertisement columns during twelve months of the year. Still, there was something impressive in this unasked-for renunciation of possibly latent enormities.

Lady Anne showed no sign of being impressed.

Egbert looked at her nervously through his glasses. To get the worst of an argument with her was no new experience. To get the worst of a monologue was a humiliating novelty.

"I shall go and dress for dinner," he announced in a voice into which he intended some shade of sternness to creep.

At the door a final access of weakness impelled him to make a further appeal.

"Aren't we being very silly?"

"A fool" was Don Tarquinio's mental comment as the door closed on Egbert's retreat. Then he lifted his velvet forepaws in the air and leapt lightly on to a book-shelf immediately under the bullfinch's cage. It was the first time he had seemed to notice the bird's existence, but he was carrying out a long-formed theory of action with the precision of mature deliberation. The bullfinch, who had fancied himself something of a despot, depressed himself of a sudden into a third of his normal displacement; then he fell to a helpless wing-beating and shrill cheeping. He had cost twenty-seven shillings without the cage, but Lady Anne made no sign of interfering. She had been dead for two hours.

Esmé

"All hunting stories are the same," said Clovis; "just as all Turf stories are the same, and all—"

"My hunting story isn't a bit like any you've ever heard," said the Baroness. "It happened quite a while ago, when I was about twenty-three. I wasn't living apart from my husband then; you see, neither of us could afford to make the other a separate allowance. In spite of everything that proverbs may say, poverty keeps together more homes than it breaks up. But we always hunted with different packs. All this has nothing to do with the story."

"We haven't arrived at the meet yet. I suppose there was a meet," said Clovis.

"Of course there was a meet," said the Baroness; "all the usual crowd were there, especially Constance Broddle. Constance is one of those strapping florid girls that go so well with autumn scenery or Christmas decorations in church. 'I feel a presentiment that something dreadful is going to happen,' she said to me; 'am I looking pale?'

"She was looking about as pale as a beetroot that has suddenly heard bad news.

"'You're looking nicer than usual,' I said, 'but that's so easy for you.' Before she had got the right bearings of this remark we had settled down to business; hounds had found a fox lying out in some gorse-bushes."

"I knew it," said Clovis; "in every fox-hunting story that I've ever heard there's been a fox and some gorse-bushes."

"Constance and I were well mounted," continued the Baroness serenely, "and we had no difficulty in keeping ourselves in the first flight, though it was a fairly stiff run. Towards the finish, however, we must have held rather too independent a line, for we lost the hounds, and found ourselves plodding aimlessly along miles away from anywhere. It was fairly exasperating, and my temper was beginning to let itself go by inches, when on pushing our way through an accommodating hedge we were gladdened by the sight of hounds in full cry in a hollow just beneath us.

"'There they go,' cried Constance, and then added in a gasp, 'In Heaven's name, what are they hunting?'

"It was certainly no mortal fox. It stood more than twice as high, had a short, ugly head, and an enormous thick neck.

"'It's a hyæna,' I cried; 'it must have escaped from Lord Pabham's Park.'

"At that moment the hunted beast turned and faced its pursuers, and the hounds (there were only about six couple of them) stood round in a half-circle and looked foolish. Evidently they had broken away from the rest of the pack on the trail of this alien scent, and were not quite sure how to treat their quarry now they had got him.

"The hyæna hailed our approach with unmistakable relief and demonstrations of friendliness. It had probably been accustomed to uniform kindness from humans, while its first experience of a pack of hounds had left a bad impression. The hounds looked more than ever embarrassed as their quarry paraded its sudden intimacy with us, and the faint toot of a horn in the distance was seized on as a welcome signal for unobtrusive departure. Constance and I and the hyæna were left alone in the gathering twilight.

" 'What are we to do?' asked Constance.

" 'What a person you are for questions,' I said.

" 'Well, we can't stay here all night with a hyæna,' she retorted.

" 'I don't know what your ideas of comfort are,' I said; 'but I shouldn't think of staying here all night even without a hyæna. My home may be an unhappy one, but at least it has hot and cold water laid on, and domestic service, and other conveniences which we shouldn't find here. We had better make for that ridge of trees to the right; I imagine the Crowley road is just beyond.'

"We trotted off slowly along a faintly marked cart-track, with the beast following cheerfully at our heels.

" 'What on earth are we to do with the hyæna?' came the inevitable question.

" 'What does one generally do with hyænas?' I asked crossly.

" 'I've never had anything to do with one before,' said Constance.

" 'Well, neither have I. If we even knew its sex we might give it a name. Perhaps we might call it Esmé. That would do in either case.'

"There was still sufficient daylight for us to distinguish wayside objects, and our listless spirits gave

24

an upward perk as we came upon a small half-naked gipsy brat picking blackberries from a low-growing bush. The sudden apparition of two horsewomen and a hyæna set it off crying, and in any case we should scarcely have gleaned any useful geographical information from that source; but there was a probability that we might strike a gipsy encampment somewhere along our route. We rode on hopefully but uneventfully for another mile or so.

"'I wonder what the child was doing there,' said Constance presently.

"'Picking blackberries. Obviously.'

"'I don't like the way it cried,' pursued Constance; 'somehow its wail keeps ringing in my ears.'

"I did not chide Constance for her morbid fancies; as a matter of fact the same sensation, of being pursued by a persistent fretful wail, had been forcing itself on my rather over-tired nerves. For company's sake I hullooed to Esmé, who had lagged somewhat behind. With a few springy bounds he drew up level, and then shot past us.

"The wailing accompaniment was explained. The gipsy child was firmly, and I expect painfully, held in his jaws.

"'Merciful Heaven!' screamed Constance, 'what on earth shall we do? What are we to do?'

"I am perfectly certain that at the Last Judgment Constance will ask more questions than any of the examining Seraphs.

"'Can't we do something?' she persisted tearfully, as Esmé cantered easily along in front of our tired horses.

"Personally I was doing everything that occurred to

me at the moment. I stormed and scolded and coaxed in English and French and gamekeeper language; I made absurd, ineffectual cuts in the air with my thongless hunting-crop; I hurled my sandwich case at the brute; in fact, I really don't know what more I could have done. And still we lumbered on through the deepening dusk, with that dark uncouth shape lumbering ahead of us, and a drone of lugubrious music floating in our ears. Suddenly Esmé bounded aside into some thick bushes, where we could not follow; the wail rose to a shriek and then stopped altogether. This part of the story I always hurry over, because it is really rather horrible. When the beast joined us again, after an absence of a few minutes, there was an air of patient understanding about him, as though he knew that he had done something of which we disapproved, but which he felt to be thoroughly justifiable.

" 'How can you let that ravening beast trot by your side?' asked Constance. She was looking more than ever like an albino beetroot.

" 'In the first place, I can't prevent it,' I said; 'and in the second place, whatever else he may be, I doubt if he's ravening at the present moment.'

"Constance shuddered. 'Do you think the poor little thing suffered much?' came another of her futile questions.

" 'The indications were all that way,' I said; 'on the other hand, of course, it may have been crying from sheer temper. Children sometimes do.'

"It was nearly pitch-dark when we emerged suddenly into the high road. A flash of lights and the whir of a motor went past us at the same moment at uncomfortably close quarters. A thud and a sharp screeching yell followed a second later. The car drew up, and when I had ridden back to the spot I found a young man bending over a dark motionless mass lying by the roadside.

" 'You have killed my Esmé,' I exclaimed bitterly.

" 'I'm so awfully sorry,' said the young man; 'I keep dogs myself, so I know what you must feel about it. I'll do anything I can in reparation.'

" 'Please bury him at once,' I said; 'that much I think I may ask of you.'

" 'Bring the spade, William,' he called to the chauffeur. Evidently hasty roadside interments were contingencies that had been provided against.

"The digging of a sufficiently large grave took some little time. 'I say, what a magnificent fellow,' said the motorist as the corpse was rolled over into the trench. 'I'm afraid he must have been rather a valuable animal.'

" 'He took second in the puppy class at Birmingham last year,' I said resolutely.

"Constance snorted loudly.

" 'Don't cry, dear,' I said brokenly; 'it was all over in a moment, He couldn't have suffered much.'

" 'Look here,' said the young fellow desperately, 'you simply must let me do something by way of reparation.'

"I refused sweetly, but as he persisted I let him have my address.

"Of course, we kept our own counsel as to the earlier episodes of the evening. Lord Pabham never advertised the loss of his hyæna; when a strictly fruit-eating animal strayed from his park a year or two previously he was called upon to give compensation in eleven cases of

27

sheep-worrying and practically to re-stock his neighbours' poultry-yards, and an escaped hyæna would have mounted up to something on the scale of a Government grant. The gipsies were equally unobtrusive over their missing offspring; I don't suppose in large encampments they really know to a child or two how many they've got."

The Baroness paused reflectively, and then continued:

"There was a sequel to the adventure, though. I got through the post a charming little diamond brooch, with the name Esmé set in a sprig of rosemary. Incidentally, too, I lost the friendship of Constance Broddle. You see, when I sold the brooch I quite properly refused to give her any share of the proceeds. I pointed out that the Esmé part of the affair was my own invention, and the hyæna part of it belonged to Lord Pabham, if it really was his hyæna, of which, of course, I've no proof."

The Match-Maker

The grill-room clock struck eleven with the respectful unobtrusiveness of one whose mission in life is to be ignored. When the flight of time should really have rendered abstinence and migration imperative the lighting apparatus would signal the fact in the usual way.

Six minutes later Clovis approached the supper-table, in the blessed expectancy of one who has dined sketchily and long ago.

"I'm starving," he announced, making an effort to sit down gracefully and read the menu at the same time.

"So I gathered," said his host, "from the fact that you were nearly punctual. I ought to have told you that I'm a Food Reformer. I've ordered two bowls of bread-and-milk and some health biscuits. I hope you don't mind."

Clovis pretended afterwards that he didn't go white above the collar-line for the fraction of a second.

"All the same," he said, "you ought not to joke about such things. There really are such people. I've known people who've met them. To think of all the adorable things there are to eat in the world, and then to go through life munching sawdust and being proud of it."

"They're like the Flagellants of the Middle Ages,

who went about mortifying themselves."

"They had some excuse," said Clovis. "They did it to save their immortal souls, didn't they? You needn't tell me that a man who doesn't love oysters and asparagus and good wines has got a soul, or a stomach either. He's simply got the instinct for being unhappy highly developed."

Clovis relapsed for a few golden moments into tender intimacies with a succession of rapidly disappearing oysters.

"I think oysters are more beautiful than any religion," he resumed presently. "They not only forgive our unkindness to them; they justify it, they incite us to go on being perfectly horrid to them. Once they arrive at the supper-table they seem to enter thoroughly into the spirit of the thing. There's nothing in Christianity or Buddhism that quite matches the sympathetic unselfishness of an oyster. Do you like my new waistcoat? I'm wearing it for the first time tonight."

"It looks like a great many others you've had lately, only worse. New dinner waistcoats are becoming a habit with you."

"They say one always pays for the excesses of one's youth; mercifully that isn't true about one's clothes. My mother is thinking of getting married."

"Again!"

"It's the first time."

"Of course, you ought to know. I was under the impression that she'd been married once or twice at least."

"Three times, to be mathematically exact. I meant that it was the first time she'd thought about getting married; the other times she did it without thinking. As a matter of fact, it's really I who am doing the thinking for her in this case. You see, it's quite two years since her last husband died."

"You evidently think that brevity is the soul of widowhood."

"Well, it struck me that she was getting moped, and beginning to settle down, which wouldn't suit her a bit. The first symptom that I noticed was when she began to complain that we were living beyond our income. All decent people live beyond their incomes nowadays, and those who aren't respectable live beyond other people's. A few gifted individuals manage to do both."

"It's hardly so much a gift as an industry."

"The crisis came," returned Clovis, "when she suddenly started the theory that late hours were bad for one, and wanted me to be in by one o'clock every night. Imagine that sort of thing for me, who was eighteen on my last birthday."

"On your last two birthdays, to be mathematically exact."

"Oh, well, that's not my fault. I'm not going to arrive at nineteen as long as my mother remains at thirty-seven. One must have some regard for appearances."

"Perhaps your mother would age a little in the process of settling down."

"That's the last thing she'd think of. Feminine reformations always start in on the failings of other people. That's why I was so keen on the husband idea."

"Did you go as far as to select the gentleman, or did you merely throw out a general idea, and trust to the force of suggestion?"

"If one wants a thing done in a hurry one must see to it oneself. I found a military Johnny hanging round on a loose end at the club, and took him home to lunch once or twice. He'd spent most of his life on the Indian frontier, building roads, and relieving famines and minimizing earthquakes, and all that sort of thing that one does do on frontiers. He could talk sense to a peevish cobra in fifteen native languages, and probably knew what to do if you found a rogue elephant on your croquet-lawn; but he was shy and diffident with women. I told my mother privately that he was an absolute woman-hater; so, of course, she laid herself out to flirt all she knew, which isn't a little."

"And was the gentleman responsive?"

"I hear he told some one at the club that he was looking out for a Colonial job, with plenty of hard work, for a young friend of his, so I gather that he has some idea of marrying into the family."

"You seem destined to be the victim of the reformation, after all."

Clovis wiped the trace of Turkish coffee and the beginnings of a smile from his lips, and slowly lowered his dexter eyelid. Which, being interpreted, probably meant, "I *don't* think!"

Tobermory

It was a chill, rain-washed afternoon of a late August day, that indefinite season when partridges are still in security or cold storage, and there is nothing to hunt—unless one is bounded on the north by the Bristol Channel, in which case one may lawfully gallop after fat red stags. Lady Blemley's house-party was not bounded on the north by the Bristol Channel, hence there was a full gathering of her guests round the tea-table on this particular afternoon. And, in spite of the blankness of the season and the triteness of the occasion, there was no trace in the company of that fatigued restlessness which means a dread of the pianola and a subdued hankering for auction bridge. The undisguised open-mouthed attention of the entire party was fixed on the homely negative personality of Mr. Cornelius Appin. Of all her guests, he was the one who had come to Lady Blemley with the vaguest reputation. Some one had said he was "clever", and he had got his invitation in the moderate expectation, on the part of his hostess, that some portion at least of his cleverness would be contributed to the general entertainment. Until tea-time that day she had been unable to discover in what direction, if any, his cleverness lay. He was neither a wit nor a croquet champion, a hypnotic force nor a begetter of amateur theatricals. Neither did his exterior suggest the sort of man in whom women are willing to pardon a generous measure of mental deficiency. He had subsided into mere Mr. Appin, and the Cornelius seemed a piece of transparent baptismal bluff. And now he was claiming to have launched on the world a discovery beside which the invention of gunpowder, of the printing-press, and of steam locomotion were inconsiderable trifles. Science had made bewildering strides in many directions during recent decades, but this thing seemed to belong to the domain of miracle rather than to scientific achievement.

"And do you really ask us to believe," Sir Wilfrid was saying, "that you have discovered a means for instructing animals in the art of human speech, and that dear old Tobermory has proved your first successful pupil?"

"It is a problem at which I have worked for the last seventeen years," said Mr. Appin, "but only during the last eight or nine months have I been rewarded with glimmerings of success. Of course I have experimented with thousands of animals, but latterly only with cats, those wonderful creatures which have assimilated themselves so marvellously with our civilization while retaining all their highly developed feral instincts. Here and there among cats one comes across an outstanding superior intellect, just as one does among the ruck of human beings, and when I made the acquaintance of Tobermory a week ago I saw at once that I was in contact with a 'Beyond-cat' of extraordinary intelligence. I had gone far along the road to success in recent experiments; with Tobermory, as you call him, I have reached the goal."

Mr. Appin concluded his remarkable statement in a voice which he strove to divest of a triumphant inflection. No one said "Rats", though Clovis's lips moved in a monosyllabic contortion which probably invoked those rodents of disbelief.

"And do you mean to say," asked Miss Resker, after a slight pause, "that you have taught Tobermory to say and understand easy sentences of one syllable?"

"My dear Miss Resker," said the wonder-worker patiently, "one teaches little children and savages and backward adults in that piecemeal fashion; when one has once solved the problem of making a beginning with an animal of highly developed intelligence one has no need for those halting methods. Tobermory can speak our language with perfect correctness."

This time Clovis very distinctly said, "Beyond-rats!" Sir Wilfrid was more polite, but equally sceptical.

"Hadn't we better have the cat in and judge for ourselves?" suggested Lady Blemley.

Sir Wilfrid went in search of the animal, and the company settled themselves down to the languid expectation of witnessing some more or less adroit drawing-room ventriloquism.

In a minute Sir Wilfrid was back in the room, his face white beneath its tan and his eyes dilated with excitement.

"By Gad, it's true!"

His agitation was unmistakably genuine, and his hearers started forward in a thrill of awakened interest.

Collapsing into an armchair, he continued breathlessly: "I found him dozing in the smoking-room and called out to him to come for his tea. He blinked at me in his usual way, and I said, 'Come on, Toby; don't keep us waiting'; and, by Gad! he drawled out in a most horribly natural voice that he'd come when he dashed well pleased! I nearly jumped out of my skin!"

Appin had preached to absolutely incredulous hearers; Sir Wilfrid's statement carried instant conviction. A Babel-like chorus of startled exclamation arose, amid which the scientist sat mutely enjoying the first fruit of his stupendous discovery.

In the midst of the clamour Tobermory entered the room and made his way with velvet tread and studied unconcern across to the group seated round the tea-table.

A sudden hush of awkwardness and constraint fell on the company. Somehow there seemed an element of embarrassment in addressing on equal terms a domestic cat of acknowledged dental ability.

"Will you have some milk, Tobermory?" asked Lady Blemley in a rather strained voice.

"I don't mind if I do," was the response, couched in a tone of even indifference. A shiver of suppressed excitement went through the listeners, and Lady Blemley might be excused for pouring out the saucerful of milk rather unsteadily.

"I'm afraid I've spilt a good deal of it," she said apologetically.

"After all, it's not my Axminster," was Tobermory's rejoinder.

Another silence fell on the group, and then Miss Resker, in her best district-visitor manner, asked if the human language had been difficult to learn.

Tobermory looked squarely at her for a moment and then fixed his gaze serenely on the middle distance. It was obvious that boring questions lay outside his scheme of life.

"What do you think of human intelligence?" asked Mavis Pellington lamely.

"Of whose intelligence in particular?" asked Tobermory coldly.

"Oh, well, mine for instance," said Mavis, with a feeble laugh.

"You put me in an embarrassing position," said Tobermory, whose tone and attitude certainly did not suggest a shred of embarrassment. "When your inclusion in this house-party was suggested Sir Wilfrid protested that you were the most brainless woman of his acquaintance, and that there was a wide distinction between hospitality and the care of the feeble-minded. Lady Blemley replied that your lack of brain-power was the precise quality which had earned you your invitation, as you were the only person she could think of who might be idiotic enough to buy their old car. You know, the one they call 'The Envy of Sisyphus', because it goes quite nicely up-hill if you push it."

Lady Blemley's protestations would have had greater effect if she had not casually suggested to Mavis only that morning that the car in question would be just the thing for her down at her Devonshire home.

Major Barfield plunged in heavily to effect a diversion.

"How about your carryings-on with the tortoise-shell puss up at the stables, eh?"

The moment he had said it every one realized the blunder.

"One does not usually discuss these matters in public," said Tobermory frigidly. "From a slight observation of your ways since you've been in this house I should imagine you'd find it inconvenient if I were to shift the conversation on to your own little affairs."

The panic which ensued was not confined to the Major.

"Would you like to go and see if cook has got your dinner ready?" suggested Lady Blemley hurriedly, affecting to ignore the fact that it wanted at least two hours to Tobermory's dinner-time.

"Thanks," said Tobermory, "not quite so soon after my tea. I don't want to die of indigestion."

"Cats have nine lives, you know," said Sir Wilfrid heartily.

"Possibly," answered Tobermory; "but only one liver."

"Adelaide!" said Mrs. Cornett, "do you mean to encourage that cat to go out and gossip about us in the servants' hall?"

The panic had indeed become general. A narrow ornamental balustrade ran in front of most of the bedroom windows at the Towers, and it was recalled with dismay that this had formed a favourite prom-enade for Tobermory at all hours, whence he could watch the pigeons—and heaven knew what else besides. If he intended to become reminiscent in his present outspoken strain the effect would be something more than disconcerting. Mrs. Cornett, who spent much time at her toilet table, and whose complexion was reputed to be of a nomadic though punctual dis-position, looked as ill at ease as the Major. Miss Scrawen, who wrote fiercely sensuous poetry and led a blameless life, merely displayed irritation; if you are methodical and virtuous in private you don't necessarily want every one to know it. Bertie van Tahn, who was so depraved at seventeen that he had long ago given up trying to be any worse, turned a dull shade of gardenia white, but he did not commit the error of dashing out of the room like Odo Finsberry, a young gentleman who was understood to be reading for the Church and who was possibly disturbed at the thought of scandals he might hear concerning other people. Clovis had the presence of mind to maintain a composed exterior; privately he was calculating how long it would take to procure a box of fancy mice through the agency of the *Exchange and Mart* as a species of hush-money.

Even in a delicate situation like the present, Agnes Resker could not endure to remain too long in the background.

"Why did I ever come down here?" she asked dramatically.

Tobermory immediately accepted the opening.

"Judging by what you said to Mrs. Cornett on the croquet-lawn yesterday, you were out for food. You described the Blemleys as the dullest people to stay with that you knew, but said they were clever enough to employ a first-rate cook; otherwise they'd find it difficult to get any one to come down a second time."

"There's not a word of truth in it! I appeal to Mrs. Cornett—" exclaimed the discomfited Agnes.

"Mrs. Cornett repeated your remark afterwards to Bertie van Tahn," continued Tobermory, "and said, 'That woman is a regular Hunger Marcher; she'd go

39

anywhere for four square meals a day,' and Bertie van Tahn said—"

At this point the chronicle mercifully ceased. Tobermory had caught a glimpse of the big yellow Tom from the Rectory working his way through the shrubbery towards the stable wing. In a flash he had vanished through the open French window.

With the disappearance of his too brilliant pupil Cornelius Appin found himself beset by a hurricane of bitter upbraiding, anxious inquiry, and frightened entreaty. The responsibility for the situation lay with him, and he must prevent matters from becoming worse. Could Tobermory impart his dangerous gift to other cats? was the first question he had to answer. It was possible, he replied, that he might have initiated his intimate friend the stable puss into his new accomplishment, but it was unlikely that his teaching could have taken a wider range as yet.

"Then," said Mrs. Cornett, "Tobermory may be a valuable cat and a great pet; but I'm sure you'll agree, Adelaide, that both he and the stable cat must be done away with without delay."

"You don't suppose I've enjoyed the last quarter of an hour, do you?" said Lady Blemley bitterly. "My husband and I are very fond of Tobermory—at least, we were before this horrible accomplishment was infused into him; but now, of course, the only thing is to have him destroyed as soon as possible."

"We can put some strychnine in the scraps he always gets at dinner-time," said Sir Wilfrid, "and I will go and drown the stable cat myself. The coachman will be very sore at losing his pet, but I'll say a very catching form of mange has broken out in both cats and we're afraid of its spreading to the kennels."

"But my great discovery!" expostulated Mr. Appin; "after all my years of research and experiment—"

"You can go and experiment on the short-horns at the farm, who are under proper control," said Mrs. Cornett, "or the elephants at the Zoological Gardens. They're said to be highly intelligent, and they have this recommendation, that they don't come creeping about our bedrooms and under chairs, and so forth."

An archangel ecstatically proclaiming the Millennium, and then finding that it clashed unpardonably with Henley and would have to be indefinitely postponed, could hardly have felt more crestfallen than Cornelius Appin at the reception of his wonderful achievement. Public opinion, however, was against him—in fact, had the general voice been consulted on the subject it is probable that a strong minority vote would have been in favour of including him in the strychnine diet.

Defective train arrangements and a nervous desire to see matters brought to a finish prevented an immediate dispersal of the party, but dinner that evening was not a social success. Sir Wilfrid had had rather a trying time with the stable cat and subsequently with the coachman. Agnes Resker ostentatiously limited her repast to a morsel of dry toast, which she bit as though it were a personal enemy; while Mavis Pellington maintained a vindictive silence throughout the meal. Lady Blemley kept up a flow of what she hoped was conversation, but her attention was fixed on the doorway. A plateful of carefully dosed fish scraps was in readiness on the sideboard, but sweets and savoury and dessert went their way, and no Tobermory appeared either in the dining-room or kitchen.

The sepulchral dinner was cheerful compared with the subsequent vigil in the smoking-room. Eating and drinking had at least supplied a distraction and cloak to the prevailing embarrassment. Bridge was out of the question in the general tension of nerves and tempers, and after Odo Finsberry had given a lugubrious rendering of "Mélisande in the Wood" to a frigid audience, music was tacitly avoided. At eleven the servants went to bed, announcing that the small window in the pantry had been left open as usual for Tobermory's private use. The guests read steadily through the current batch of magazines, and fell back gradually on the "Badminton Library" and bound volumes of *Punch*. Lady Blemley made periodic visits to the pantry, returning each time with an expression of listless depression which forestalled questioning.

At two o'clock Clovis broke the dominating silence.

"He won't turn up tonight. He's probably in the local newspaper office at the present moment, dictating the first instalment of his reminiscences. Lady What's-her-name's book won't be in it. It will be the event of the day."

Having made this contribution to the general cheerfulness, Clovis went to bed. At long intervals the various members of the house-party followed his example.

The servants taking round the early tea made a uniform announcement in reply to a uniform question. Tobermory had not returned.

Breakfast was, if anything, a more unpleasant

function than dinner had been, but before its conclusion the situation was relieved. Tobermory's corpse was brought in from the shrubbery, where a gardener had just discovered it. From the bites on his throat and the yellow fur which coated his claws it was evident that he had fallen in unequal combat with the big Tom from the Rectory.

By midday most of the guests had quitted the Towers, and after lunch Lady Blemley had sufficiently recovered her spirits to write an extremely nasty letter to the Rectory about the loss of her valuable pet.

Tobermory had been Appin's one successful pupil, and he was destined to have no successor. A few weeks later an elephant in the Dresden Zoological Garden, which had shown no previous signs of irritability, broke loose and killed an Englishman who had apparently been teasing it. The victim's name was variously reported in the papers as Oppin and Eppelin, but his front name was faithfully rendered Cornelius.

"If he was trying German irregular verbs on the poor beast," said Clovis, "he deserved all he got."

Mrs. Packletide's Tiger

It was Mrs. Packletide's pleasure and intention that she should shoot a tiger. Not that the lust to kill had suddenly descended on her, or that she felt that she would leave India safer and more wholesome than she had found it, with one fraction less of wild beast per million of inhabitants. The compelling motive for her sudden deviation towards the footsteps of Nimrod was the fact that Loona Bimberton had recently been carried eleven miles in an aeroplane by an Algerian aviator, and talked of nothing else; only a personally procured tiger-skin and a heavy harvest of Press photographs could successfully counter that sort of thing. Mrs. Packletide had already arranged in her mind the lunch she would give at her house in Curzon Street, ostensibly in Loona Bimberton's honour, with a tiger-skin rug occupying most of the foreground and all of the conversation. She had also already designed in her mind the tiger-claw brooch that she was going to give Loona Bimberton on her next birthday. In a world that is supposed to be chiefly swayed by hunger and by love Mrs. Packletide was an exception; her movements and motives were largely governed by dislike of Loona Bimberton.

Circumstances proved propitious. Mrs. Packletide

had offered a thousand rupees for the opportunity of shooting a tiger without overmuch risk or exertion, and it so happened that a neighbouring village could boast of being the favoured rendezvous of an animal of respectable antecedents, which had been driven by the increasing infirmities of age to abandon game-killing and confine its appetite to the smaller domestic animals. The prospect of earning the thousand rupees had stimulated the sporting and commercial instinct of the villagers; children were posted night and day on the outskirts of the local jungle to head the tiger back in the unlikely event of his attempting to roam away to fresh hunting-grounds, and the cheaper kinds of goats were left about with elaborate carelessness to keep him satisfied with his present quarters. The one great anxiety was lest he should die of old age before the date appointed for the memsahib's shoot. Mothers carrying their babies home through the jungle after the day's work in the fields hushed their singing lest they might curtail the restful sleep of the venerable herd-robber.

The great night duly arrived, moonlit and cloudless. A platform had been constructed in a comfortable and conveniently placed tree, and thereon crouched Mrs. Packletide and her paid companion, Miss Mebbin. A goat, gifted with a particularly persistent bleat, such as even a partially deaf tiger might be reasonably expected to hear on a still night, was tethered at the correct distance. With an accurately sighted rifle and a thumb-nail pack of patience cards the sportswoman awaited the coming of the quarry.

"I suppose we are in some danger?" said Miss Mebbin.

She was not actually nervous about the wild beast, but she had a morbid dread of performing an atom more service than she had been paid for.

"Nonsense," said Mrs. Packletide; "it's a very old tiger. It couldn't spring up here even if it wanted to."

"If it's an old tiger I think you ought to get it cheaper. A thousand rupees is a lot of money."

Louisa Mebbin adopted a protective elder-sister attitude towards money in general, irrespective of nationality or denomination. Her energetic intervention had saved many a rouble from dissipating itself in tips in some Moscow hotel, and francs and centimes clung to her instinctively under circumstances which would have driven them headlong from less sympathetic hands. Her speculations as to the market depreciation of tiger remnants were cut short by the appearance on the scene of the animal itself. As soon as it caught sight of the tethered goat it lay flat on the earth, seemingly less from a desire to take advantage of all available cover than for the purpose of snatching a short rest before commencing the grand attack.

"I believe it's ill," said Louisa Mebbin, loudly in Hindustani, for the benefit of the village headman, who was in ambush in a neighbouring tree.

"Hush!" said Mrs. Packletide, and at that moment the tiger commenced ambling towards his victim.

"Now, now!" urged Miss Mebbin with some excitement; "if he doesn't touch the goat we needn't pay for it." (The bait was an extra.)

The rifle flashed out with a loud report, and the great tawny beast sprang to one side and then rolled over in the stillness of death. In a moment a crowd of excited natives had swarmed on to the scene, and their shouting speedily carried the glad news to the village, where a thumping of tom-toms took up the chorus of triumph. And their triumph and rejoicing found a ready echo in the heart of Mrs. Packletide; already that luncheon-party in Curzon Street seemed immeasurably nearer.

It was Louisa Mebbin who drew attention to the fact that the goat was in death-throes from a mortal bullet-wound, while no trace of the rifle's deadly work could be found on the tiger. Evidently the wrong animal had been hit, and the beast of prey had succumbed to heart-failure, caused by the sudden report of the rifle, accelerated by senile decay. Mrs. Packletide was pardonably annoyed at the discovery; but, at any rate, she was the possessor of a dead tiger, and the villagers, anxious for their thousand rupees, gladly connived at the fiction that she had shot the beast. And Miss Mebbin was a paid companion. Therefore did Mrs. Packletide face the cameras with a light heart, and her pictured fame reached from the pages of the *Texas Weekly Snapshot* to the illustrated Monday supplement of the *Novoe Vremya*. As for Loona Bimberton, she refused to look at an illustrated paper for weeks, and her letter of thanks for the gift of a tiger-claw brooch was a model of repressed emotions. The luncheon-party she declined; there are limits beyond which repressed emotions become dangerous.

From Curzon Street the tiger-skin rug travelled down to the Manor House, and was duly inspected and admired by the county, and it seemed a fitting and appropriate thing when Mrs. Packletide went to the County Costume Ball in the character of Diana. She refused to fall in, however, with Clovis's tempting suggestion of a primeval dance party, at which every one should wear the skins of beasts they had recently slain. "I should be in rather a Baby Bunting condition," confessed Clovis, "with a miserable rabbit-skin or two to wrap up in, but then," he added, with a rather malicious glance at Diana's proportions, "my figure is quite as good as that Russian dancing boy's."

"How amused every one would be if they knew what really happened," said Louisa Mebbin a few days after the ball.

"What do you mean?" asked Mrs. Packletide quickly.

"How you shot the goat and frightened the tiger to death," said Miss Mebbin, with her disagreeably pleasant laugh.

"No one would believe it," said Mrs. Packletide, her face changing colour as rapidly as though it were going through a book of patterns before post-time.

"Loona Bimberton would," said Miss Mebbin. Mrs. Packletide's face settled on an unbecoming shade of greenish white.

"You surely wouldn't give me away?" she asked.

"I've seen a week-end cottage near Dorking that I should rather like to buy," said Miss Mebbin with seeming irrelevance. "Six hundred and eighty, freehold. Quite a bargain, only I don't happen to have the money.

Louisa Mebbin's pretty week-end cottage, christened by her "Les Fauves", and gay in summer-time with its garden borders of tiger-lilies, is the wonder and admiration of her friends.

"It is a marvel how Louisa manages to do it," is the general verdict.

Mrs. Packletide indulges in no more big-game shooting.

"The incidental expenses are so heavy," she confides to inquiring friends.

The Stampeding of Lady Bastable

"It would be rather nice if you would put Clovis up for another six days while I go up north to the Mac-Gregors'," said Mrs. Sangrail sleepily across the breakfast-table. It was her invariable plan to speak in a sleepy, comfortable voice whenever she was unusually keen about anything; it put people off their guard, and they frequently fell in with her wishes before they had realized that she was really asking for anything. Lady Bastable, however, was not so easily taken unawares; possibly she knew that voice and what it betokened—at any rate, she knew Clovis.

She frowned at a piece of toast and ate it very slowly, as though she wished to convey the impression that the process hurt her more than it hurt the toast; but no extension of hospitality on Clovis's behalf rose to her lips.

"It would be a great convenience to me," pursued Mrs. Sangrail, abandoning the careless tone. "I particularly don't want to take him to the MacGregors', and it will only be for six days."

"It will seem longer," said Lady Bastable dismally. "The last time he stayed here for a week—"

"I know," interrupted the other hastily, "but that was nearly two years ago. He was younger then."

"But he hasn't improved," said her hostess; "it's no use growing older if you only learn new ways of misbehaving yourself."

Mrs. Sangrail was unable to argue the point; since Clovis had reached the age of seventeen she had never ceased to bewail his irrepressible waywardness to all her circle of acquaintances, and a polite scepticism would have greeted the slightest hint at a prospective reformation. She discarded the fruitless effort at cajolery and resorted to undisguised bribery.

"If you'll have him here for these six days I'll cancel that outstanding bridge account."

It was only for forty-nine shillings, but Lady Bastable loved shillings with a great, strong love. To lose money at bridge and not to have to pay it was one of those rare experiences which gave the card-table a glamour in her eyes which it could never otherwise have possessed. Mrs. Sangrail was almost equally devoted to her card winnings, but the prospect of conveniently warehousing her offspring for six days, and incidentally saving his railway fare to the north, reconciled her to the sacrifice; when Clovis made a belated appearance at the breakfast-table the bargain had been struck.

"Just think," said Mrs. Sangrail sleepily; "Lady Bastable has very kindly asked you to stay on here while I go to the MacGregors'."

Clovis said suitable things in a highly unsuitable manner, and proceeded to make punitive expeditions among the breakfast dishes with a scowl on his face that would have driven the purr out of a peace conference. The arrangement that had been concluded behind his back was doubly distasteful to him. In the first place, he particularly wanted to teach the MacGregor boys, who could well afford the knowledge, how to play poker-patience; secondly, the Bastable catering was of the kind that is classified as a rude plenty, which Clovis translated as a plenty that gives rise to rude remarks. Watching him from behind ostentatiously sleepy lids, his mother realized, in the light of long experience, that any rejoicing over the success of her manoeuvre would be distinctly premature. It was one thing to fit Clovis into a convenient niche of the domestic jigsaw puzzle; it was quite another matter to get him to stay there.

Lady Bastable was wont to retire in state to the morning room immediately after breakfast and spend a quiet hour in skimming through the papers; they were there, so she might as well get their money's worth out of them. Politics did not greatly interest her, but she was obsessed with a favourite foreboding that one of these days there would be a great social upheaval, in which everybody would be killed by everybody else. "It will come sooner than we think," she would observe darkly; a mathematical expert of exceptionally high powers would have been puzzled to work out the approximate date from the slender and confusing groundwork which this assertion afforded.

On this particular morning the sight of Lady Bastable enthroned among her papers gave Clovis the hint towards which his mind had been groping all breakfast time. His mother had gone upstairs to supervise packing operations, and he was alone on the ground-floor with his hostess—and the servants. The latter were the key to the situation. Bursting wildly into the kitchen quarters, Clovis screamed a frantic though strictly non-committal summons: "Poor Lady Bastable! In the morning room! Oh, quick!" The next moment the butler, cook, page-boy, two or three maids, and a gardener who had happened to be in one of the outer kitchens were following in a hot scurry after Clovis as he headed back for the morning room. Lady Bastable was roused from the world of newspaper lore by hearing a Japanese screen in the hall go down with a crash. Then the door leading from the hall flew open and her young guest tore madly through the room, shrieked at her in passing, "The jacquerie! They're on us!" and dashed like an escaping hawk out through the French window. The scared mob of servants burst in on his heels, the gardener still clutching the sickle with which he had been trimming hedges, and the impetus of their headlong haste carried them, slipping and sliding, over the smooth parquet flooring towards the chair where their mistress sat in panic-stricken amazement. If she had had a moment granted her for reflection she would have behaved, as she afterwards explained, with considerable dignity. It was probably the sickle which decided her, but anyway she followed the lead that Clovis had given her through the French window, and ran well and far across the lawn before the eyes of her astonished retainers.

Lost dignity is not a possession which can be restored at a moment's notice, and both Lady Bastable and the butler found the process of returning to normal conditions almost as painful as a slow recovery from drowning. A jacquerie, even if carried out with the most respectful of intentions, cannot fail to leave some traces of embarrassment behind it. By lunch-time, however, decorum had reasserted itself with enhanced rigour as a natural rebound from its recent overthrow, and the meal was served in a frigid stateliness that might have been framed on a Byzantine model. Half-way through its duration Mrs. Sangrail was solemnly presented with an envelope lying on a silver salver. It contained a cheque for forty-nine shillings.

The MacGregor boys learned how to play poker-patience; after all, they could afford to.

The Unrest-Cure

On the rack in the railway carriage immediately opposite Clovis was a solidly wrought travelling bag, with a carefully written label, on which was inscribed, "J. P. Huddle, The Warren, Tilfield, near Slowborough." Immediately below the rack sat the human embodiment of the label, a solid, sedate individual, sedately dressed, sedately conversational. Even without his conversation (which was addressed to a friend seated by his side, and touched chiefly on such topics as the backwardness of Roman hyacinths and the prevalence of measles at the Rectory), one could have gauged fairly accurately the temperament and mental outlook of the travelling bag's owner. But he seemed unwilling to leave anything to the imagination of a casual observer, and his talk grew presently personal and introspective.

"I don't know how it is," he told his friend, "I'm not much over forty, but I seem to have settled down into a deep groove of elderly middle age. My sister shows the same tendency. We like everything to be exactly in its accustomed place; we like things to happen exactly at their appointed times; we like everything to be usual, orderly, punctual, methodical, to a hair's breadth, to a minute. It distresses and upsets us if it is not so. For instance, to take a very trifling matter, a thrush has built its nest year after year in the catkin-tree on the lawn; this year, for no obvious reason, it is building in the ivy on the garden wall. We have said very little about it, but I think we both feel that the change is unnecessary, and just a little irritating."

"Perhaps," said the friend, "it is a different thrush."

"We have suspected that," said J. P. Huddle, "and I think it gives us even more cause for annoyance. We don't feel that we want a change of thrush at our time of life; and yet, as I have said, we have scarcely reached an age when these things should make themselves seriously felt."

"What you want," said the friend, "is an Unrest-cure."

"An Unrest-cure? I've never heard of such a thing."

"You've heard of Rest-cures for people who've broken down under stress of too much worry and strenuous living; well, you're suffering from overmuch repose and placidity, and you need the opposite kind of treatment."

"But where would one go for such a thing?"

"Well, you might stand as an Orange candidate for Kilkenny, or do a course of district visiting in one of the Apache quarters of Paris, or give lectures in Berlin to prove that most of Wagner's music was written by Gambetta; and there's always the interior of Morocco to travel in. But, to be really effective, the Unrest-cure ought to be tried in the home. How you would do it I haven't the faintest idea."

It was at this point in the conversation that Clovis became galvanized into alert attention. After all, his two days' visit to an elderly relative at Slowborough did not promise much excitement. Before the train had stopped he had decorated his sinister shirt-cuff with the inscription, "J. P. Huddle, The Warren, Tilfield, near Slowborough."

Two mornings later Mr. Huddle broke in on his sister's privacy as she sat reading *Country Life* in the morning room. It was her day and hour and place for reading *Country Life*, and the intrusion was absolutely irregular; but he bore in his hand a telegram, and in that household telegrams were recognized as happening by the hand of God. This particular telegram partook of the nature of a thunderbolt. "Bishop examining confirmation class in neighbourhood unable stay rectory on account measles invokes your hospitality sending secretary arrange."

"I scarcely know the Bishop; I've only spoken to him once," exclaimed J. P. Huddle, with the exculpating air of one who realizes too late the indiscretion of speaking to strange Bishops. Miss Huddle was the first to rally; she disliked thunderbolts as fervently as her brother did, but the womanly instinct in her told her that thunderbolts must be fed.

"We can curry the cold duck," she said. It was not the appointed day for curry, but the little orange envelope involved a certain departure from rule and custom. Her brother said nothing, but his eyes thanked her for being brave.

"A young gentleman to see you," announced the parlour-maid.

"The secretary!" murmured the Huddles in unison;

they instantly stiffened into a demeanour which proclaimed that, though they held all strangers to be guilty, they were willing to hear anything they might have to say in their defence. The young gentleman, who came into the room with a certain elegant haughtiness, was not at all Huddle's idea of a bishop's secretary; he had not supposed that the episcopal establishment could have afforded such an expensively upholstered article when there were so many other claims on its resources. The face was fleetingly familiar; if he had bestowed more attention on the fellow-traveller sitting opposite him in the railway carriage two days before he might have recognized Clovis in his present visitor.

"You are the Bishop's secretary?" asked Huddle, becoming consciously deferential.

"His confidential secretary," answered Clovis. "You may call me Stanislaus; my other name doesn't matter. The Bishop and Colonel Alberti may be here to lunch. I shall be here in any case."

It sounded rather like the programme of a Royal visit.

"The Bishop is examining a confirmation class in the neighbourhood, isn't he?" asked Miss Huddle.

"Ostensibly," was the dark reply, followed by a request for a large-scale map of the locality.

Clovis was still immersed in a seemingly profound study of the map when another telegram arrived. It was addressed to "Prince Stanislaus, care of Huddle, The Warren, etc." Clovis glanced at the contents and announced: "The Bishop and Alberti won't be here till late in the afternoon." Then he returned to his scrutiny of the map.

The luncheon was not a very festive function. The

princely secretary ate and drank with fair appetite, but severely discouraged conversation. At the finish of the meal he broke suddenly into a radiant smile, thanked his hostess for a charming repast, and kissed her hand with deferential rapture. Miss Huddle was unable to decide in her mind whether the action savoured of Louis Quatorzian courtliness or the reprehensible Roman attitude towards the Sabine women. It was not her day for having a headache, but she felt that the circumstances excused her, and retired to her room to have as much headache as was possible before the Bishop's arrival. Clovis, having asked the way to the nearest telegraph office, disappeared presently down the carriage drive. Mr. Huddle met him in the hall some two hours later, and asked when the Bishop would arrive.

"He is in the library with Alberti," was the reply.

"But why wasn't I told? I never knew he had come!" exclaimed Huddle.

"No one knows he is here," said Clovis; "the quieter we can keep matters the better. And on no account disturb him in the library. Those are his orders."

"But what is all this mystery about? And who is Alberti? And isn't the Bishop going to have tea?"

"The Bishop is out for blood, not tea."

"Blood!" gasped Huddle, who did not find that the thunderbolt improved on acquaintance.

"Tonight is going to be a great night in the history of Christendom," said Clovis. "We are going to massacre every Jew in the neighbourhood."

"To massacre the Jews!" said Huddle indignantly. "Do you mean to tell me there's a general rising against

59

them?"

"No, it's the Bishop's own idea. He's in there arranging all the details now."

"But—the Bishop is such a tolerant, humane man."

"That is precisely what will heighten the effect of his action. The sensation will be enormous."

That at least Huddle could believe.

"He will be hanged!" he exclaimed with conviction.

"A motor is waiting to carry him to the coast, where a steam yacht is in readiness."

"But there aren't thirty Jews in the whole neighbourhood," protested Huddle, whose brain, under the repeated shocks of the day, was operating with the uncertainty of a telegraph wire during earthquake disturbances.

"We have twenty-six on our list," said Clovis, referring to a bundle of notes. "We shall be able to deal with them all the more thoroughly."

"Do you mean to tell me that you are meditating violence against a man like Sir Leon Birberry," stammered Huddle; "he's one of the most respected men in the country."

"He's down on our list," said Clovis carelessly; "after all, we've got men we can trust to do our job, so we shan't have to rely on local assistance. And we've got some Boy Scouts helping us as auxiliaries."

"Boy Scouts!"

"Yes; when they understood there was real killing to be done they were even keener than the men."

"This thing will be a blot on the Twentieth Century!"

"And your house will be the blotting-pad. Have you realized that half the papers of Europe and the United

States will publish pictures of it? By the way, I've sent some photographs of you and your sister, that I found in the library, to the *Martin* and *Die Woche*; I hope you don't mind. Also a sketch of the staircase; most of the killing will probably be done on the staircase."

The emotions that were surging in J. P. Huddle's brain were almost too intense to be disclosed in speech, but he managed to gasp out: "There aren't any Jews in this house."

"Not at present," said Clovis.

"I shall go to the police," shouted Huddle with sudden energy.

"In the shrubbery," said Clovis, "are posted ten men, who have orders to fire on any one who leaves the house without my signal of permission. Another armed picquet is in ambush near the front gate. The Boy Scouts watch the back premises."

At this moment the cheerful hoot of a motor-horn was heard from the drive. Huddle rushed to the hall door with the feeling of a man half-awakened from a nightmare, and beheld Sir Leon Birberry, who had driven himself over in his car. "I got your telegram," he said; "what's up?"

Telegram? It seemed to be a day of telegrams.

"Come here at once. Urgent. James Huddle," was the purport of the message displayed before Huddle's bewildered eyes.

"I see it all!" he exclaimed suddenly in a voice shaken with agitation, and with a look of agony in the direction of the shrubbery he hauled the astonished Birberry into the house. Tea had just been laid in the hall, but the now thoroughly panic-stricken Huddle dragged his protesting guest upstairs, and in a few minutes' time the entire household had been summoned to that region of momentary safety. Clovis alone graced the tea-table with his presence; the fanatics in the library were evidently too immersed in their monstrous machinations to dally with the solace of teacup and hot toast. Once the youth rose, in answer to the summons of the front-door bell, and admitted Mr. Paul Isaacs, shoemaker and parish councillor, who had also received a pressing invitation to The Warren. With an atrocious assumption of courtesy, which a Borgia could hardly have outdone, the secretary escorted this new captive of his net to the head of the stairway, where his involuntary host awaited him.

And then ensued a long ghastly vigil of watching and waiting. Once or twice Clovis left the house to stroll across to the shrubbery, returning always to the library, for the purpose evidently of making a brief report. Once he took in the letters from the evening postman, and brought them to the top of the stairs with punctilious politeness. After his next absence he came half-way up the stairs to make an announcement.

"The Boy Scouts mistook my signal, and have killed the postman. I've had very little practice in this sort of thing, you see. Another time I shall do better."

The housemaid, who was engaged to be married to the evening postman, gave way to clamorous grief.

"Remember that your mistress has a headache," said J. P. Huddle. (Miss Huddle's headache was worse.)

Clovis hastened downstairs, and after a short visit to the library returned with another message:

"The Bishop is sorry to hear that Miss Huddle has a headache. He is issuing orders that as far as possible no firearms shall be used near the house; any killing that is necessary on the premises will be done with cold steel. The Bishop does not see why a man should not be a gentleman as well as a Christian."

That was the last they saw of Clovis; it was nearly seven o'clock, and his elderly relative liked him to dress for dinner. But, though he had left them for ever, the lurking suggestion of his presence haunted the lower regions of the house during the long hours of the wakeful night, and every creak of the stairway, every rustle of wind through the shrubbery, was fraught with horrible meaning. At about seven next morning the gardener's boy and the early postman finally convinced the watchers that the Twentieth Century was still unblotted.

"I don't suppose," mused Clovis, as an early train bore him townwards, "that they will be in the least grateful for the Unrest-cure."

The Jesting of Arlington Stringham

Arlington Stringham made a joke in the House of Commons. It was a thin House, and a very thin joke; something about the Anglo-Saxon race having a great many angles. It is possible that it was unintentional, but a fellow-member, who did not wish it to be supposed that he was asleep because his eyes were shut, laughed. One or two of the papers noted "a laugh" in brackets, and another, which was notorious for the carelessness of its political news, mentioned "laughter". Things often begin in that way.

"Arlington made a joke in the House last night," said Eleanor Stringham to her mother; "in all the years we've been married neither of us has made jokes, and I don't like it now. I'm afraid it's the beginning of the rift in the lute."

"What lute?" said her mother.

"It's a quotation," said Eleanor.

To say that anything was a quotation was an excellent method, in Eleanor's eyes, for withdrawing it from discussion, just as you could always defend indifferent lamb late in the season by saying "It's mutton."

And, of course, Arlington Stringham continued to tread the thorny path of conscious humour into which Fate had beckoned him.

"The country's looking very green, but, after all, that's what it's there for," he remarked to his wife two days later.

"That's very modern, and I dare say very clever, but I'm afraid it's wasted on me," she observed coldly. If she had known how much effort it had cost him to make the remark she might have greeted it in a kinder spirit. It is the tragedy of human endeavour that it works so often unseen and unguessed.

Arlington said nothing, not from injured pride, but because he was thinking hard for something to say. Eleanor mistook his silence for an assumption of tolerant superiority, and her anger prompted her to a further gibe.

"You had better tell it to Lady Isobel. I've no doubt she would appreciate it."

Lady Isobel was seen everywhere with a fawn-coloured collie at a time when every one else kept nothing but Pekingese, and she had once eaten four green apples at an afternoon tea in the Botanical Gardens, so she was widely credited with a rather unpleasant wit. The censorious said she slept in a hammock and understood Yeats's poems, but her family denied both stories.

"The rift is widening to an abyss," said Eleanor to her mother that afternoon.

"I should not tell that to any one," remarked her mother, after long reflection.

"Naturally, I should not talk about it very much," said Eleanor, "but why shouldn't I mention it to any one?"

"Because you can't have an abyss in a lute. There isn't room."

Eleanor's outlook on life did not improve as the afternoon wore on. The page-boy had brought from the library *By Mere and Wold* instead of *By Mere*

Chance, the book which every one denied having read. The unwelcome substitute appeared to be a collection of nature notes contributed by the author to the pages of some Northern weekly, and when one had been prepared to plunge with disapproving mind into a regrettable chronicle of ill-spent lives it was intensely irritating to read "the dainty yellow-hammers are now with us, and flaunt their jaundiced livery from every bush and hillock". Besides, the thing was so obviously untrue; either there must be hardly any bushes or hillocks in those parts or the country must be fearfully overstocked with yellow-hammers. The thing scarcely seemed worth telling such a lie about. And the page-boy stood there, with his sleekly brushed and parted hair, and his air of chaste and callous indifference to the desires and passions of the world. Eleanor hated boys, and she would have liked to have whipped this one long and often. It was perhaps the yearning of a woman who had no children of her own.

She turned at random to another paragraph. "Lie quietly concealed in the fern and bramble in the gap by the old rowan tree, and you may see, almost every evening during early summer, a pair of lesser whitethroats creeping up and down the nettles and hedge-growth that mask their nesting-place."

The insufferable monotony of the proposed recreation! Eleanor would not have watched the most brilliant performance at His Majesty's Theatre for a single evening under such uncomfortable circumstances, and to be asked to watch lesser whitethroats creeping up and down a nettle "almost every evening" during the height of the season struck her as an imputation on her intelligence that was positively offensive. Impatiently she transferred her attention to the dinner menu, which the boy had thoughtfully brought in as an alternative to the more solid literary fare. "Rabbit curry", met her eye, and the lines of disapproval deepened on her already puckered brow. The cook was a great believer in the influence of environment, and nourished an obstinate conviction that if you brought rabbit and curry-powder together in one dish a rabbit curry would be the result. And Clovis and the odious Bertie van Tahn were coming to dinner. Surely, thought Eleanor, if Arlington knew how much she had had that day to try her, he would refrain from joke-making.

At dinner that night it was Eleanor herself who mentioned the name of a certain statesman, who may be decently covered under the disguise of X.

"X.," said Arlington Stringham, "has the soul of a meringue."

It was a useful remark to have on hand, because it applied equally well to four prominent statesmen of the day, which quadrupled the opportunities for using it.

"Meringues haven't got souls," said Eleanor's mother.

"It's a mercy that they haven't," said Clovis; "they would be always losing them, and people like my aunt would get up missions to meringues, and say it was wonderful how much one could teach them and how much more one could learn from them."

"What could you learn from a meringue?" asked Eleanor's mother.

"My aunt has been known to learn humility from an ex-Viceroy," said Clovis.

"I wish cook would learn to make curry, or have the sense to leave it alone," said Arlington, suddenly and savagely.

Eleanor's face softened. It was like one of his old remarks in the days when there was no abyss between them.

It was during the debate on the Foreign Office vote that Stringham made his great remark that "the people of Crete unfortunately make more history than they can consume locally". It was not brilliant, but it came in the middle of a dull speech, and the House was quite pleased with it. Old gentlemen with bad memories said it reminded them of Disraeli.

It was Eleanor's friend, Gertrude Ilpton, who drew her attention to Arlington's newest outbreak. Eleanor in these days avoided the morning papers.

"It's very modern, and I suppose very clever," she observed.

"Of course it's clever," said Gertrude; "all Lady Isobel's sayings are clever, and luckily they bear repeating."

"Are you sure it's one of her sayings?" asked Eleanor.

"My dear, I've heard her say it dozens of times."

"So that is where he gets his humour," said Eleanor slowly, and the hard lines deepened round her mouth.

The death of Eleanor Stringham from an overdose of chloral, occurring at the end of a rather uneventful season, excited a certain amount of unobtrusive speculation. Clovis, who perhaps exaggerated the importance of curry in the home, hinted at domestic sorrow.

And of course Arlington never knew. It was the tragedy of his life that he should miss the fullest effect of his jesting.

Adrian

His baptismal register spoke of him pessimistically as John Henry, but he had left that behind with the other maladies of infancy, and his friends knew him under the front-name of Adrian. His mother lived in Bethnal Green, which was not altogether his fault; one can discourage too much history in one's family, but one cannot always prevent geography. And, after all, the Bethnal Green habit has this virtue—that it is seldom transmitted to the next generation. Adrian lived in a roomlet which came under the auspicious constellation of W.

How he lived was to a great extent a mystery even to himself; his struggle for existence probably coincided in many material details with the rather dramatic accounts he gave of it to sympathetic acquaintances. All that is definitely known is that he now and then emerged from the struggle to dine at the Ritz or Carlton, correctly garbed and with a correctly critical appetite. On these occasions he was usually the guest of Lucas Croyden, an amiable worldling, who had three thousand a year and a taste for introducing impossible people to irreproachable cookery. Like most men who combine three thousand a year with an uncertain digestion, Lucas was a Socialist, and he argued that you cannot

hope to elevate the masses until you have brought
plovers' eggs into their lives and taught them to
appreciate the difference between coupe Jacques and
Macédoine de fruits. His friends pointed out that it was
a doubtful kindness to initiate a boy from behind a
drapery counter into the blessedness of the higher
catering, to which Lucas invariably replied that all
kindnesses were doubtful. Which was perhaps true.

It was after one of his Adrian evenings that Lucas
met his aunt, Mrs. Mebberley, at a fashionable teashop,
where the lamp of family life is still kept burning and
you meet relatives who might otherwise have slipped
your memory.

"Who was that good-looking boy who was dining
with you last night?" she asked. "He looked much too
nice to be thrown away upon you."

Susan Mebberley was a charming woman, but she
was also an aunt.

"Who are his people?" she continued, when the
protégé's name (revised version) had been given her.

"His mother lives at Beth—"

Lucas checked himself on the threshold of what was
perhaps a social indiscretion.

"Beth? Where is it? It sounds like Asia Minor. Is she
mixed up with Consular people?"

"Oh, no. Her work lies among the poor."

This was a side-slip into truth. The mother of Adrian
was employed in a laundry.

"I see," said Mrs. Mebberley, "mission work of some
sort. And meanwhile the boy has no one to look after
him. It's obviously my duty to see that he doesn't come
to harm. Bring him to call on me."

"My dear Aunt Susan," expostulated Lucas, "I really know very little about him. He may not be at all nice, you know, on further acquaintance."

"He has delightful hair and a weak mouth. I shall take him with me to Homburg or Cairo."

"It's the maddest thing I ever heard of," said Lucas angrily.

"Well, there is a strong strain of madness in our family. If you haven't noticed it yourself all your friends must have."

"One is so dreadfully under everybody's eyes at Homburg. At least you might give him a preliminary trial at Etretat."

"And be surrounded by Americans trying to talk French? No, thank you. I love Americans, but not when they try to talk French. What a blessing it is that they never try to talk English. Tomorrow at five you can bring your young friend to call on me."

And Lucas, realizing that Susan Mebberley was a woman as well as an aunt, saw that she would have to be allowed to have her own way.

Adrian was duly carried abroad under the Mebberley wing; but as a reluctant concession to sanity Homburg and other inconveniently fashionable resorts were given a wide berth, and the Mebberley establishment planted itself down in the best hotel at Dohledorf, an Alpine townlet somewhere at the back of the Engadine. It was the usual kind of resort, with the usual type of visitors, that one finds over the greater part of Switzerland during the summer season, but to Adrian it was all unusual. The mountain air, the certainty of regular and abundant meals, and in particular the social atmosphere, affected him much as the undiscriminating fervour of a forcing-house might affect a weed that had strayed within its limits. He had been brought up in a world where breakages were regarded as crimes and expiated as such; it was something new and altogether exhilarating to find that you were considered rather amusing if you smashed things in the right manner and at the recognized hours. Susan Mebberley had expressed the intention of showing Adrian a bit of the world; the particular bit of the world represented by Dohledorf began to be shown a good deal of Adrian.

Lucas got occasional glimpses of the Alpine sojourn, not from his aunt or Adrian, but from the industrious pen of Clovis, who was also moving as a satellite in the Mebberley constellation.

"The entertainment which Susan got up last night ended in disaster. I thought it would. The Grobmayer child, a particularly loathsome five-year-old, had appeared as 'Bubbles' during the early part of the evening, and been put to bed during the interval. Adrian watched his opportunity and kidnapped it when the nurse was downstairs, and introduced it during the second half of the entertainment, thinly disguised as a performing pig. It certainly *looked* very like a pig, and grunted and slobbered just like the real article; no one knew exactly what it was, but every one said it was awfully clever, especially the Grobmayers. At the third curtain Adrian pinched it too hard, and it yelled 'Marmar!' I am supposed to be good at descriptions, but don't ask me to describe the sayings and doings of the Grobmayers at that moment; it was like one of the angrier Psalms set to Strauss's music. We have moved to an hotel higher up the valley."

Clovis's next letter arrived five days later, and was written from the Hotel Steinbock.

"We left the Hotel Victoria this morning. It was fairly comfortable and quiet—at least there was an air of repose about it when we arrived. Before we had been in residence twenty-four hours most of the repose had vanished 'like a dutiful bream', as Adrian expressed it. However, nothing unduly outrageous happened till last night, when Adrian had a fit of insomnia and amused himself by unscrewing and transposing all the bedroom numbers on his floor. He transferred the bathroom label to the adjoining bedroom door, which happened to be that of Frau Hofrath Schilling, and this morning from seven o'clock onwards the old lady had a stream of involuntary visitors; she was too horrified and scandalized it seems to get up and lock her door. The would-be bathers flew back in confusion to their rooms, and, of course, the change of numbers led them astray again, and the corridor gradually filled with panic-stricken, scantily robed humans, dashing wildly about like rabbits in a ferret-infested warren. It took nearly an hour before the guests were all sorted into their respective rooms, and Frau Hofrath's condition was still causing some anxiety when we left. Susan is beginning to look a little worried. She can't very well turn the boy adrift, as he hasn't got any money, and she can't send him to his people as she doesn't know where they are. Adrian says his mother moves about a good deal and he's lost her address. Probably, if the truth were known, he's had a row at home. So many boys nowadays seem to think that quarrelling with one's family is a recognized occupation."

Lucas's next communication from the travellers took the form of a telegram from Mrs. Mebberley herself. It was sent "reply prepaid", and consisted of a single sentence: "In Heaven's name, where is Beth?"

The Chaplet

A strange stillness hung over the restaurant; it was one of those rare moments when the orchestra was not discoursing the strains of the Ice-cream Sailor waltz.

"Did I ever tell you," asked Clovis of his friend, "the tragedy of music at mealtimes?

"It was a gala evening at the Grand Sybaris Hotel, and a special dinner was being served in the Amethyst dining-hall. The Amethyst dining-hall had almost a European reputation, especially with that section of Europe which is historically identified with the Jordan Valley. Its cooking was beyond reproach, and its orchestra was sufficiently highly salaried to be above criticism. Thither came in shoals the intensely musical and the almost intensely musical, who are very many, and in still greater numbers the merely musical, who know how Tschaikowsky's name is pronounced and can recognize several of Chopin's nocturnes if you give them due warning; these eat in the nervous, detached manner of roebuck feeding in the open, and keep anxious ears cocked towards the orchestra for the first hint of a recognizable melody.

"'Ah, yes, Pagliacci,' they murmur, as the opening strains follow hot upon the soup, and if no contradiction is forthcoming from any better-informed quarter they break forth into subdued humming by way of supplementing the efforts of the musicians. Sometimes the melody starts on level terms with the soup, in which case the banqueters contrive somehow to hum between the spoonfuls; the facial expression of enthusiasts who are punctuating potage St. Germain with Pagliacci is not beautiful, but it should be seen by those who are bent on observing all sides of life. One cannot discount the unpleasant things of this world merely by looking the other way.

"In addition to the aforementioned types the restaurant was patronized by a fair sprinkling of the absolutely non-musical; their presence in the dining-hall could only be explained on the supposition that they had come there to dine.

"The earlier stages of the dinner had worn off. The wine lists had been consulted, by some with the blank embarrassment of a schoolboy suddenly called on to locate a Minor Prophet in the tangled hinterland of the Old Testament, by others with the severe scrutiny which suggests that they have visited most of the higher-priced wines in their own homes and probed their family weaknesses. The diners who chose their wine in the latter fashion always gave their orders in a penetrating voice, with a plentiful garnishing of stage directions. By insisting on having your bottle pointing to the north when the cork is being drawn, and calling the waiter Max, you may induce an impression on your guests which hours of laboured boasting might be powerless to achieve. For this purpose, however, the guests must be chosen as carefully as the wine.

"Standing aside from the revellers in the shadow of a

massive pillar was an interested spectator who was assuredly of the feast, and yet not in it. Monsieur Aristide Saucourt was the *chef* of the Grand Sybaris Hotel, and if he had an equal in his profession he had never acknowledged the fact. In his own domain he was a potentate, hedged around with the cold brutality that Genius expects rather than excuses in her children; he never forgave, and those who served him were careful that there should be little to forgive. In the outer world, the world which devoured his creations, he was an influence; how profound or how shallow an influence he never attempted to guess. It is the penalty and the safeguard of genius that it computes itself by troy weight in a world that measures by vulgar hundredweights.

"Once in a way the great man would be seized with a desire to watch the effect of his master-efforts, just as the guiding brain of Krupp's might wish at a supreme moment to intrude into the firing line of an artillery duel. And such an occasion was the present. For the first time in the history of the Grand Sybaris Hotel, he was presenting to its guests the dish which he had brought to that pitch of perfection which almost amounts to scandal. Canetons à la mode d'Amblève. In thin gilt lettering on the creamy white of the menu how little those words conveyed to the bulk of the imperfectly educated diners. And yet how much specialized effort had been lavished, how much carefully treasured lore had been ungarnered, before those six words could be written. In the Department of Deux-Sèvres ducklings had lived peculiar and beautiful lives and died in the odour of satiety to furnish the main theme of the dish; champignons, which even a purist for Saxon English would have hesitated to address as mushrooms, had contributed their languorous atrophied bodies to the garnishing, and a sauce devised in the twilight reign of the Fifteenth Louis had been summoned back from the imperishable past to take its part in the wonderful confection. Thus far had human effort laboured to achieve the desired result; the rest had been left to human genius—the genius of Aristide Saucourt.

"And now the moment had arrived for the serving of the great dish, the dish which world-weary Grand Dukes and market-obsessed money magnates counted among their happiest memories. And at the same moment something else happened. The leader of the highly salaried orchestra placed his violin caressingly against his chin, lowered his eyelids, and floated into a sea of melody.

"'Hark!' said most of the diners, 'he is playing "The Chaplet".'

"They knew it was "The Chaplet" because they had heard it played at luncheon and afternoon tea, and at supper the night before, and had not had time to forget.

"'Yes, he is playing "The Chaplet",' they reassured one another. The general voice was unanimous on the subject. The orchestra had already played it eleven times that day, four times by desire and seven times from force of habit, but the familiar strains were greeted with the rapture due to a revelation. A murmur of much humming rose from half the tables in the room, and some of the more overwrought listeners laid down knife and fork in order to be able to burst in with loud clappings at the earliest permissible moment.

"And the Canetons à la mode d'Amblève? In

stupefied, sickened wonder Aristide watched them grow cold in total neglect, or suffer the almost worse indignity of perfunctory pecking and listless munching while the banqueters lavished their approval and applause on the music-makers. Calves' liver and bacon, with parsley sauce, could hardly have figured more ignominiously in the evening's entertainment. And while the master of culinary art leaned back against the sheltering pillar, choking with a horrible brain-searing rage that could find no outlet for its agony, the orchestra leader was bowing his acknowledgments of the hand-clappings that rose in a storm around him. Turning to his colleagues he nodded the signal for an encore. But before the violin had been lifted anew into position there came from the shadow of the pillar an explosive negative.

" 'Noh! Noh! You do not play thot again!'

"The musician turned in furious astonishment. Had he taken warning from the look in the other man's eyes he might have acted differently. But the admiring plaudits were ringing in his ears, and he snarled out sharply, 'That is for me to decide.'

" 'Noh! You play thot never again,' shouted the *chef*, and the next moment he had flung himself violently upon the loathed being who had supplanted him in the world's esteem. A large metal tureen, filled to the brim with steaming soup, had just been placed on a side table in readiness for a late party of diners; before the waiting staff or the guests had time to realize what was happening, Aristide had dragged his struggling victim up to the table and plunged his head deep down into the almost boiling contents of the tureen. At the further end of the room the diners were still spasmodically applauding in view of an encore.

"Whether the leader of the orchestra died from drowning by soup, or from the shock to his professional vanity, or was scalded to death, the doctors were never wholly able to agree. Monsieur Aristide Saucourt, who now lives in complete retirement, always inclined to the drowning theory."

The Quest

An unwonted peace hung over the Villa Elsinore, broken, however, at frequent intervals, by clamorous lamentations suggestive of bewildered bereavement. The Momebys had lost their infant child; hence the peace which its absence entailed; they were looking for it in wild, undisciplined fashion, giving tongue the whole time, which accounted for the outcry which swept through house and garden whenever they returned to try the home coverts anew. Clovis, who was temporarily and unwillingly a paying guest at the villa, had been dozing in a hammock at the far end of the garden when Mrs. Momeby had broken the news to him.

"We've lost Baby," she screamed.

"Do you mean that it's dead, or stampeded, or that you staked it at cards and lost it that way?" asked Clovis lazily.

"He was toddling about quite happily on the lawn," said Mrs. Momeby tearfully, "and Arnold had just come in, and I was asking him what sort of sauce he would like with the asparagus—"

"I hope he said hollandaise," interrupted Clovis, with a show of quickened interest, "because if there's anything I hate—"

"And all of a sudden I missed Baby," continued Mrs.

Momeby in a shriller tone. "We've hunted high and low, in house and garden and outside the gates, and he's nowhere to be seen."

"Is he anywhere to be heard?" asked Clovis; "if not, he must be at least two miles away."

"But where? And how?" asked the distracted mother.

"Perhaps an eagle or a wild beast has carried him off," suggested Clovis.

"There aren't eagles and wild beasts in Surrey," said Mrs. Momeby, but a note of horror had crept into her voice.

"They escape now and then from travelling shows. Sometimes I think they let them get loose for the sake of the advertisement. Think what a sensational headline it would make in the local papers: 'Infant son of prominent Nonconformist devoured by spotted hyæna.' Your husband isn't a prominent Nonconformist, but his mother came of Wesleyan stock, and you must allow the newspapers some latitude."

"But we should have found his remains," sobbed Mrs. Momeby.

"If the hyæna was really hungry and not merely toying with his food there wouldn't be much in the way of remains. It would be like the small-boy-and-apple story—there ain't going to be no core."

Mrs. Momeby turned away hastily to seek comfort and counsel in some other direction. With the selfish absorption of young motherhood she entirely disregarded Clovis's obvious anxiety about the asparagus sauce. Before she had gone a yard, however, the click of the side gate caused her to pull up sharp. Miss Gilpet, from the Villa Peterhof, had come over to hear details of the bereavement. Clovis was already rather bored with the story, but Mrs. Momeby was equipped with that merciless faculty which finds as much joy in the nine-tieth time of telling as in the first.

"Arnold had just come in; he was complaining of rheumatism—"

"There are so many things to complain of in this household that it would never have occurred to me to complain of rheumatism," murmured Clovis.

"He was complaining of rheumatism," continued Mrs. Momeby, trying to throw a chilling inflection into a voice that was already doing a good deal of sobbing and talking at high pressure as well.

She was again interrupted.

"There is no such thing as rheumatism," said Miss Gilpet. She said it with the conscious air of defiance that a waiter adopts in announcing that the cheapest-priced claret in the wine-list is no more. She did not proceed, however, to offer the alternative of some more expensive malady, but denied the existence of them all.

Mrs. Momeby's temper began to shine out through her grief.

"I suppose you'll say next that Baby hasn't really disappeared."

"He has disappeared," conceded Miss Gilpet, "but only because you haven't sufficient faith to find him. It's only lack of faith on your part that prevents him from being restored to you safe and well."

"But if he's been eaten in the meantime by a hyæna and partly digested," said Clovis, who clung affectionately to his wild beast theory, "surely some ill-effects would be noticeable?"

Miss Gilpet was rather staggered by this complication of the question.

"I feel sure that a hyæna has not eaten him," she said lamely.

"The hyæna may be equally certain that it has. You see, it may have just as much faith as you have, and more special knowledge as to the present whereabouts of the baby."

Mrs. Momeby was in tears again. "If you have faith," she sobbed, struck by a happy inspiration, "won't you find our little Erik for us? I am sure you have powers that are denied to us."

Rose-Marie Gilpet was thoroughly sincere in her adherence to Christian Science principles; whether she understood or correctly expounded them the learned in such manners may best decide. In the present case she was undoubtedly confronted with a great opportunity, and as she started forth on her vague search she strenuously summoned to her aid every scrap of faith that she possessed. She passed out into the bare and open high road, followed by Mrs. Momeby's warning, "It's no use going there, we've searched there a dozen times." But Rose-Marie's ears were already deaf to all things save self-congratulation; for sitting in the middle of the highway, playing contentedly with the dust and some faded buttercups, was a white-pinafored baby with a mop of tow-coloured hair tied over one temple with a pale-blue ribbon. Taking first the usual feminine precaution of looking to see that no motor-car was on the distant horizon, Rose-Marie dashed at the child and bore it, despite its vigorous opposition, in through the portals of Elsinore. The child's furious screams had already announced the fact of its discovery, and the almost hysterical parents raced down the lawn to meet their restored offspring. The æsthetic value of the scene was marred in some degree by Rose-Marie's difficulty in holding the struggling infant, which was borne wrong-end foremost towards the agitated bosom of its family. "Our own little Erik come back to us," cried the Momebys in unison; as the child had rammed its fists tightly into its eye-sockets and nothing could be seen of its face but a widely gaping mouth, the recognition was in itself almost an act of faith.

"Is he glad to get back to Daddy and Mummy again?" crooned Mrs. Momeby; the preference which the child was showing for its dust and buttercup distractions was so marked that the question struck Clovis as being unnecessarily tactless.

"Give him a ride on the roly-poly," suggested the father brilliantly, as the howls continued with no sign of early abatement. In a moment the child had been placed astride the big garden roller and a preliminary tug was given to set it in motion. From the hollow depths of the cylinder came an ear-splitting roar, drowning even the vocal efforts of the squalling baby, and immediately afterwards there crept forth a white-pinafored infant with a mop of tow-coloured hair tied over one temple with a pale-blue ribbon. There was no mistaking either the features or the lung-power of the new arrival.

"Our own little Erik," screamed Mrs. Momeby, pouncing on him and nearly smothering him with kisses; "did he hide in the roly-poly to give us all a big fright?"

This was the obvious explanation of the child's

sudden disappearance and equally abrupt discovery. There remained, however, the problem of the interloping baby, which now sat whimpering on the lawn in a disfavour as chilling as its previous popularity had been unwelcome. The Momebys glared at it as though it had wormed its way into their short-lived affections by heartless and unworthy pretences. Miss Gilpet's face took on an ashen tinge as she stared helplessly at the bunched-up figure that had been such a gladsome sight to her eyes a few moments ago.

"When love is over, how little of love even the lover understands," quoted Clovis to himself.

Rose-Marie was the first to break the silence.

"If that is Erik you have in your arms, who is—that?"

"That, I think, is for you to explain," said Mrs. Momeby stiffly.

"Obviously," said Clovis, "it's a duplicate Erik that your powers of faith called into being. The question is: What are you going to do with him?"

The ashen pallor deepened in Rose-Marie's cheeks. Mrs. Momeby clutched the genuine Erik closer to her side, as though she feared that her uncanny neighbour might out of sheer pique turn him into a bowl of gold-fish.

"I found him sitting in the middle of the road," said Rose-Marie weakly.

"You can't take him back and leave him there," said Clovis; "the highway is meant for traffic, not to be used as a lumber-room for disused miracles."

Rose-Marie wept. The proverb "Weep and you weep alone" broke down as badly on application as most of its kind. Both babies were wailing lugubriously, and the parent Momebys had scarcely recovered from their earlier lachrymose condition. Clovis alone maintained an unruffled cheerfulness.

"Must I keep him always?" asked Rose-Marie dolefully.

"Not always," said Clovis consolingly; "he can go into the Navy when he's thirteen." Rose-Marie wept afresh.

"Of course," added Clovis, "there may be no end of a bother about his birth certificate. You'll have to explain matters to the Admiralty, and they're dreadfully hide-bound."

It was rather a relief when a breathless nursemaid from the Villa Charlottenburg over the way came running across the lawn to claim little Percy, who had slipped out of the front gate and disappeared like a twinkling from the high road.

And even then Clovis found it necessary to go in person to the kitchen to make sure about the asparagus sauce.

The Way to the Dairy

The Baroness and Clovis sat in a much-frequented corner of the Park exchanging biographical confidences about the long succession of passers-by.

"Who are those depressed-looking young women who have just gone by?" asked the Baroness; "they have the air of people who have bowed to destiny and are not quite sure whether the salute will be returned."

"Those," said Clovis, "are the Brimley Bomefields. I dare say you would look depressed if you had been through their experiences."

"I'm always having depressing experiences," said the Baroness, "but I never give them outward expression. It's as bad as looking one's age. Tell me about the Brimley Bomefields."

"Well," said Clovis, "the beginning of their tragedy was that they found an aunt. The aunt had been there all the time, but they had very nearly forgotten her existence until a distant relative refreshed their memory by remembering her very distinctly in his will; it is wonderful what the force of example will accomplish. The aunt, who had been unobtrusively poor, became quite pleasantly rich, and the Brimley Bomefields grew suddenly concerned at the loneliness of her life and took her under their collective wings. She had as many wings around her at this time as one of those beast-things in Revelation."

"So far I don't see any tragedy from the Brimley Bomefields' point of view," said the Baroness.

"We haven't got to it yet," said Clovis. "The aunt had been used to living very simply, and had seen next to nothing of what we should consider life, and her nieces didn't encourage her to do much in the way of making a splash with her money. Quite a good deal of it would come to them at her death, and she was a fairly old woman, but there was one circumstance which cast a shadow of gloom over the satisfaction they felt in the discovery and acquisition of this desirable aunt: she openly acknowledged that a comfortable slice of her little fortune would go to a nephew on the other side of her family. He was rather a deplorable thing in rotters, and quite hopelessly top-hole in the way of getting through money, but he had been more or less decent to the old lady in her unremembered days, and she wouldn't hear anything against him. At least, she wouldn't pay any attention to what she did hear, but her nieces took care that she should have to listen to a good deal in that line. It seemed such a pity, they said among themselves, that good money should fall into such worthless hands. They habitually spoke of their aunt's money as 'good money,' as though other people's aunts dabbled for the most part in spurious currency.

"Regularly after the Derby, St. Leger, and other notable racing events they indulged in audible speculations as to how much money Roger had squandered in unfortunate betting transactions.

" 'His travelling expenses must come to a big sum,'

said the eldest Brimley Bomefield one day; 'they say he attends every race-meeting in England, besides others abroad. I shouldn't wonder if he went all the way to India to see the race for the Calcutta Sweepstake that one hears so much about.'

"'Travel enlarges the mind, my dear Christine,' said her aunt.

"'Yes, dear aunt, travel undertaken in the right spirit,' agreed Christine; 'but travel pursued merely as a means towards gambling and extravagant living is more likely to contract the purse than to enlarge the mind. However, as long as Roger enjoys himself, I suppose he doesn't care how fast or unprofitably the money goes, or where he is to find more. It seems a pity, that's all.'

"The aunt by that time had begun to talk of something else, and it was doubtful if Christine's moralizing had been even accorded a hearing. It was her remark, however—the aunt's remark, I mean—about travel enlarging the mind, that gave the youngest Brimley Bomefield her great idea for the showing-up of Roger.

"'If aunt could only be taken somewhere to see him gambling and throwing away money,' she said, 'it would open her eyes to his character more effectually than anything we can say.'

"'My dear Veronique,' said her sisters, 'we can't go following him to race-meetings.'

"'Certainly not to race-meetings,' said Veronique, 'but we might go to some place where one can look on at gambling without taking part in it.'

"'Do you mean Monte Carlo?' they asked her, beginning to jump rather at the idea.

"'Monte Carlo is a long way off, and has a dreadful

90

reputation,' said Veronique; 'I shouldn't like to tell our friends that we were going to Monte Carlo. But I believe Roger usually goes to Dieppe about this time of year, and some quite respectable English people go there, and the journey wouldn't be expensive. If aunt could stand the Channel crossing the change of scene might do her a lot of good.'

"And that was how the fateful idea came to the Brimley Bomefields.

"From the very first set-off disaster hung over the expedition, as they afterwards remembered. To begin with, all the Brimley Bomefields were extremely unwell during the crossing, while the aunt enjoyed the sea air and made friends with all manner of strange travelling companions. Then, although it was many years since she had been on the Continent, she had served a very practical apprenticeship there as a paid companion, and her knowledge of colloquial French beat theirs to a standstill. It became increasingly difficult to keep under their collective wings a person who knew what she wanted and was able to ask for it and to see that she got it. Also, as far as Roger was concerned, they drew Dieppe blank; it turned out that he was staying at Pourville, a little watering-place a mile or two further west. The Brimley Bomefields discovered that Dieppe was too crowded and frivolous, and persuaded the old lady to migrate to the comparative seclusion of Pourville.

"'You won't find it dull, you know,' they assured her; 'there is a little casino attached to the hotel, and you can watch the people dancing and throwing away their money at *petits chevaux*.'

"It was just before *petits chevaux* had been supplanted by *boule*.

"Roger was not staying in the same hotel, but they knew that the casino would be certain of his patronage on most afternoons and evenings.

"On the first evening of their visit they wandered into the casino after a fairly early dinner, and hovered near the tables. Bertie van Tahn was staying there at the time, and he described the whole incident to me. The Brimley Bomefields kept a furtive watch on the doors as though they were expecting some one to turn up, and the aunt got more and more amused and interested watching the little horses whirl round and round the board.

" 'Do you know, poor little number eight hasn't won for the last thirty-two times,' she said to Christine; 'I've been keeping count. I shall really have to put five francs on him to encourage him.'

" 'Come and watch the dancing, dear,' said Christine nervously. It was scarcely a part of their strategy that Roger should come in and find the old lady backing her fancy at the *petits chevaux* table.

" 'Just wait while I put five francs on number eight,' said the aunt, and in another moment her money was lying on the table. The horses commenced to move round; it was a slow race this time, and number eight crept up at the finish like some crafty demon and placed his nose just a fraction in front of number three, who had seemed to be winning easily. Recourse had to be had to measurement, and the number eight was proclaimed the winner. The aunt picked up thirty-five francs. After that the Brimley Bomefields would have had to have used concerted force to get her away from the tables. When

Roger appeared on the scene she was fifty-two francs to the good; her nieces were hovering forlornly in the background, like chickens that have been hatched out by a duck and are despairingly watching their parent disporting herself in a dangerous and uncongenial element. The supper-party which Roger insisted on standing that night in honour of his aunt and the three Miss Brimley Bomefields was remarkable for the unrestrained gaiety of two of the participants and the funereal mirthlessness of the remaining guests.

"'I do not think,' Christine confided afterwards to a friend, who re-confided it to Bertie van Tahn, 'that I shall ever be able to touch *pâté de foie gras* again. It would bring back memories of that awful evening.'

"For the next two or three days the nieces made plans for returning to England or moving on to some other resort where there was no casino. The aunt was busy making a system for winning at *petits chevaux*. Number eight, her first love, had been running rather unkindly for her, and a series of plunges on number five had turned out even worse.

"'Do you know, I dropped over seven hundred francs at the tables this afternoon,' she announced cheerfully at dinner on the fourth evening of their visit.

"'Aunt! Twenty-eight pounds! And you were losing last night too.'

"'Oh, I shall get it all back,' she said optimistically; 'but not here. These silly little horses are no good. I shall go somewhere where one can play comfortably at roulette. You needn't look so shocked. I've always felt that, given the opportunity, I should be an inveterate gambler, and now you darlings have put the opportunity in my way. I must drink your very good healths. Waiter, a bottle of *Pontet Canet*. Ah, it's number seven on the wine list; I shall plunge on number seven tonight. It won four times running this afternoon when I was backing that silly number five.'

"Number seven was not in a winning mood that evening. The Brimley Bomefields, tired of watching disaster from a distance, drew near to the table where their aunt was now an honoured habituée, and gazed mournfully at the successive victories of one and five and eight and four, which swept 'good money' out of the purse of seven's obstinate backer. The day's losses totalled something very near two thousand francs.

" 'You incorrigible gamblers,' said Roger chaffingly to them, when he found them at the tables.

" 'We are not gambling,' said Christine freezingly; 'we are looking on.'

" 'I *don't* think,' said Roger knowingly; 'of course you're a syndicate and aunt is putting the stakes on for all of you. Any one can tell by your looks when the wrong horse wins that you've got a stake on.'

"Aunt and nephew had supper alone that night, or at least they would have if Bertie hadn't joined them; all the Brimley Bomefields had headaches.

"The aunt carried them all off to Dieppe the next day and set cheerily about the task of winning back some of her losses. Her luck was variable; in fact, she had some fair streaks of good fortune, just enough to keep her thoroughly amused with her new distraction; but on the whole she was a loser. The Brimley Bome-fields had a collective attack of nervous prostration on the day when she sold out a quantity of shares in

Argentine rails. 'Nothing will ever bring that money back,' they remarked lugubriously to one another.

"Veronique at last could bear it no longer, and went home; you see, it had been her idea to bring the aunt on this disastrous expedition, and though the others did not cast the fact verbally in her face, there was a certain lurking reproach in their eyes which was harder to meet than actual upbraidings. The other two remained behind, forlornly mounting guard over their aunt until such time as the waning of the Dieppe season should at last turn her in the direction of home and safety. They made anxious calculations as to how little 'good money' might, with reasonable luck, be squandered in the meantime. Here, however, their reckoning went far astray; the close of the Dieppe season merely turned their aunt's thoughts in search of some other convenient gambling resort. 'Show a cat the way to the dairy——' I forget how the proverb goes on, but it summed up the situation as far as the Brimley Bomefields' aunt was concerned. She had been introduced to unexplored pleasures, and found them greatly to her liking, and she was in no hurry to forgo the fruits of her newly acquired knowledge. You see, for the first time in her life the old thing was thoroughly enjoying herself; she was losing money, but she had plenty of fun and excitement over the process, and she had enough left to do very comfortably on. Indeed, she was only just learning to understand the art of doing oneself well. She was a popular hostess, and in return her fellow-gamblers were always ready to entertain her to dinners and suppers when their luck was in. Her nieces, who still remained in attendance on her, with the pathetic unwillingness of a crew to leave a foundering treasure

95

ship which might yet be steered into port, found little pleasure in these Bohemian festivities; to see 'good money' lavished on good living for the entertainment of a nondescript circle of acquaintances who were not likely to be in any way socially useful to them, did not attune them to a spirit of revelry. They contrived, whenever possible, to excuse themselves from participation in their aunt's deplored gaieties; the Brimley Bomefield headaches became famous.

"And one day the nieces came to the conclusion that, as they would have expressed it, 'no useful purpose would be served' by their continued attendance on a relative who had so thoroughly emancipated herself from the sheltering protection of their wings. The aunt bore the announcement of their departure with a cheerfulness that was almost disconcerting.

" 'It's time you went home and had those headaches seen to by a specialist,' was her comment on the situation.

"The homeward journey of the Brimley Bomefields was a veritable retreat from Moscow, and what made it the more bitter was the fact that the Moscow, in this case, was not overwhelmed with fire and ashes, but merely extravagantly over-illuminated.

"From mutual friends and acquaintances they sometimes get glimpses of their prodigal relative, who has settled down into a confirmed gambling maniac, living on such salvage of income as obliging moneylenders have left at her disposal.

"So you need not be surprised," concluded Clovis, "if they do wear a depressed look in public."

"Which is Veronique?" asked the Baroness.

"The most depressed-looking of the three," said Clovis.

The Talking-Out of Tarrington

"Heavens!" exclaimed the aunt of Clovis, "here's some one I know bearing down on us. I can't remember his name, but he lunched with us once in Town. Tarrington—yes, that's it. He's heard of the picnic I'm giving for the Princess, and he'll cling to me like a life belt till I give him an invitation; then he'll ask if he may bring all his wives and mothers and sisters with him. That's the worst of these small watering-places; one can't escape from anybody."

"I'll fight a rearguard action for you if you like to do a bolt now," volunteered Clovis; "you've a clear ten yards start if you don't lose time."

The aunt of Clovis responded gamely to the suggestion, and churned away like a Nile steamer, with a long brown ripple of Pekingese spaniel trailing in her wake.

"Pretend you don't know him," was her parting advice, tinged with the reckless courage of the non-combatant.

The next moment the overtures of an affably disposed gentleman were being received by Clovis with a "silent-upon-a-peak-in-Darien" stare which denoted an absence of all previous acquaintance with the object scrutinized.

"I expect you don't know me with my moustache," said the new-comer; "I've only grown it during the last two months."

"On the contrary," said Clovis, "the moustache is the only thing about you that seemed familiar to me. I felt certain that I had met it somewhere before."

"My name is Tarrington," resumed the candidate for recognition.

"A very useful kind of name," said Clovis; "with a name of that sort no one would blame you if you did nothing in particular heroic or remarkable, would they? And yet if you were to raise a troop of light horse in a moment of national emergency, 'Tarrington's Light Horse' would sound quite appropriate and pulse-quickening; whereas if you were called Spoopin, for instance, the thing would be out of the question. No one, even in a moment of national emergency, could possibly belong to Spoopin's Horse."

The new-comer smiled weakly, as one who is not to be put off by mere flippancy, and began again with patient persistence:

"I think you ought to remember my name—"

"I shall," said Clovis, with an air of immense sincerity. "My aunt was asking me only this morning to suggest names for four young owls she's just had sent her as pets. I shall call them all Tarrington; then if one or two of them die or fly away, or leave us in any of the ways that pet owls are prone to, there will be always one or two left to carry on your name. And my aunt won't *let* me forget it; she will always be asking 'Have the Tarringtons had their mice?' and questions of that sort. She says if you keep wild creatures in captivity you ought to see after their wants, and of course she's quite right there."

"I met you at luncheon at your aunt's house once—" broke in Mr. Tarrington, pale but still resolute.

"My aunt never lunches," said Clovis; "she belongs to the National Anti-Luncheon League, which is doing quite a lot of good work in a quiet, unobtrusive way. A subscription of half a crown per quarter entitles you to go without ninety-two luncheons."

"This must be something new," exclaimed Tarrington.

"It's the same aunt that I've always had," said Clovis coldly.

"I perfectly well remember meeting you at a luncheon party given by your aunt," persisted Tarrington, who was beginning to flush an unhealthy shade of mottled pink.

"What was there for lunch?" asked Clovis.

"Oh, well, I don't remember that—"

"How nice of you to remember my aunt when you can no longer recall the names of the things you ate. Now my memory works quite differently. I can remember a menu long after I've forgotten the hostess that accompanied it. When I was seven years old I recollect being given a peach at a garden-party by some Duchess or other; I can't remember a thing about her, except that I imagine our acquaintance must have been of the slightest, as she called me a 'nice little boy', but I have unfading memories of that peach. It was one of those exuberant peaches that meet you halfway, so to speak, and are all over you in a moment. It was a beautiful unspoiled product of a hothouse, and yet it managed quite successfully to give itself the airs of a compote. You had to bite it and imbibe it at the same time. To me there has always been something charming and mystic in the thought of that delicate velvet globe of fruit, slowly ripening and warming to perfection through the long summer days and perfumed nights, and then coming suddenly athwart my life in the supreme moment of its existence. I can never forget it, even if I wished to. And when I had devoured all that was edible of it, there still remained the stone, which a heedless, thoughtless child would doubtless have thrown away; I put it down the neck of a young friend who was wearing a very *décolleté* sailor suit. I told him it was a scorpion, and from the way he wriggled and screamed he evidently believed it, though where the silly kid imagined I could procure a live scorpion at a garden-party I don't know. Altogether, that peach is for me an unfading and happy memory—"

The defeated Tarrington had by this time retreated out of earshot, comforting himself as best he might with the reflection that a picnic which included the presence of Clovis might prove a doubtfully agreeable experience.

"I shall certainly go in for a Parliamentary career," said Clovis to himself as he turned complacently to rejoin his aunt. "As a talker-out of inconvenient bills I should be invaluable."

The Secret Sin of Septimus Brope

"Who and what is Mr. Brope?" demanded the aunt of Clovis suddenly.

Mrs. Riversedge, who had been snipping off the heads of defunct roses, and thinking of nothing in particular, sprang hurriedly to mental attention. She was one of those old-fashioned hostesses who consider that one ought to know something about one's guests, and that the something ought to be to their credit.

"I believe he comes from Leighton Buzzard," she observed by way of preliminary explanation.

"In these days of rapid and convenient travel," said Clovis, who was dispersing a colony of green-fly with visitations of cigarette smoke, "to come from Leighton Buzzard does not necessarily denote any great strength of character. It might only mean mere restlessness. Now if he had left it under a cloud, or as a protest against the incurable and heartless frivolity of its inhabitants, that would tell us something about the man and his mission in life."

"What does he do?" pursued Mrs. Troyle magisterially.

"He edits the *Cathedral Monthly*," said her hostess, "and he's enormously learned about memorial brasses and transepts and the influence of Byzantine worship on modern liturgy, and all those sort of things. Perhaps he is just a little bit heavy and immersed in one range of subjects, but it takes all sorts to make a good house-party, you know. You don't find him *too* dull, do you?"

"Dulness I could overlook," said the aunt of Clovis: "what I cannot forgive is his making love to my maid."

"My dear Mrs. Troyle," gasped the hostess, "what an extraordinary idea! I assure you Mr. Brope would not dream of doing such a thing."

"His dreams are a matter of indifference to me; for all I care his slumbers may be one long indiscretion of unsuitable erotic advances, in which the entire servants' hall may be involved. But in his waking hours he shall not make love to my maid. It's no use arguing about it, I'm firm on the point."

"But you must be mistaken," persisted Mrs. Riversedge; "Mr. Brope would be the last person to do such a thing."

"He is the first person to do such a thing, as far as my information goes, and if I have any voice in the matter he certainly shall be the last. Of course, I am not referring to respectably intentioned lovers."

"I simply cannot think that a man who writes so charmingly and informingly about transepts and Byzantine influences would behave in such an unprincipled manner," said Mrs. Riversedge; "what evidence have you that he's doing anything of the sort? I don't want to doubt your word, of course, but we mustn't be too ready to condemn him unheard, must we?"

"Whether we condemn him or not, he has certainly not been unheard. He has the room next to my dressing-room, and on two occasions, when I dare say he thought I was absent, I have plainly heard him announcing through the wall, 'I love you, Florrie.' Those partition walls upstairs are very thin; one can almost hear a watch ticking in the next room."

"Is your maid called Florence?"

"Her name is Florinda."

"What an extraordinary name to give a maid!"

"I did not give it to her; she arrived in my service already christened."

"What I mean is," said Mrs. Riversedge, "that when I get maids with unsuitable names I call them Jane; they soon get used to it."

"An excellent plan," said the aunt of Clovis coldly; "unfortunately I have got used to being called Jane myself. It happens to be my name."

She cut short Mrs. Riversedge's flood of apologies by abruptly remarking:

"The question is not whether I'm to call my maid Florinda, but whether Mr. Brope is to be permitted to call her Florrie. I am strongly of opinion that he shall not."

"He may have been repeating the words of some song," said Mrs. Riversedge hopefully; "there are lots of those sorts of silly refrains with girls' names," she continued, turning to Clovis as a possible authority on the subject. " 'You mustn't call me Mary—' "

"I shouldn't think of doing so," Clovis assured her; "in the first place, I've always understood that your name was Henrietta; and then I hardly know you well enough to take such a liberty."

"I mean there's a *song* with that refrain," hurriedly explained Mrs. Riversedge, "and there's 'Rhoda, Rhoda kept a pagoda', and 'Maisie is a daisy', and heaps of others. Certainly it doesn't sound like Mr. Brope to be singing such songs, but I think we ought to give him the benefit of the doubt."

"I had already done so," said Mrs. Troyle, "until further evidence came my way."

She shut her lips with the resolute finality of one who enjoys the blessed certainty of being implored to open them again.

"Further evidence!" exclaimed her hostess; "do tell me!"

"As I was coming upstairs after breakfast Mr. Brope was just passing my room. In the most natural way in the world a piece of paper dropped out of a packet that he held in his hand and fluttered to the ground just at my door. I was going to call out to him 'You've dropped something,' and then for some reason I held back and didn't show myself till he was safely in his room. You see it occurred to me that I was very seldom in my room just at that hour, and that Florinda was almost always there tidying up things about that time. So I picked up that innocent-looking piece of paper."

Mrs. Troyle paused again, with the self-applauding air of one who has detected an asp lurking in an apple-charlotte.

Mrs. Riversedge snipped vigorously at the nearest rose bush, incidentally decapitating a Viscountess Folkestone that was just coming into bloom.

"What was on the paper?" she asked.

"Just the words in pencil, 'I love you, Florrie,' and then underneath, crossed out with a faint line, but perfectly plain to read, 'Meet me in the garden by the yew.'"

"There *is* a yew tree at the bottom of the garden," admitted Mrs. Riversedge.

"At any rate he appears to be truthful," commented Clovis.

"To think that a scandal of this sort should be going on under my roof!" said Mrs. Riversedge indignantly.

"I wonder why it is that scandal seems so much worse under a roof," observed Clovis; "I've always regarded it as a proof of the superior delicacy of the cat tribe that it conducts most of its scandals above the slates."

"Now I come to think of it," resumed Mrs. Riversedge, "there are things about Mr. Brope that I've never been able to account for. His income, for instance: he only gets two hundred a year as editor of the *Cathedral Monthly*, and I know that his people are quite poor, and he hasn't any private means. Yet he manages to afford a flat somewhere in Westminster, and he goes abroad to Bruges and those sorts of places every year, and always dresses well, and gives quite nice luncheon-parties in the season. You can't do all that on two hundred a year, can you?"

"Does he write for any other papers?" queried Mrs. Troyle.

"No, you see he specializes so entirely on liturgy and ecclesiastical architecture that his field is rather restricted. He once tried the *Sporting and Dramatic* with an article on church edifices in famous fox-hunting centres, but it wasn't considered of sufficient general interest to be accepted. No, I don't see how he can support himself in his present style merely by what he writes."

"Perhaps he sells spurious transepts to American enthusiasts," suggested Clovis.

"How could you sell a transept?" said Mrs. Riversedge; "such a thing would be impossible."

"Whatever he may do to eke out his income," interrupted Mrs. Troyle, "he is certainly not going to fill in his leisure moments by making love to my maid."

"Of course not," agreed her hostess; "that must be put a stop to at once. But I don't quite know what we ought to do."

"You might put a barbed wire entanglement round the yew tree as a precautionary measure," said Clovis.

"I don't think that the disagreeable situation that has arisen is improved by flippancy," said Mrs. Riversedge; "a good maid is a treasure—"

"I am sure I don't know what I should do without Florinda," admitted Mrs. Troyle; "she understands my hair. I've long ago given up trying to do anything with it myself. I regard one's hair as I regard husbands: as long as one is seen together in public one's private divergences don't matter. Surely that was the luncheon gong."

Septimus Brope and Clovis had the smoking-room to themselves after lunch. The former seemed restless and preoccupied, the latter quietly observant.

"What is a lorry?" asked Septimus suddenly; "I don't mean the thing on wheels, of course I know what that is, but isn't there a bird with a name like that, the larger form of a lorikeet?"

"I fancy it's a lory, with one 'r'," said Clovis lazily, "in which case it's no good to you."

Septimus Brope stared in some astonishment.

"How do you mean, no good to me?" he asked, with more than a trace of uneasiness in his voice.

"Won't rhyme with Florrie," explained Clovis briefly.

Septimus sat upright in his chair, with unmistakable alarm on his face.

"How did you find out? I mean how did you know I was trying to get a rhyme to Florrie?" he asked sharply.

"I didn't know," said Clovis, "I only guessed. When you wanted to turn the prosaic lorry of commerce into a feathered poem flitting through the verdure of a tropical forest, I knew you must be working up a sonnet, and Florrie was the only female name that suggested itself as rhyming with lorry."

Septimus still looked uneasy.

"I believe you know more," he said.

Clovis laughed quietly, but said nothing.

"How much do you know?" Septimus asked desperately.

"The yew tree in the garden," said Clovis.

"There! I felt certain I'd dropped it somewhere. But you must have guessed something before. Look here, you have surprised my secret. You won't give me away, will you? It is nothing to be ashamed of, but it wouldn't do for the editor of the *Cathedral Monthly* to go in openly for that sort of thing, would it?"

"Well, I suppose not," admitted Clovis.

"You see," continued Septimus, "I get quite a decent lot of money out of it. I could never live in the style I do on what I get as editor of the *Cathedral Monthly*."

Clovis was even more startled than Septimus had been earlier in the conversation, but he was better skilled in repressing surprise.

"Do you mean to say you get money out of— Florrie?" he asked.

"Not out of Florrie, as yet," said Septimus; "in fact, I don't mind saying that I'm having a good deal of trouble over Florrie. But there are a lot of others."

Clovis's cigarette went out.

"This is *very* interesting," he said slowly. And then, with Septimus Brope's next words, illumination dawned on him.

"There are heaps of others; for instance:

> "'Cora with the lips of coral,
>   You and I will never quarrel.'

That was one of my earliest successes, and it still brings me in royalties. And then there is—'Esmeralda, when I first beheld her', and 'Fair Teresa, how I love to please her', both of those have been fairly popular. And there is one rather dreadful one," continued Septimus, flushing deep carmine, "which has brought me in more money than any of the others:

> "'Lively little Lucie
>   With her naughty nez retrousee.'

Of course, I loathe the whole lot of them; in fact, I'm rapidly becoming something of a woman-hater under their influence, but I can't afford to disregard the financial aspect of the matter. And at the same time you can understand that my position as an authority on ecclesiastical architecture and liturgical subjects would be weakened, if not altogether ruined, if it once got about that I was the author of 'Cora with the lips of coral' and all the rest of them."

Clovis had recovered sufficiently to ask in a sympathetic, if rather unsteady, voice what was the special trouble with "Florrie".

"I can't get her into lyric shape, try as I will," said Septimus mournfully. "You see, one has to work in a lot of sentimental, sugary compliment with a catchy rhyme, and a certain amount of personal biography or prophecy. They've all of them got to have a long string of past successes recorded about them, or else you've got to foretell blissful things about them and yourself in the future. For instance, there is:

> " 'Dainty little girlie Mavis,
> She is such a rara avis.
> All the money I can save is
> All to be for Mavis mine.'

It goes to a sickening namby-pamby waltz tune, and for months nothing else was sung and hummed in Blackpool and other popular centres."

This time Clovis's self-control broke down badly.

"Please excuse me," he gurgled, "but I can't help it when I remember the awful solemnity of that article of yours that you so kindly read us last night, on the Coptic Church in its relation to early Christian worship."

Septimus groaned.

"You see how it would be," he said; "as soon as people knew me to be the author of that miserable sentimental twaddle, all respect for the serious labours of my life would be gone. I dare say I know more about memorial brasses than any one living, in fact I hope one day to publish a monograph on the subject, but I should be pointed out everywhere as the man whose ditties were in the mouths of nigger minstrels along the entire coast-line of our Island home. Can you wonder that I positively hate Florrie all the time that I'm trying to grind out sugar-coated rhapsodies about her?"

"Why not give free play to your emotions, and be brutally abusive? An uncomplimentary refrain would have an instant success as a novelty if you were sufficiently outspoken."

"I've never thought of that," said Septimus, "and I'm afraid I couldn't break away from the habit of fulsome adulation and suddenly change my style."

"You needn't change your style in the least," said Clovis; "merely reverse the sentiment and keep to the inane phraseology of the thing. If you'll do the body of the song I'll knock off the refrain, which is the thing that principally matters, I believe. I shall charge half-shares in the royalties, and throw in my silence as to your guilty secret. In the eyes of the world you shall still be the man who has devoted his life to the study of transepts and Byzantine ritual; only sometimes, in the long winter evenings, when the wind howls drearily down the chimney and the rain beats against the windows, I shall think of you as the author of 'Cora with the lips of coral'. Of course, if in sheer gratitude at my silence you like to take me for a much-needed holiday to the Adriatic or somewhere equally interesting, paying all expenses, I shouldn't dream of refusing."

Later in the afternoon Clovis found his aunt and Mrs. Riversedge indulging in gentle exercise in the Jacobean garden.

"I've spoken to Mr. Brope about F.," he announced.

"How splendid of you! What did he say?" came in a quick chorus from the two ladies.

"He was quite frank and straightforward with me when he saw that I knew his secret," said Clovis, "and it seems that his intentions were quite serious, if slightly unsuitable. I tried to show him the impracticability of the course that he was following. He said he wanted to be understood, and he seemed to think that Florinda would excel in that requirement, but I pointed out that there were probably dozens of delicately nurtured, pure-hearted young English girls who would be capable of understanding him, while Florinda was the only person in the world who understood my aunt's hair. That rather weighed with him, for he's not really a selfish animal, if you take him in the right way, and when I appealed to the memory of his happy childish days, spent amid the daisied fields of Leighton Buzzard (I suppose daisies do grow there), he was obviously affected. Anyhow, he gave me his word that he would put Florinda absolutely out of his mind, and he has agreed to go for a short trip abroad as the best distraction for his thoughts. I am going with him as far as Ragusa. If my aunt should wish to give me a really nice scarf-pin (to be chosen by myself), as a small recognition of the very considerable service I had done her, I shouldn't dream of refusing. I'm not one of those who think that because one is abroad one can go about dressed anyhow."

A few weeks later in Blackpool and places where they sing, the following refrain held undisputed sway:

"How you bore me, Florrie,

With those eyes of vacant blue;
You'll be very sorry, Florrie,
If I marry you.
Though I'm easy-goin', Florrie,
This I swear is true,
I'll throw you down a quarry, Florrie,
If I marry you."

The Remoulding of Groby Lington

"A man is known by the company he keeps."

In the morning-room of his sister-in-law's house Groby Lington fidgeted away the passing minutes with the demure restlessness of advanced middle age. About a quarter of an hour would have to elapse before it would be time to say his good-byes and make his way across the village green to the station, with a selected escort of nephews and nieces. He was a good-natured, kindly dispositioned man, and in theory he was delighted to pay periodical visits to the wife and children of his dead brother William; in practice, he infinitely preferred the comfort and seclusion of his own house and garden, and the companionship of his books and his parrot to these rather meaningless and tiresome incursions into a family circle with which he had little in common. It was not so much the spur of his own conscience that drove him to make the occasional short journey by rail to visit his relatives, as an obedient concession to the more insistent but vicarious conscience of his brother, Colonel John, who was apt to accuse him of neglecting poor old William's family. Groby usually forgot or ignored the existence of his neighbour kinsfolk until such time as he was threatened with a visit from the Colonel, when he would put matters straight by a hurried pilgrimage across the few miles of intervening country to renew his acquaintance with the young people and assume a kindly if rather forced interest in the well-being of his sister-in-law. On this occasion he had cut matters so fine between the timing of his exculpatory visit and the coming of Colonel John, that he would scarcely be home before the latter was due to arrive. Anyhow, Groby had got it over, and six or seven months might decently elapse before he need again sacrifice his comforts and inclinations on the altar of family sociability. He was inclined to be distinctly cheerful as he hopped about the room, picking up first one object, then another, and subjecting each to a brief bird-like scrutiny.

Presently his cheerful listlessness changed sharply to an attitude of vexed attention. In a scrap-book of drawings and caricatures belonging to one of his nephews he had come across an unkindly clever sketch of himself and his parrot, solemnly confronting each other in postures of ridiculous gravity and repose, and bearing a likeness to one another that the artist had done his utmost to accentuate. After the first flush of annoyance had passed away, Groby laughed good-naturedly and admitted to himself the cleverness of the drawing. Then the feeling of resentment repossessed him, resentment not against the caricaturist who had embodied the idea in pen and ink, but against the possible truth that the idea represented. Was it really the case that people grew in time to resemble the animals they kept as pets, and had he unconsciously become more and more like the comically solemn bird that was his constant companion? Groby was unusually silent as he walked to the train with his escort of chattering nephews and nieces, and during the short railway journey his mind was more and more possessed with an introspective conviction that he had gradually settled down into a sort of parrot-like existence. What, after all, did his daily routine amount to but a sedate meandering and pecking and perching, in his garden, among his fruit trees, in his wicker chair on the lawn, or by the fireside in his library? And what was the sum total of his conversation with chance-encountered neighbours? "Quite a Spring day, isn't it?" "It looks as though we should have some rain." "Glad to see you about again; you must take care of yourself." "How the young folk shoot up, don't they?" Strings of stupid, inevitable perfunctory remarks came to his mind, remarks that were certainly not the mental exchange of human intelligences, but mere empty parrot-talk. One might really just as well salute one's acquaintances with "Pretty Polly. Puss, puss, miaow!" Groby began to fume against the picture of himself as a foolish feathered fowl which his nephew's sketch had first suggested, and which his own accusing imagination was filling in with such unflattering detail.

"I'll give the beastly bird away," he said resentfully; though he knew at the same time that he would do no such thing. It would look so absurd after all the years that he had kept the parrot and made much of it suddenly to try and find it a new home.

"Has my brother arrived?" he asked of the stable-boy, who had come with the pony-carriage to meet him.

"Yessir, came down by the two-fifteen. Your parrot's dead." The boy made the latter announcement with the relish which his class finds in proclaiming a catastrophe.

115

"My parrot dead?" said Groby. "What caused its death?"

"The ipe," said the boy briefly.

"The ipe?" queried Groby. "Whatever's that?"

"The ipe what the Colonel brought down with him," came the rather alarming answer.

"Do you mean to say my brother is ill?" asked Groby. "Is it something infectious?"

"Th' Colonel's so well as ever he was," said the boy; and as no further explanation was forthcoming Groby had to possess himself in mystified patience till he reached home. His brother was waiting for him at the hall door.

"Have you heard about the parrot?" he asked at once. "'Pon my soul I'm awfully sorry. The moment he saw the monkey I'd brought down as a surprise for you he squawked out, 'Rats to you, sir!' and the blessed monkey made one spring at him, got him by the neck and whirled him round like a rattle. He was as dead as mutton by the time I'd got him out of the little beggar's paws. Always been such a friendly little beast, the monkey has, should never have thought he'd got it in him to see red like that. Can't tell you how sorry I feel about it, and now of course you'll hate the sight of the monkey."

"Not at all," said Groby sincerely. A few hours earlier the tragic end which had befallen his parrot would have presented itself to him as a calamity; now it arrived almost as a polite attention on the part of the Fates.

"The bird was getting old, you know," he went on, in explanation of his obvious lack of decent regret at the loss of his pet. "I was really beginning to wonder if it was an unmixed kindness to let him go on living till he succumbed to old age. What a charming little monkey!" he added, when he was introduced to the culprit.

The new-comer was a small, long-tailed monkey from the Western Hemisphere, with a gentle, half-shy, half-trusting manner that instantly captured Groby's confidence; a student of simian character might have seen in the fitful red light in its eyes some indication of the underlying temper which the parrot had so rashly put to the test with such dramatic consequences for itself. The servants, who had come to regard the defunct bird as a regular member of the household, and one who gave really very little trouble, were scandalized to find his bloodthirsty aggressor installed in his place as an honoured domestic pet.

"A nasty heathen ipe what don't never say nothing sensible and cheerful, same as pore Polly did," was the unfavourable verdict of the kitchen quarters.

One Sunday morning, some twelve or fourteen months after the visit of Colonel John and the parrot-tragedy, Miss Wepley sat decorously in her pew in the parish church, immediately in front of that occupied by Groby Lington. She was, comparatively speaking, a new-comer in the neighbourhood, and was not personally acquainted with her fellow-worshipper in the seat behind, but for the past two years the Sunday morning service had brought them regularly within each other's sphere of consciousness. Without having paid particular attention to the subject, she could probably have given a correct rendering of the way in which he pronounced certain words occurring in the responses, while he was well aware of the trivial fact that, in addition to her prayer book and handkerchief, a small paper packet of throat lozenges always reposed on the seat beside her. Miss Wepley rarely had recourse to her lozenges, but in case she should be taken with a fit of coughing she wished to have the emergency duly provided for. On this particular Sunday the lozenges occasioned an unusual diversion in the even tenor of her devotions, far more disturbing to her personally than a prolonged attack of coughing would have been. As she rose to take part in the singing of the first hymn, she fancied that she saw the hand of her neighbour, who was alone in the pew behind her, make a furtive downward grab at the packet lying on the seat; on turning sharply round she found that the packet had certainly disappeared, but Mr. Lington was to all outward seeming serenely intent on his hymn-book. No amount of interrogatory glaring on the part of the despoiled lady could bring the least shade of conscious guilt to his face.

"Worse was to follow," as she remarked afterwards to a scandalized audience of friends and acquaintances. "I had scarcely knelt in prayer when a lozenge, one of *my* lozenges, came whizzing into the pew, just under my nose. I turned round and stared, but Mr. Lington had his eyes closed and his lips moving as though engaged in prayer. The moment I resumed my devotions another lozenge came rattling in, and then another. I took no notice for a while, and then turned round suddenly just as the dreadful man was about to flip another one at me. He hastily pretended to be turning over the leaves of his book, but I was not to be taken in that time. He saw that he had been discovered and no more lozenges came. Of course I have changed my pew."

"No gentleman would have acted in such a disgraceful manner," said one of her listeners; "and yet Mr. Lington used to be so respected by everybody. He seems to have behaved like a little ill-bred schoolboy."

"He behaved like a monkey," said Miss Wepley.

Her unfavourable verdict was echoed in other quarters about the same time. Groby Lington had never been a hero in the eyes of his personal retainers, but he had shared the approval accorded to his defunct parrot as a cheerful, well-dispositioned body, who gave no particular trouble. Of late months, however, this character would hardly have been endorsed by the members of his domestic establishment. The stolid stable-boy, who had first announced to him the tragic end of his feathered pet, was one of the first to give voice to the murmurs of disapproval which became rampant and general in the servants' quarters, and he had fairly substantial grounds for his disaffection. In a burst of hot summer weather he had obtained permission to bathe in a modest-sized pond in the orchard, and thither one afternoon Groby had bent his steps, attracted by loud imprecations of anger mingled with the shriller chattering of monkey-language. He beheld his plump diminutive servitor, clad only in a waistcoat and a pair of socks, storming ineffectually at the monkey which was seated on a low branch of an apple tree, abstractedly fingering the remainder of the boy's outfit, which he had removed just out of his reach.

"The ipe's been an' took my clothes," whined the

boy, with the passion of his kind for explaining the obvious. His incomplete toilet effect rather embarrassed him, but he hailed the arrival of Groby with relief, as promising moral and material support in his efforts to get back his raided garments. The monkey had ceased its defiant jabbering, and doubtless with a little coaxing from its master it would hand back the plunder.

"If I lift you up," suggested Groby, "you will just be able to reach the clothes."

The boy agreed, and Groby clutched him firmly by the waistcoat, which was about all there was to catch hold of, and lifted him clear of the ground. Then, with a deft swing he sent him crashing into a clump of tall nettles, which closed receptively round him. The victim had not been brought up in a school which teaches one to repress one's emotions—if a fox had attempted to gnaw at his vitals he would have flown to complain to the nearest hunt committee rather than have affected an attitude of stoical indifference. On this occasion the volume of sound which he produced under the stimulus of pain and rage and astonishment was generous and sustained, but above his bellowings he could distinctly hear the triumphant chattering of his enemy in the tree, and a peal of shrill laughter from Groby.

When the boy had finished an improvised St. Vitus caracole, which would have brought him fame on the boards of the Coliseum, and which indeed met with ready appreciation and applause from the retreating figure of Groby Lington, he found that the monkey had also discreetly retired, while his clothes were scattered on the grass at the foot of the tree.

"They'm two ipes, that's what they be," he muttered angrily, and if his judgment was severe, at least he spoke under the sting of considerable provocation.

It was a week or two later that the parlour-maid gave notice, having been terrified almost to tears by an outbreak of sudden temper on the part of the master anent some under done cutlets. "'E gnashed 'is teeth at me, 'e did reely," she informed a sympathetic kitchen audience.

"I'd like to see 'im talk like that to me, I would," said the cook defiantly, but her cooking from that moment showed a marked improvement.

It was seldom that Groby Lington so far detached himself from his accustomed habits as to go and form one of a house-party, and he was not a little piqued that Mrs. Glenduff should have stowed him away in the musty old Georgian wing of the house, in the next room, moreover, to Leonard Spabbink, the eminent pianist.

"He plays Liszt like an angel," had been the hostess's enthusiastic testimonial.

"He may play him like a trout for all I care," had been Groby's mental comment, "but I wouldn't mind betting that he snores. He's just the sort and shape that would. And if I hear him snoring through those ridiculous thin-panelled walls, there'll be trouble."

He did, and there was.

Groby stood it for about two and a quarter minutes, and then made his way through the corridor into Spabbink's room. Under Groby's vigorous measures the musician's flabby, redundant figure sat up in bewildered semi-consciousness like an ice-cream that has been taught to beg. Groby prodded him into complete wakefulness, and then the pettish self-satisfied pianist fairly lost his temper and slapped his domineering visitant on the hand. In another moment Spabbink was being nearly stifled and very effectually gagged by a pillow-case tightly bound round his head, while his plump pyjama'd limbs were hauled out of bed and smacked, pinched, kicked, and bumped in a catch-as-catch-can progress across the floor, towards the flat shallow bath in whose utterly inadequate depths Groby perseveringly strove to drown him. For a few moments the room was almost in darkness: Groby's candle had overturned in an early stage of the scuffle, and its flicker scarcely reached to the spot where splashings, smacks, muffled cries, and splutterings, and a chatter of ape-like rage told of the struggle that was being waged round the shores of the bath. A few instants later the one-sided combat was brightly lit up by the flare of blazing curtains and rapidly kindling panelling.

When the hastily aroused members of the house-party stampeded out on to the lawn, the Georgian wing was well alight and belching forth masses of smoke, but some moments elapsed before Groby appeared with the half-drowned pianist in his arms, having just bethought him of the superior drowning facilities offered by the pond at the bottom of the lawn. The cool night air sobered his rage, and when he found that he was innocently acclaimed as the heroic rescuer of poor Leonard Spabbink, and loudly commended for his presence of mind in tying a wet cloth round his head to protect him from smoke suffocation, he accepted the situation, and subsequently gave a graphic account of his finding the musician asleep with an overturned candle by his side and the conflagration well started. Spabbink gave *his* version some days later, when he had partially recovered from the shock of his midnight castigation and immersion, but the gentle pitying smiles and evasive comments with which his story was greeted warned him that the public ear was not at his disposal. He refused, however, to attend the ceremonial presentation of the Royal Humane Society's life-saving medal.

It was about this time that Groby's pet monkey fell a victim to the disease which attacks so many of its kind when brought under the influence of a northern climate. Its master appeared to be profoundly affected by its loss, and never quite recovered the level of spirits that he had recently attained. In company with the tortoise, which Colonel John presented to him on his last visit, he potters about his lawn and kitchen garden, with none of his erstwhile sprightliness; and his nephews and nieces are fairly well justified in alluding to him as "Old Uncle Groby".

The She-Wolf

Leonard Bilsiter was one of those people who have failed to find this world attractive or interesting, and who have sought compensation in an "unseen world" of their own experience or imagination—or invention. Children do that sort of thing successfully, but children are content to convince themselves, and do not vulgarise their beliefs by trying to convince other people. Leonard Bilsiter's beliefs were for "the few", that is to say, any one who would listen to him.

His dabblings in the unseen might not have carried him beyond the customary platitudes of the drawing room visionary if accident had not reinforced his stock-in-trade of mystical lore. In company with a friend, who was interested in a Ural mining concern, he had made a trip across Eastern Europe at a moment when the great Russian railway strike was developing from a threat to a reality; its outbreak caught him on the return journey, somewhere on the further side of Perm, and it was while waiting for a couple of days at a wayside station in a state of suspended locomotion that he made the acquaintance of a dealer in harness and metalware, who profitably whiled away the tedium of the long halt by initiating his English travelling companion in a fragmentary system of folklore that he had picked up from Trans-Baikal traders and natives. Leonard returned to his home circle garrulous about his Russian strike experiences, but oppressively reticent about certain dark mysteries, which he alluded to under the resounding title of Siberian Magic. The reticence wore off in a week or two under the influence of an entire lack of general curiosity, and Leonard began to make more detailed allusions to the enormous powers which this new esoteric force, to use his own description of it, conferred on the initiated few who knew how to wield it. His aunt, Cecilia Hoops, who loved sensation perhaps rather better than she loved the truth, gave him as clamorous an advertisement as any one could wish for by retailing an account of how he had turned a vegetable marrow into a wood pigeon before her very eyes. As a manifestation of the possession of supernatural powers, the story was discounted in some quarters by the respect accorded to Mrs. Hoops's powers of imagination.

However divided opinion might be on the question of Leonard's status as a wonder-worker or a charlatan, he certainly arrived at Mary Hampton's house-party with a reputation for pre-eminence in one or other of those professions, and he was not disposed to shun such publicity as might fall to his share. Esoteric forces and unusual powers figured largely in whatever conversation he or his aunt had a share in, and his own performances, past and potential, were the subject of mysterious hints and dark avowals.

"I wish you would turn me into a wolf, Mr. Bilsiter," said his hostess at luncheon the day after his arrival.

"My dear Mary," said Colonel Hampton, "I never knew you had a craving in that direction."

"A she-wolf, of course," continued Mrs. Hampton; "it would be too confusing to change one's sex as well as one's species at a moment's notice."

"I don't think one should jest on these subjects," said Leonard.

"I'm not jesting, I'm quite serious, I assure you. Only don't do it today; we have only eight available bridge players, and it would break up one of our tables. To-morrow we shall be a larger party. Tomorrow night, after dinner— "

"In our present imperfect understanding of these hidden forces I think one should approach them with humbleness rather than mockery," observed Leonard, with such severity that the subject was forthwith dropped.

Clovis Sangrail had sat unusually silent during the discussion on the possibilities of Siberian Magic; after lunch he side-tracked Lord Pabham into the comparative seclusion of the billiard-room and delivered himself of a searching question.

"Have you such a thing as a she-wolf in your collection of wild animals? A she-wolf of moderately good temper?"

Lord Pabham considered. "There is Loiusa," he said, "a rather fine specimen of the timber-wolf. I got her two years ago in exchange for some Arctic foxes. Most of my animals get to be fairly tame before they've been with me very long; I think I can say Louisa has an angelic temper, as she-wolves go. Why do you ask?"

"I was wondering whether you would lend her to me for tomorrow night," said Clovis, with the careless solicitude of one who borrows a collar stud or a tennis racquet.

"Tomorrow night?"

"Yes, wolves are nocturnal animals, so the late hours won't hurt her," said Clovis, with the air of one who has taken everything into consideration; "one of your men could bring her over from Pabham Park after dusk, and with a little help he ought to be able to smuggle her into the conservatory at the same moment that Mary Hampton makes an unobtrusive exit."

Lord Pabham stared at Clovis for a moment in pardonable bewilderment; then his face broke into a wrinkled network of laughter.

"Oh, that's your game, is it? You are going to do a little Siberian Magic on your own account. And is Mrs. Hampton willing to be a fellow-conspirator?"

"Mary is pledged to see me through with it, if you will guarantee Louisa's temper."

"I'll answer for Louisa," said Lord Pabham.

By the following day the house-party had swollen to larger proportions, and Bilsiter's instinct for self-advertisement expanded duly under the stimulant of an increased audience. At dinner that evening he held forth at length on the subject of unseen forces and untested powers, and his flow of impressive eloquence continued unabated while coffee was being served in the drawing room preparatory to a general migration to the card-room. His aunt ensured a respectful hearing for his utterances, but her sensation-loving soul hankered after something more dramatic than mere vocal demonstration.

"Won't you do something to *convince* them of your powers, Leonard?" she pleaded. "Change something into another shape. He can, you know, if he only chooses to," she informed the company.

"Oh, do," said Mavis Pellington earnestly, and her request was echoed by nearly every one present. Even those who were not open to conviction were perfectly willing to be entertained by an exhibition of amateur conjuring.

Leonard felt that something tangible was expected of him.

"Has any one present," he asked, "got a three-penny bit or some small object of no particular value—?"

"You're surely not going to make coins disappear, or something primitive of that sort?" said Clovis contemptuously.

"I think it very unkind of you not to carry out my suggestion of turning me into a wolf," said Mary Hampton, as she crossed over to the conservatory to give her macaws their usual tribute from the dessert dishes.

"I have already warned you of the danger of treating these powers in a mocking spirit," said Leonard solemnly.

"I don't believe you can do it," laughed Mary provocatively from the conservatory; "I dare you to do it if you can. I defy you to turn me into a wolf."

As she said this she was lost to view behind a clump of azaleas.

"Mrs. Hampton—" began Leonard with increased solemnity, but he got no further. A breath of chill air seemed to rush across the room, and at the same time the macaws broke forth into ear-splitting screams.

"What on earth is the matter with those confounded birds, Mary?" exclaimed Colonel Hampton; at the same moment an even more piercing scream from Mavis Pellington stampeded the entire company from their seats. In various attitudes of helpless horror or instinctive defence they confronted the evil-looking grey beast that was peering at them from amid a setting of fern and azalea.

Mrs. Hoops was the first to recover from the general chaos of fright and bewilderment.

"Leonard!" she screamed shrilly to her nephew, "turn it back into Mrs. Hampton at once! It may fly at us at any moment. Turn it back!"

"I—I don't know how to," faltered Leonard, who looked more scared and horrified than any one.

"What!" shouted Colonel Hampton, "you've taken the abominable liberty of turning my wife into a wolf, and now you stand there calmly and say you can't turn her back again!"

To do strict justice to Leonard, calmness was not a distinguishing feature of his attitude at the moment.

"I assure you I didn't turn Mrs. Hampton into a wolf; nothing was farther from my intentions," he protested.

"Then where is she, and how came that animal into the conservatory?" demanded the Colonel.

"Of course we must accept your assurance that you didn't turn Mrs. Hampton into a wolf," said Clovis politely, "but you will agree that appearances are against you."

"Are we to have all these recriminations with that beast standing there ready to tear us to pieces?" wailed Mavis indignantly.

"Lord Pabham, you know a good deal about wild beasts—" suggested Colonel Hampton.

"The wild beasts that I have been accustomed to," said Lord Pabham, "have come with proper credentials from well-known dealers, or have been bred in my own menagerie. I've never before been confronted with an animal that walks unconcernedly out of an azalea bush, leaving a charming and popular hostess unaccounted for. As far as one can judge from *outward* characteristics," he continued, "it has the appearance of a well-grown female of the North American timber-wolf, a variety of the common species *canis lupus*."

"Oh, never mind its Latin name," screamed Mavis, as the beast came a step or two further into the room; "can't you entice it away with food, and shut it up where it can't do any harm?"

"If it is really Mrs. Hampton, who has just had a very good dinner, I don't suppose food will appeal to it very strongly," said Clovis.

"Leonard," beseeched Mrs. Hoops tearfully, "even if this *is* none of your doing can't you use your great powers to turn this dreadful beast into something harmless before it bites us all—a rabbit or something?"

"I don't suppose Colonel Hampton would care to have his wife turned into a succession of fancy animals as though we were playing a round game with her," interposed Clovis.

"I absolutely forbid it," thundered the Colonel.

"Most wolves that I've had anything to do with have been inordinately fond of sugar," said Lord Pabham; "if you like I'll try the effect on this one."

He took a piece of sugar from the saucer of his coffee cup and flung it to the expectant Louisa, who snapped it in mid-air. There was a sigh of relief from the company; a wolf that ate sugar when it might at the least have been employed in tearing macaws to pieces had already shed some of its terrors. The sigh deepened to a gasp of thanksgiving when Lord Pabham decoyed the animal out of the room by a pretended largesse of further sugar. There was an instant rush to the vacated conservatory. There was no trace of Mrs. Hampton except the plate containing the macaws' supper.

"The door is locked on the inside!" exclaimed Clovis, who had deftly turned the key as he affected to test it.

Every one turned towards Bilsiter.

"If you haven't turned my wife into a wolf," said Colonel Hampton, "will you kindly explain where she has disappeared to, since she obviously could not have gone through a locked door? I will not press you for an explanation of how a North American timber-wolf suddenly appeared in the conservatory, but I think I have some right to inquire what has become of Mrs. Hampton."

Bilsiter's reiterated disclaimer was met with a general murmur of impatient disbelief.

"I refuse to stay another hour under this roof," declared Mavis Pellington.

"If our hostess has really vanished out of human form," said Mrs. Hoops, "none of the ladies of the party can very well remain. I absolutely decline to be chaperoned by a wolf!"

"It's a she-wolf," said Clovis soothingly.

The correct etiquette to be observed under the unusual circumstances received no further elucidation. The sudden entry of Mary Hampton deprived the discussion of its immediate interest.

"Some one has mesmerised me," she exclaimed

crossly; "I found myself in the game larder, of all places, being fed with sugar by Lord Pabham. I hate being mesmerised, and the doctor has forbidden me to touch sugar."

The situation was explained to her, as far as it permitted of anything that could be called explanation.

"Then you *really* did turn me into a wolf, Mr. Bilsiter?" she exclaimed excitedly.

But Leonard had burned the boat in which he might now have embarked on a sea of glory. He could only shake his head feebly.

"It was I who took that liberty," said Clovis; "you see, I happen to have lived for a couple of years in North-eastern Russia, and I have more than a tourist's acquaintance with the magic craft of that region. One does not care to speak about these strange powers, but once in a way, when one hears a lot of nonsense being talked about them, one is tempted to show what Siberian Magic can accomplish in the hands of some one who really understands it. I yielded to that temptation. May I have some brandy? the effort has left me rather faint."

If Leonard Bilsiter could at that moment have transformed Clovis into a cockroach and then have stepped on him he would gladly have performed both operations.

Laura

"You are not really dying, are you?" asked Amanda.

"I have the doctor's permission to live till Tuesday," said Laura.

"But today is Saturday; this is serious!" gasped Amanda.

"I don't know about it being serious; it is certainly Saturday," said Laura.

"Death is always serious," said Amanda.

"I never said I was going to die. I am presumably going to leave off being Laura, but I shall go on being something. An animal of some kind, I suppose. You see, when one hasn't been very good in the life one has just lived, one reincarnates in some lower organism. And I haven't been very good, when one comes to think of it. I've been petty and mean and vindictive and all that sort of thing when circumstances have seemed to warrant it."

"Circumstances never warrant that sort of thing," said Amanda hastily.

"If you don't mind my saying so," observed Laura, "Egbert is a circumstance that would warrant any amount of that sort of thing. You're married to him—that's different; you've sworn to love, honour, and endure him: I haven't."

"I don't see what's wrong with Egbert," protested Amanda.

"Oh, I dare say the wrongness has been on my part," admitted Laura dispassionately; "he has merely been the extenuating circumstance. He made a thin, peevish kind of fuss, for instance, when I took the collie puppies from the farm out for a run the other day."

"They chased his young broods of speckled Sussex and drove two sitting hens off their nests, besides running all over the flower beds. You know how devoted he is to his poultry and garden."

"Anyhow, he needn't have gone on about it for the entire evening and then have said, 'Let's say no more about it' just when I was beginning to enjoy the discussion. That's where one of my petty vindictive revenges came in," added Laura with an unrepentant chuckle; "I turned the entire family of speckled Sussex into his seedling shed the day after the puppy episode."

"How could you?" exclaimed Amanda.

"It came quite easy," said Laura; "two of the hens pretended to be laying at the time, but I was firm."

"And we thought it was an accident!"

"You see," resumed Laura, "I really *have* some grounds for supposing that my next incarnation will be in a lower organism. I shall be an animal of some kind. On the other hand, I haven't been a bad sort in my way, so I think I may count on being a nice animal, some thing elegant and lively, with a love of fun. An otter, perhaps."

"I can't imagine you as an otter," said Amanda.

"Well, I don't suppose you can imagine me as an angel, if it comes to that," said Laura.

Amanda was silent. She couldn't.

"Personally I think an otter life would be rather enjoyable," continued Laura; "salmon to eat all the year round, and the satisfaction of being able to fetch the trout in their own homes without having to wait for hours till they condescend to rise to the fly you've been dangling before them; and an elegant svelte figure—"

"Think of the otter hounds," interposed Amanda; "how dreadful to be hunted and harried and finally worried to death!"

"Rather fun with half the neighbourhood looking on, and anyhow not worse than this Saturday-to-Tuesday business of dying by inches; and then I should go on into something else. If I had been a moderately good otter I suppose I should get back into human shape of some sort; probably something rather primitive—a little brown, unclothed Nubian boy, I should think."

"I wish you would be serious," sighed Amanda; "you really ought to be if you're only going to live till Tuesday."

As a matter of fact Laura died on Monday.

"So dreadfully upsetting," Amanda complained to her uncle-in-law, Sir Lulworth Quayne. "I've asked quite a lot of people down for golf and fishing, and the rhododendrons are just looking their best."

"Laura always was inconsiderate," said Sir Lulworth; "she was born during Goodwood week, with an Ambassador staying in the house who hated babies."

"She had the maddest kind of ideas," said Amanda; "do you know if there was any insanity in her family?"

"Insanity? No, I never heard of any. Her father lives in West Kensington, but I believe he's sane on all other subjects."

"She had an idea that she was going to be reincarnated as an otter," said Amanda.

"One meets with those ideas of reincarnation so frequently, even in the West," said Sir Lulworth, "that one can hardly set them down as being mad. And Laura was such an unaccountable person in this life that I should not like to lay down definite rules as to what she might be doing in an after state."

"You think she really might have passed into some animal form?" asked Amanda. She was one of those who shape their opinions rather readily from the standpoint of those around them.

Just then Egbert entered the breakfast-room, wearing an air of bereavement that Laura's demise would have been insufficient, in itself, to account for.

"Four of my speckled Sussex have been killed," he exclaimed; "the very four that were to go to the show on Friday. One of them was dragged away and eaten right in the middle of that new carnation bed that I've been to such trouble and expense over. My best flower bed and my best fowls singled out for destruction; it almost seems as if the brute that did the deed had special knowledge how to be as devastating as possible in a short space of time."

"Was it a fox, do you think?" asked Amanda.

"Sounds more like a polecat," said Sir Lulworth.

"No," said Egbert, "there were marks of webbed feet all over the place, and we followed the tracks down to the stream at the bottom of the garden; evidently an otter."

Amanda looked quickly and furtively across at Sir Lulworth.

Egbert was too agitated to eat any breakfast, and went

out to superintend the strengthening of the poultry yard defences.

"I think she might at least have waited till the funeral was over," said Amanda in a scandalised voice.

"It's her own funeral, you know," said Sir Lulworth; "it's a nice point in etiquette how far one ought to show respect to one's own mortal remains."

Disregard for mortuary convention was carried to further lengths next day; during the absence of the family at the funeral ceremony the remaining survivors of the speckled Sussex were massacred. The marauder's line of retreat seemed to have embraced most of the flower beds on the lawn, but the strawberry beds in the lower garden had also suffered.

"I shall get the otter hounds to come here at the earliest possible moment," said Egbert savagely.

"On no account! You can't dream of such a thing!" exclaimed Amanda. "I mean, it wouldn't do, so soon after a funeral in the house."

"It's a case of necessity," said Egbert; "once an otter takes to that sort of thing it won't stop."

"Perhaps it will go elsewhere now there are no more fowls left," suggested Amanda.

"One would think you wanted to shield the beast," said Egbert.

"There's been so little water in the stream lately," objected Amanda; "it seems hardly sporting to hunt an animal when it has so little chance of taking refuge anywhere."

"Good gracious!" fumed Egbert, "I'm not thinking about sport. I want to have the animal killed as soon as possible."

Even Amanda's opposition weakened when, during church time on the following Sunday, the otter made its way into the house, raided half a salmon from the larder and worried it into scaly fragments on the Persian rug in Egbert's studio.

"We shall have it hiding under our beds and biting pieces out of our feet before long," said Egbert, and from what Amanda knew of this particular otter she felt that the possibility was not a remote one.

On the evening preceding the day fixed for the hunt Amanda spent a solitary hour walking by the banks of the stream, making what she imagined to be hound noises. It was charitably supposed by those who overheard her performance, that she was practising for farmyard imitations at the forthcoming village entertainment.

It was her friend and neighbour, Aurora Burret, who brought her news of the day's sport.

"Pity you weren't out; we had quite a good day. We found at once, in the pool just below your garden."

"Did you—kill?" asked Amanda.

"Rather. A fine she-otter. Your husband got rather badly bitten in trying to 'tail it'. Poor beast, I felt quite sorry for it, it had such a human look in its eyes when it was killed. You'll call me silly, but do you know who the look reminded me of? My dear woman, what is the matter?"

When Amanda had recovered to a certain extent from her attack of nervous prostration Egbert took her to the Nile Valley to recuperate. Change of scene speedily brought about the desired recovery of health and mental balance. The escapades of an adventurous otter in search of a variation of diet were viewed in their proper light. Amanda's normally placid temperament reasserted itself. Even a hurricane of shouted curses, coming from her husband's dressing-room, in her husband's voice, but hardly in his usual vocabulary, failed to disturb her serenity as she made a leisurely toilet one evening in a Cairo hotel.

"What is the matter? What has happened?" she asked in amused curiosity.

"The little beast has thrown all my clean shirts into the bath! Wait till I catch you, you little—"

"What little beast?" asked Amanda, suppressing a desire to laugh; Egbert's language was so hopelessly inadequate to express his outraged feelings.

"A little beast of a naked brown Nubian boy," spluttered Egbert.

And now Amanda is seriously ill.

The Boar-Pig

"There is a back way on to the lawn," said Mrs. Phili-
dore Stossen to her daughter, "through a small grass
paddock and then through a walled fruit garden full of
gooseberry bushes. I went all over the place last year
when the family were away. There is a door that opens
from the fruit garden into a shrubbery, and once we
emerge from there we can mingle with the guests as if
we had come in by the ordinary way. It's much safer
than going in by the front entrance and running the risk
of coming bang up against the hostess; that would be so
awkward when she doesn't happen to have invited us."

"Isn't it a lot of trouble to take for getting admittance
to a garden party?"

"To a garden party, yes; to *the* garden party of the
season, certainly not. Every one of any consequence in
the county, with the exception of ourselves, has been
asked to meet the Princess, and it would be far more
troublesome to invent explanations as to why we
weren't there than to get in by a roundabout way. I
stopped Mrs. Cuvering in the road yesterday and talked
very pointedly about the Princess. If she didn't choose
to take the hint and send me an invitation it's not my
fault, is it? Here we are: we just cut across the grass and
through that little gate into the garden."

Mrs. Stossen and her daughter, suitably arrayed for a county garden party function with an infusion of Almanack de Gotha, sailed through the narrow grass paddock and the ensuing gooseberry garden with the air of state barges making an unofficial progress along a rural trout stream. There was a certain amount of furtive haste mingled with the stateliness of their advance, as though hostile searchlights might be turned on them at any moment; and, as a matter of fact, they were not unobserved. Matilda Cuvering, with the alert eyes of thirteen years and the added advantage of an exalted position in the branches of a medlar tree, had enjoyed a good view of the Stossen flanking movement and had foreseen exactly where it would break down in execution.

"They'll find the door locked, and they'll jolly well have to go back the way they came," she remarked to herself. "Serves them right for not coming in by the proper entrance. What a pity Tarquin Superbus isn't loose in the paddock. After all, as every one else is enjoying themselves, I don't see why Tarquin shouldn't have an afternoon out."

Matilda was of an age when thought is action; she slid down from the branches of the medlar tree, and when she clambered back again Tarquin, the huge white Yorkshire boar-pig, had exchanged the narrow limits of his sty for the wider range of the grass paddock. The discomfited Stossen expedition, returning in recriminatory but otherwise orderly retreat from the unyielding obstacle of the locked door, came to a sudden halt at the gate dividing the paddock from the gooseberry garden.

"What a villainous-looking animal," exclaimed Mrs. Stossen; "it wasn't there when we came in."

"It's there now, anyhow," said her daughter. "What on earth are we to do? I wish we had never come."

The boar-pig had drawn nearer to the gate for a closer inspection of the human intruders, and stood champing his jaws and blinking his small red eyes in a manner that was doubtless intended to be disconcerting, and, as far as the Stossens were concerned, thoroughly achieved that result.

"Shoo! Hish! Hish! Shoo!" cried the ladies in chorus.

"If they think they're going to drive him away by reciting lists of the kings of Israel and Judah they're laying themselves out for disappointment," observed Matilda from her seat in the medlar tree. As she made the observation aloud Mrs. Stossen became for the first time aware of her presence. A moment or two earlier she would have been anything but pleased at the discovery that the garden was not as deserted as it looked, but now she hailed the fact of the child's presence on the scene with absolute relief.

"Little girl, can you find some one to drive away—" she began hopefully.

"*Comment? Comprends pas*," was the response.

"Oh, are you French? *Etes vous française?*"

"*Pas de tous. 'Suis anglaise.*"

"Then why not talk English? I want to know if—"

"*Permettez-moi expliquer*. You see, I'm rather under a cloud," said Matilda. "I'm staying with my aunt, and I was told I must behave particularly well today, as lots of people were coming for a garden party, and I was told to imitate Claude, that's my young cousin, who never does anything wrong except by accident, and then is always apologetic about it. It seems they thought I ate too much raspberry trifle at lunch, and they said Claude never eats too much raspberry trifle. Well, Claude always goes to sleep for half an hour after lunch, because he's told to, and I waited till he was asleep, and tied his hands and started forcible feeding with a whole bucketful of raspberry trifle that they were keeping for the garden party. Lots of it went on to his sailor-suit and some of it on to the bed, but a good deal went down Claude's throat, and they can't say again that he has never been known to eat too much raspberry trifle. That is why I am not allowed to go to the party, and as an additional punishment I must speak French all the afternoon. I've had to tell you all this in English, as there were words like 'forcible feeding' that I didn't know the French for; of course I could have invented them, but if I had said *nourriture obligatoire* you wouldn't have had the least idea what I was talking about. *Mais maintenant, nous parlons français.*"

"Oh, very well, *trés bien*," said Mrs. Stossen reluctantly; in moments of flurry such French as she knew was not under very good control. "*Là, à l'autre côté de la porte, est un cochon—*"

"*Un cochon? Ah, le petit charmant!*" exclaimed Matilda with enthusiasm.

"*Mais non, pas du tout petit, et pas du tout charmant; un bête féroce—*"

"*Une bête,*" corrected Matilda; "a pig is masculine as long as you call it a pig, but if you lose your temper with it and call it a ferocious beast it becomes one of us at once. French is a dreadfully unsexing language."

"For goodness' sake let us talk English then," said Mrs. Stossen. "Is there any way out of this garden except through the paddock where the pig is?"

"I always go over the wall, by way of the plum tree," said Matilda.

"Dressed as we are we could hardly do that," said Mrs. Stossen; it was difficult to imagine her doing it in any costume.

"Do you think you could go and get some one who would drive the pig away?" asked Miss Stossen.

"I promised my aunt I would stay here till five o'clock; it's not four yet."

"I am sure, under the circumstances, your aunt would permit—"

"My conscience would not permit," said Matilda with cold dignity.

"We can't stay here till five o'clock," exclaimed Mrs. Stossen with growing exasperation.

"Shall I recite to you to make the time pass quicker?" asked Matilda obligingly. " 'Belinda, the little Bread-winner', is considered my best piece, or, perhaps, it ought to be something in French. Henri Quatre's address to his soldiers is the only thing I really know in that language."

"If you will go and fetch some one to drive that animal away I will give you something to buy yourself a nice present," said Mrs. Stossen.

Matilda came several inches lower down the medlar tree.

"That is the most practical suggestion you have made yet for getting out of the garden," she remarked cheerfully; "Claude and I are collecting money for the

Children's Fresh Air Fund, and we are seeing which of us can collect the biggest sum."

"I shall be very glad to contribute half a crown, very glad indeed," said Mrs. Stossen, digging that coin out of the depths of a receptacle which formed a detached outwork of her toilet.

"Claude is a long way ahead of me at present," continued Matilda, taking no notice of the suggested offering; "you see, he's only eleven, and has golden hair, and those are enormous advantages when you're on the collecting job. Only the other day a Russian lady gave him ten shillings. Russians understand the art of giving far better than we do. I expect Claude will net quite twenty-five shillings this afternoon; he'll have the field to himself, and he'll be able to do the pale, fragile, not-long-for-this-world business to perfection after his raspberry trifle experience. Yes, he'll be *quite* two pounds ahead of me by now."

With much probing and plucking and many regretful murmurs the beleaguered ladies managed to produce seven-and-sixpence between them.

"I am afraid this is all we've got," said Mrs. Stossen.

Matilda showed no sign of coming down either to the earth or to their figure.

"I could not do violence to my conscience for anything less than ten shillings," she announced stiffly.

Mother and daughter muttered certain remarks under their breath, in which the word "beast" was prominent, and probably had no reference to Tarquin.

"I find I *have* got another half-crown," said Mrs. Stossen in a shaking voice; "here you are. Now please fetch some one quickly."

Matilda slipped down from the tree, took possession of the donation, and proceeded to pick up a handful of over-ripe medlars from the grass at her feet. Then she climbed over the gate and addressed herself affectionately to the boar-pig.

"Come, Tarquin, dear old boy; you know you can't resist medlars when they're rotten and squashy."

Tarquin couldn't. By dint of throwing the fruit in front of him at judicious intervals Matilda decoyed him back to his sty, while the delivered captives hurried across the paddock.

"Well, I never! The little minx!" exclaimed Mrs. Stossen when she was safely on the high road. "The animal wasn't savage at all, and as for the ten shillings, I don't believe the Fresh Air Fund will see a penny of it!"

There she was unwarrantably harsh in her judgment. If you examine the books of the fund you will find the acknowledgment: "Collected by Miss Matilda Cuvering, 2s. 6d."

The Brogue

The hunting season had come to an end, and the Mullets had not succeeded in selling the Brogue. There had been a kind of tradition in the family for the past three or four years, a sort of fatalistic hope, that the Brogue would find a purchaser before the hunting was over; but seasons came and went without anything happening to justify such ill-founded optimism. The animal had been named Berserker in the earlier stages of its career; it had been rechristened the Brogue later on, in recognition of the fact that, once acquired, it was extremely difficult to get rid of. The unkinder wits of the neighbourhood had been known to suggest that the first letter of its name was superfluous. The Brogue had been variously described in sale catalogues as a light-weight hunter, a lady's hack, and, more simply, but still with a touch of imagination, as a useful brown gelding, standing 15.1. Toby Mullet had ridden him for four seasons with the West Wessex; you can ride almost any sort of horse with the West Wessex as long as it is an animal that knows the country. The Brogue knew the country intimately, having personally created most of the gaps that were to be met with in banks and hedges for many miles round. His manners and characteristics were not ideal in the hunting field, but he was probably rather safer to ride to hounds than he was as a hack on country roads. According to the Mullet family, he was not really road-shy, but there were one or two objects of dislike that brought on sudden attacks of what Toby called the swerving sickness. Motors and cycles he treated with tolerant disregard, but pigs, wheelbarrows, piles of stones by the roadside, perambulators in a village street, gates painted too aggressively white, and sometimes, but not always, the newer kind of beehives, turned him aside from his tracks in vivid imitation of the zigzag course of forked lightning. If a pheasant rose noisily from the other side of a hedgerow the Brogue would spring into the air at the same moment, but this may have been due to a desire to be companionable. The Mullet family contradicted the widely prevalent report that the horse was a confirmed crib-biter.

It was about the third week in May that Mrs. Mullet, relict of the late Sylvester Mullet, and mother of Toby and a bunch of daughters, assailed Clovis Sangrail on the outskirts of the village with a breathless catalogue of local happenings.

"You know our new neighbour, Mr. Penricarde?" she vociferated; "awfully rich, owns tin mines in Cornwall, middle-aged and rather quiet. He's taken the Red House on a long lease and spent a lot of money on alterations and improvements. Well, Toby's sold him the Brogue!"

Clovis spent a moment or two in assimilating the astonishing news; then he broke out into unstinted congratulation. If he had belonged to a more emotional race he would probably have kissed Mrs. Mullet.

"How wonderfully lucky to have pulled it off at last!

Now you can buy a decent animal. I've always said that Toby was clever. Ever so many congratulations."

"Don't congratulate me. It's the most unfortunate thing that could have happened!" said Mrs. Mullet dramatically.

Clovis stared at her in amazement.

"Mr. Penricarde," said Mrs. Mullet, sinking her voice to what she imagined to be an impressive whisper, though it rather resembled a hoarse, excited squeak, "Mr. Penricarde has just begun to pay attentions to Jessie. Slight at first, but now unmistakable. I was a fool not to have seen it sooner. Yesterday, at the Rectory garden party, he asked her what her favourite flowers were, and she told him carnations, and today a whole stack of carnations has arrived, clove and malmaison and lovely dark red ones, regular exhibition blooms, and a box of chocolates that he must have got on purpose from London. And he's asked her to go round the links with him tomorrow. And now, just at this critical moment, Toby has sold him that animal. It's a calamity!"

"But you've been trying to get the horse off your hands for years," said Clovis.

"I've got a houseful of daughters," said Mrs. Mullet, "and I've been trying—well, not to get them off my hands, of course, but a husband or two wouldn't be amiss among the lot of them; there are six of them, you know."

"I don't know," said Clovis, "I've never counted, but I expect you're right as to the number; mothers generally know these things."

"And now," continued Mrs. Mullet, in her tragic

whisper, "when there's a rich husband-in-prospect imminent on the horizon Toby goes and sells him that miserable animal. It will probably kill him if he tries to ride it; anyway it will kill any affection he might have felt towards any member of our family. What is to be done? We can't very well ask to have the horse back; you see, we praised it up like anything when we thought there was a chance of his buying it, and said it was just the animal to suit him."

"Couldn't you steal it out of his stable and send it to grass at some farm miles away?" suggested Clovis; "write 'Votes for Women' on the stable door, and the thing would pass for a Suffragette outrage. No one who knew the horse could possibly suspect you of wanting to get it back again."

"Every newspaper in the country would ring with the affair," said Mrs. Mullet; "can't you imagine the headline, 'Valuable Hunter Stolen by Suffragettes'? The police would scour the countryside till they found the animal."

"Well, Jessie must try and get it back from Penricarde on the plea that it's an old favourite. She can say it was only sold because the stable had to be pulled down under the terms of an old repairing lease, and that now it has been arranged that the stable is to stand for a couple of years longer."

"It sounds a queer proceeding to ask for a horse back when you've just sold him," said Mrs. Mullet, "but something must be done, and done at once. The man is not used to horses, and I believe I told him it was as quiet as a lamb. After all, lambs go kicking and twisting about as if they were demented, don't they?"

"The lamb has an entirely unmerited character for sedateness," agreed Clovis.

Jessie came back from the golf links next day in a state of mingled elation and concern.

"It's all right about the proposal," she announced, "he came out with it at the sixth hole. I said I must have time to think it over. I accepted him at the seventh."

"My dear," said her mother, "I think a little more maidenly reserve and hesitation would have been advisable, as you've known him so short a time. You might have waited till the ninth hole."

"The seventh is a very long hole," said Jessie; "besides, the tension was putting us both off our game. By the time we'd got to the ninth hole we'd settled lots of things. The honeymoon is to be spent in Corsica, with perhaps a flying visit to Naples if we feel like it, and a week in London to wind up with. Two of his nieces are to be asked to be bridesmaids, so with our lot there will be seven, which is rather a lucky number. You are to wear your pearl grey, with any amount of Honiton lace jabbed into it. By the way, he's coming over this evening to ask your consent to the whole affair. So far all's well, but about the Brogue it's a different matter. I told him the legend about the stable, and how keen we were about buying the horse back, but he seems equally keen on keeping it. He said he must have horse exercise now that he's living in the country, and he's going to start riding tomorrow. He's ridden a few times in the Row, on an animal that was accustomed to carry octogenarians and people undergoing rest-cures, and that's about all his experience in the saddle—oh, and he rode a pony once in Norfolk, when he was fifteen and the pony twenty-four; and tomorrow he's going to ride the Brogue! I shall be a widow before I'm married, and I do so want to see what Corsica's like; it looks so silly on the map."

Clovis was sent for in haste, and the developments of the situation put before him.

"Nobody can ride that animal with any safety," said Mrs. Mullet, "except Toby, and he knows by long experience what it is going to shy at, and manages to swerve at the same time."

"I did hint to Mr. Penricarde—to Vincent, I should say—that the Brogue didn't like white gates," said Jessie.

"White gates!" exclaimed Mrs. Mullet; "did you mention what effect a pig has on him? He'll have to go past Lockyer's farm to get to the high road, and there's sure to be a pig or two grunting about in the lane."

"He's taken rather a dislike to turkeys lately," said Toby.

"It's obvious that Penricarde mustn't be allowed to go out on that animal," said Clovis, "at least not till Jessie has married him, and tired of him. I tell you what: ask him to a picnic tomorrow, starting at an early hour; he's not the sort to go out for a ride before breakfast. The day after I'll get the rector to drive him over to Crowleigh before lunch, to see the new cottage hospital they're building there. The Brogue will be standing idle in the stable and Toby can offer to exercise it; then it can pick up a stone or something of the sort and go conveniently lame. If you hurry on the wedding a bit the lameness fiction can be kept up till the ceremony is safely over."

Mrs. Mullet belonged to an emotional race, and she kissed Clovis.

It was nobody's fault that the rain came down in torrents the next morning, making a picnic a fantastic impossibility. It was also nobody's fault, but sheer ill-luck, that the weather cleared up sufficiently in the afternoon to tempt Mr. Penricarde to make his first essay with the Brogue. They did not get as far as the pigs at Lockyer's farm; the rectory gate was painted a dull unobtrusive green, but it had been white a year or two ago, and the Brogue never forgot that he had been in the habit of making a violent curtsey, a back-pedal and a swerve at this particular point of the road. Subsequently, there being apparently no further call on his services, he broke his way into the rectory orchard, where he found a hen turkey in a coop; later visitors to the orchard found the coop almost intact, but very little left of the turkey.

Mr. Penricarde, a little stunned and shaken, and suffering from a bruised knee and some minor damages, good-naturedly ascribed the accident to his own inexperience with horses and country roads, and allowed Jessie to nurse him back into complete recovery and golf-fitness within something less than a week.

In the list of wedding presents which the local newspaper published a fortnight or so later appeared the following item:

"Brown saddle-horse, 'The Brogue', bridegroom's gift to bride."

"Which shows," said Toby Mullet, "that he knew nothing."

"Or else," said Clovis, "that he has a very pleasing wit."

The Hen

"Dora Bittholz is coming on Thursday," said Mrs. Sangrail.

"This next Thursday?" asked Clovis.

His mother nodded.

"You've rather done it, haven't you?" he chuckled. "Jane Martlet has only been here five days, and she never stays less than a fortnight, even when she's asked definitely for a week. You'll never get her out of the house by Thursday."

"Why should I?" asked Mrs. Sangrail. "She and Dora are good friends, aren't they? They used to be, as far as I remember."

"They used to be; that's what makes them all the more bitter now. Each feels that she has nursed a viper in her bosom. Nothing fans the flame of human resentment so much as the discovery that one's bosom has been utilised as a snake sanatorium."

"But what has happened? Has some one been making mischief?"

"Not exactly," said Clovis; "a hen came between them."

"A hen? What hen?"

"It was a bronze Leghorn or some such exotic breed, and Dora sold it to Jane at a rather exotic price. They both go in for prize poultry, you know, and Jane thought she was going to get her money back in a large family of pedigree chickens. The bird turned out to be an abstainer from the egg habit, and I'm told that the letters which passed between the two women were a revelation as to how much invective could be got on to a sheet of notepaper."

"How ridiculous!" said Mrs. Sangrail. "Couldn't some of their friends compose the quarrel?"

"People tried," said Clovis, "but it must have been rather like composing the storm music of the 'Fliegende Holländer'. Jane was willing to take back some of her most libellous remarks if Dora would take back the hen, but Dora said that would be owning herself in the wrong, and you know she'd as soon think of owning slum property in Whitechapel as do that."

"It's a most awkward situation," said Mrs. Sangrail. "Do you suppose they won't speak to one another?"

"On the contrary, the difficulty will be to get them to leave off. Their remarks on each other's conduct and character have hitherto been governed by the fact that only four ounces of plain speaking can be sent through the post for a penny."

"I can't put Dora off," said Mrs. Sangrail. "I've already postponed her visit once, and nothing short of a miracle would make Jane leave before her self-allotted fortnight is over."

"Miracles are rather in my line," said Clovis. "I don't pretend to be very hopeful in this case but I'll do my best."

"As long as you don't drag me into it—" stipulated his mother.

"Servants are a bit of a nuisance," muttered Clovis, as he sat in the smoking-room after lunch, talking fitfully to Jane Martlet in the intervals of putting together the materials of a cocktail, which he had irreverently patented under the name of an Ella Wheeler Wilcox. It was partly compounded of old brandy and partly of curaçoa; there were other ingredients, but they were never indiscriminately revealed.

"Servants a nuisance!" exclaimed Jane, bounding into the topic with the exuberant plunge of a hunter when it leaves the high road and feels turf under its hoofs; "I should think they were! The trouble I've had in getting suited this year you would hardly believe. But I don't see what you have to complain of—your mother is so wonderfully lucky in her servants. Sturridge, for instance—he's been with you for years, and I'm sure he's a paragon as butlers go."

"That's just the trouble," said Clovis. "It's when servants have been with you for years that they become a really serious nuisance. The 'here today and gone tomorrow' sort don't matter—you've simply got to replace them; it's the stayers and the paragons that are the real worry."

"But if they give satisfaction—"

"That doesn't prevent them from giving trouble. Now, you've mentioned Sturridge—it was Sturridge I was particularly thinking of when I made the observation about servants being a nuisance."

"The excellent Sturridge a nuisance! I can't believe it."

"I know he's excellent, and we just couldn't get along without him; he's the one reliable element in this rather haphazard household. But his very orderliness has had an effect on him. Have you ever considered what it must be like to go on unceasingly doing the correct thing in the correct manner in the same surroundings for the greater part of a lifetime? To know and ordain and superintend exactly what silver and glass and table linen shall be used and set out on what occasions, to have cellar and pantry and plate-cupboard under a minutely devised and undeviating administration, to be noiseless, impalpable, omnipresent, and, as far as your own department is concerned, omniscient?"

"I should go mad," said Jane with conviction.

"Exactly," said Clovis thoughtfully, swallowing his completed Ella Wheeler Wilcox.

"But Sturridge hasn't gone mad," said Jane with a flutter of inquiry in her voice.

"On most points he's thoroughly sane and reliable," said Clovis, "but at times he is subject to the most obstinate delusions, and on those occasions he becomes not merely a nuisance but a decided embarrassment."

"What sort of delusions?"

"Unfortunately they usually centre round one of the guests of the house party, and that is where the awkwardness comes in. For instance, he took it into his head that Matilda Sheringham was the Prophet Elijah, and as all that he remembered about Elijah's history was the episode of the ravens in the wilderness he absolutely declined to interfere with what he imagined to be Matilda's private catering arrangements, wouldn't allow any tea to be sent up to her in the morning, and if he was waiting at table he passed her over altogether in handing round the dishes."

"How very unpleasant. Whatever did you do about it?"

"Oh, Matilda got fed, after a fashion, but it was judged to be best for her to cut her visit short. It was really the only thing to be done," said Clovis with some emphasis.

"I shouldn't have done that," said Jane, "I should have humoured him in some way. I certainly shouldn't have gone away."

Clovis frowned.

"It is not always wise to humour people when they get these ideas into their heads. There's no knowing to what lengths they may go if you encourage them."

"You don't mean to say he might be dangerous, do you?" asked Jane with some anxiety.

"One can never be certain," said Clovis; "now and then he gets some idea about a guest which *might* take an unfortunate turn. That is precisely what is worrying me at the present moment."

"What, has he taken a fancy about some one here now?" asked Jane excitedly. "How thrilling! Do tell me who it is."

"You," said Clovis briefly.

"Me?"

Clovis nodded.

"Who on earth does he think I am?"

"Queen Anne," was the unexpected answer.

"Queen Anne! What an idea. But, anyhow, there's nothing dangerous about her; she's such a colourless personality."

"What does posterity chiefly say about Queen Anne?" asked Clovis rather sternly.

"The only thing that I can remember about her," said Jane, "is the saying 'Queen Anne's dead'."

"Exactly," said Clovis, staring at the glass that had held the Ella Wheeler Wilcox, "dead."

"Do you mean he takes me for the ghost of Queen Anne?" asked Jane.

"Ghost? Dear no. No one ever heard of a ghost that came down to breakfast and ate kidneys and toast and honey with a healthy appetite. No, it's the fact of you being so very much alive and flourishing that perplexes and annoys him. All his life he has been accustomed to look on Queen Anne as the personification of every-thing that is dead and done with, 'as dead as Queen Anne', you know; and now he has to fill your glass at lunch and dinner and listen to your accounts of the gay time you had at the Dublin Horse Show, and naturally he feels that something's very wrong with you."

"But he wouldn't be downright hostile to me on that account, would he?" Jane asked anxiously.

"I didn't get really alarmed about it till lunch to-day," said Clovis; "I caught him glowering at you with a very sinister look and muttering: 'Ought to be dead long ago, she ought, and some one should see to it.' That's why I mentioned the matter to you."

"This is awful," said Jane; "your mother must be told about it at once."

"My mother mustn't hear a word about it," said Clovis earnestly; "it would upset her dreadfully. She relies on Sturridge for everything."

"But he might kill me at any moment," protested Jane.

"Not at any moment; he's busy with the silver all the afternoon."

"You'll have to keep a sharp look-out all the time and be on your guard to frustrate any murderous attack," said Jane, adding in a tone of weak obstinacy: "It's a dreadful situation to be in, with a mad butler dangling over you like the sword of What's-his-name, but I'm certainly not going to cut my visit short."

Clovis swore horribly under his breath; the miracle was an obvious misfire.

It was in the hall the next morning after a late breakfast that Clovis had his final inspiration as he stood engaged in coaxing rust spots from an old putter.

"Where is Miss Martlet?" he asked the butler, who was at that moment crossing the hall.

"Writing letters in the morning-room, sir," said Sturridge, announcing a fact of which his questioner was already aware.

"She wants to copy the inscription on that old basket-hilted sabre," said Clovis, pointing to a venerable weapon hanging on the wall. "I wish you'd take it to her; my hands are all over oil. Take it without the sheath, it will be less trouble."

The butler drew the blade, still keen and bright in its well-cared-for old age, and carried it into the morning-room. There was a door near the writing-table leading to a back stairway; Jane vanished through it with such lightning rapidity that the butler doubted whether she had seen him come in. Half an hour later Clovis was driving her and her hastily packed luggage to the station.

"Mother will be awfully vexed when she comes back from her ride and finds you have gone," he observed to the departing guest, "but I'll make up some story about an urgent wire having called you away. It wouldn't do to alarm her unnecessarily about Sturridge."

Jane sniffed slightly at Clovis's ideas of unnecessary alarm, and was almost rude to the young man who came round with thoughtful inquiries as to luncheon-baskets.

The miracle lost some of its usefulness from the fact that Dora wrote the same day postponing the date of her visit, but, at any rate, Clovis holds the record as the only human being who ever hustled Jane Martlet out of the time-table of her migrations.

The Open Window

"My aunt will be down presently, Mr. Nuttel," said a very self-possessed young lady of fifteen; "in the meantime you must try and put up with me."

Framton Nuttel endeavoured to say the correct something which should duly flatter the niece of the moment without unduly discounting the aunt that was to come. Privately he doubted more than ever whether these formal visits on a succession of total strangers would do much towards helping the nerve cure which he was supposed to be undergoing.

"I know how it will be," his sister had said when he was preparing to migrate to this rural retreat; "you will bury yourself down there and not speak to a living soul, and your nerves will be worse than ever from moping. I shall just give you letters of introduction to all the people I know there. Some of them, as far as I can remember, were quite nice."

Framton wondered whether Mrs. Sappleton, the lady to whom he was presenting one of the letters of introduction, came into the nice division.

"Do you know many of the people round here?" asked the niece, when she judged that they had had sufficient silent communion.

"Hardly a soul," said Framton. "My sister was

staying here, at the rectory, you know, some four years ago, and she gave me letters of introduction to some of the people here."

He made the last statement in a tone of distinct regret.

"Then you know practically nothing about my aunt?" pursued the self-possessed young lady.

"Only her name and address," admitted the caller. He was wondering whether Mrs. Sappleton was in the married or widowed state. An undefinable something about the room seemed to suggest masculine habitation.

"Her great tragedy happened just three years ago," said the child; "that would be since your sister's time."

"Her tragedy?" asked Framton; somehow in this restful country spot tragedies seemed out of place.

"You may wonder why we keep that window wide open on an October afternoon," said the niece, indicating a large French window that opened on to a lawn.

"It is quite warm for the time of the year," said Framton; "but has that window got anything to do with the tragedy?"

"Out through that window, three years ago to a day, her husband and her two young brothers went off for their day's shooting. They never came back. In crossing the moor to their favourite snipe-shooting ground they were all three engulfed in a treacherous piece of bog. It had been that dreadful wet summer, you know, and places that were safe in other years gave way suddenly without warning. Their bodies were never recovered. That was the dreadful part of it." Here the child's voice lost its self-possessed note and became falteringly human. "Poor aunt always thinks that they will come back some day, they and the little brown spaniel that was lost with them, and walk in at that window just as they used to do. That is why the window is kept open every evening till it is quite dusk. Poor dear aunt, she has often told me how they went out, her husband with his white waterproof coat over his arm, and Ronnie, her youngest brother, singing 'Bertie, why do you bound?' as he always did to tease her, because she said it got on her nerves. Do you know, sometimes on still, quiet evenings like this, I almost get a creepy feeling that they will all walk in through that window—"

She broke off with a little shudder. It was a relief to Framton when the aunt bustled into the room with a whirl of apologies for being late in making her appearance.

"I hope Vera has been amusing you?" she said.

"She has been very interesting," said Framton.

"I hope you don't mind the open window," said Mrs. Sappleton briskly; "my husband and brothers will be home directly from shooting, and they always come in this way. They've been out for snipe in the marshes today, so they'll make a fine mess over my poor carpets. So like you men-folk, isn't it?"

She rattled on cheerfully about the shooting and the scarcity of birds, and the prospects for duck in the winter. To Framton it was all purely horrible. He made a desperate but only partially successful effort to turn the talk on to a less ghastly topic; he was conscious that his hostess was giving him only a fragment of her attention, and her eyes were constantly straying past him to the open window and the lawn beyond. It was certainly an unfortunate coincidence that he should have paid his visit on this tragic anniversary.

"The doctors agree in ordering me complete rest, an absence of mental excitement, and avoidance of anything in the nature of violent physical exercise," announced Framton, who laboured under the tolerably wide-spread delusion that total strangers and chance acquaintances are hungry for the least detail of one's ailments and infirmities, their cause and cure. "On the matter of diet they are not so much in agreement," he continued.

"No?" said Mrs. Sappleton, in a voice which only replaced a yawn at the last moment. Then she suddenly brightened into alert attention—but not to what Framton was saying.

"Here they are at last!" she cried. "Just in time for tea, and don't they look as if they were muddy up to the eyes!"

Framton shivered slightly and turned towards the niece with a look intended to convey sympathetic comprehension. The child was staring out through the open window with dazed horror in her eyes. In a chill shock of nameless fear Framton swung round in his seat and looked in the same direction.

In the deepening twilight three figures were walking across the lawn towards the window; they all carried guns under their arms, and one of them was additionally burdened with a white coat hung over his shoulders. A tired brown spaniel kept close at their heels. Noiselessly they neared the house, and then a hoarse young voice chanted out of the dusk: "I said, Bertie, why do you bound?"

Framton grabbed wildly at his stick and hat; the hall door, the gravel drive, and the front gate were dimly noted stages in his headlong retreat. A cyclist coming along the road had to run into the hedge to avoid an imminent collision.

"Here we are, my dear," said the bearer of the white mackintosh, coming in through the window; "fairly muddy, but most of it's dry. Who was that who bolted out as we came up?"

"A most extraordinary man, a Mr. Nuttel," said Mrs. Sappleton; "could only talk about his illnesses, and dashed off without a word of good-bye or apology when you arrived. One would think he had seen a ghost."

"I expect it was the spaniel," said the niece calmly; "he told me he had a horror of dogs. He was once hunted into a cemetery somewhere on the banks of the Ganges by a pack of pariah dogs, and had to spend the night in a newly dug grave with the creatures snarling and grinning and foaming just above him. Enough to make any one lose their nerve."

Romance at short notice was her speciality.

The Lull

"I've asked Latimer Springfield to spend Sunday with us and stop the night," announced Mrs. Durmot at the breakfast-table.

"I thought he was in the throes of an election," remarked her husband.

"Exactly; the poll is on Wednesday, and the poor man will have worked himself to a shadow by that time. Imagine what electioneering must be like in this awful soaking rain, going along slushy country roads and speaking to damp audiences in draughty schoolrooms, day after day for a fortnight. He'll have to put in an appearance at some place of worship on Sunday morning, and he can come to us immediately afterwards and have a thorough respite from everything connected with politics. I won't let him even think of them. I've had the picture of Cromwell dissolving the Long Parliament taken down from the staircase, and even the portrait of Lord Rosebery's 'Ladas' removed from the smoking-room. And Vera," added Mrs. Durmot, turning to her sixteen-year-old niece, "be careful what colour ribbon you wear in your hair; not blue or yellow on any account; those are the rival party colours, and emerald green or orange would be almost as bad, with this Home Rule business to the fore."

"On state occasions I always wear a black ribbon in my hair," said Vera with crushing dignity.

Latimer Springfield was a rather cheerless, oldish young man, who went into politics somewhat in the spirit in which other people might go into half mourning. Without being an enthusiast, however, he was a fairly strenuous plodder, and Mrs. Durmot had been reasonably near the mark in asserting that he was working at high pressure over this election. The restful lull which his hostess enforced on him was decidedly welcome, and yet the nervous excitement of the contest had too great a hold on him to be totally banished.

"I know he's going to sit up half the night working up points for his final speeches," said Mrs. Durmot regretfully; "however, we've kept politics at arm's length all the afternoon and evening. More than that we cannot do."

"That remains to be seen," said Vera, but she said it to herself.

Latimer had scarcely shut his bedroom door before he was immersed in a sheaf of notes and pamphlets, while a fountain-pen and pocket-book were brought into play for the due marshalling of useful facts and discreet fictions. He had been at work for perhaps thirty-five minutes, and the house was seemingly consecrated to the healthy slumber of country life, when a stifled squealing and scuffling in the passage was followed by a loud tap at his door. Before he had time to answer, a much-encumbered Vera burst into the room with the question; "I say, can I leave these here?"

"These" were a small black pig and a lusty specimen of black-red gamecock.

The Lull

Latimer was moderately fond of animals, and particularly interested in small livestock rearing from the economic point of view; in fact, one of the pamphlets on which he was at that moment engaged warmly advocated the further development of the pig and poultry industry in our rural districts; but he was pardonably unwilling to share even a commodious bedroom with samples of henroost and sty products.

"Wouldn't they be happier somewhere outside?" he asked, tactfully expressing his own preference in the matter in an apparent solicitude for theirs.

"There is no outside," said Vera impressively, "nothing but a waste of dark, swirling waters. The reservoir at Brinkley has burst."

"I didn't know there was a reservoir at Brinkley," said Latimer.

"Well, there isn't now, it's jolly well all over the place, and as we stand particularly low we're the centre of an inland sea just at present. You see the river has overflowed its banks as well."

"Good gracious! Have any lives been lost?"

"Heaps, I should say. The second housemaid has already identified three bodies that have floated past the billiard-room window as being the young man she's engaged to. Either she's engaged to a large assortment of the population round here or else she's very careless at identification. Of course it may be the same body coming round again and again in a swirl; I hadn't thought of that."

"But we ought to go out and do rescue work, oughtn't we?" said Latimer, with the instinct of a Parliamentary candidate for getting into the local limelight.

"We can't," said Vera decidedly, "we haven't any boats and we're cut off by a raging torrent from any human habitation. My aunt particularly hoped you would keep to your room and not add to the confusion, but she thought it would be so kind of you if you would take in Hartlepool's Wonder, the gamecock, you know, for the night. You see, there are eight other gamecocks, and they fight like furies if they get together, so we're putting one in each bedroom. The fowl-houses are all flooded out, you know. And then I thought perhaps you wouldn't mind taking in this wee piggie; he's rather a little love, but he has a vile temper. He gets that from his mother—not that I like to say things against her when she's lying dead and drowned in her sty, poor thing. What he really wants is a man's firm hand to keep him in order. I'd try and grapple with him myself, only I've got my chow in my room, you know, and he goes for pigs wherever he finds them."

"Couldn't the pig go in the bathroom?" asked Latimer faintly, wishing that he had taken up as determined a stand on the subject of bedroom swine as the chow had.

"The bathroom?" Vera laughed shrilly. "It'll be full of Boy Scouts till morning if the hot water holds out."

"Boy Scouts?"

"Yes, thirty of them came to rescue us while the water was only waist-high; then it rose another three feet or so and we had to rescue them. We're giving them hot baths in batches and drying their clothes in the hot-air cupboard, but, of course, drenched clothes don't dry in a minute, and the corridor and staircase are beginning to look like a bit of coast scenery by Tuke.

Two of the boys are wearing your Melton overcoat; I hope you don't mind."

"It's a new overcoat," said Latimer, with every indication of minding dreadfully.

"You'll take every care of Hartlepool's Wonder, won't you?" said Vera. "His mother took three firsts at Birmingham, and he was second in the cockerel class last year at Gloucester. He'll probably roost on the rail at the bottom of your bed. I wonder if he'd feel more at home if some of his wives were up here with him? The hens are all in the pantry, and I think I could pick out Hartlepool Helen; she's his favourite."

Latimer showed a belated firmness on the subject of Hartlepool Helen, and Vera withdrew without pressing the point, having first settled the gamecock on his extemporised perch and taken an affectionate farewell of the pigling. Latimer undressed and got into bed with all due speed, judging that the pig would abate its inquisitorial restlessness once the light was turned out. As a substitute for a cosy, straw-bedded sty the room offered, at first inspection, few attractions, but the disconsolate animal suddenly discovered an appliance in which the most luxuriously contrived piggeries were notably deficient. The sharp edge of the underneath part of the bed was pitched at exactly the right elevation to permit the pigling to scrape himself ecstatically backwards and forwards, with an artistic humping of the back at the crucial moment and an accompanying gurgle of long-drawn delight. The gamecock, who may have fancied that he was being rocked in the branches of a pine-tree, bore the motion with greater fortitude than Latimer was able to command. A series of slaps directed at the pig's body were accepted more as an additional and pleasing irritant than as a criticism of conduct or a hint to desist; evidently something more than a man's firm hand was needed to deal with the case. Latimer slipped out of bed in search of a weapon of dissuasion. There was sufficient light in the room to enable the pig to detect this manoeuvre, and the vile temper, inherited from the drowned mother, found full play. Latimer bounded back into bed, and his conqueror, after a few threatening snorts and champings of its jaws, resumed its massage operations with renewed zeal. During the long wakeful hours which ensued Latimer tried to distract his mind from his own immediate troubles by dwelling with decent sympathy on the second housemaid's bereavement, but he found himself more often wondering how many Boy Scouts were sharing his Melton overcoat. The rôle of Saint Martin *malgré lui* was not one which appealed to him.

Towards dawn the pigling fell into a happy slumber, and Latimer might have followed its example, but at about the same time Stupor Hartlepooli gave a rousing crow, clattered down to the floor and forthwith commenced a spirited combat with his reflection in the wardrobe mirror. Remembering that the bird was more or less under his care Latimer performed Hague Tribunal offices by draping a bath-towel over the provocative mirror, but the ensuing peace was local and short-lived. The deflected energies of the gamecock found new outlet in a sudden and sustained attack on the sleeping and temporarily inoffensive pigling, and the duel which followed was desperate and embittered beyond any possibility of effective intervention.

The feathered combatant had the advantage of being able, when hard pressed, to take refuge on the bed, and freely availed himself of this circumstance; the pigling never quite succeeded in hurling himself on to the same eminence, but it was not from want of trying.

Neither side could claim any decisive success, and the struggle had been practically fought to a standstill by the time that the maid appeared with the early morning tea.

"Lor, sir," she exclaimed in undisguised astonishment, "do you want those animals in your room?"

Want!

The pigling, as though aware that it might have outstayed its welcome, dashed out at the door, and the gamecock followed it at a more dignified pace.

"If Miss Vera's dog sees that pig—!" exclaimed the maid, and hurried off to avert such a catastrophe.

A cold suspicion was stealing over Latimer's mind; he went to the window and drew up the blind. A light, drizzling rain was falling, but there was not the faintest trace of any inundation.

Some half-hour later he met Vera on the way to the breakfast-room.

"I should not like to think of you as a deliberate liar," he observed coldly, "but one occasionally has to do things one does not like."

"At any rate I kept your mind from dwelling on politics all the night," said Vera.

Which was, of course, perfectly true.

The Schartz-Metterklume Method

Lady Carlotta stepped out on to the platform of the small wayside station and took a turn or two up and down its uninteresting length, to kill time till the train should be pleased to proceed on its way. Then, in the roadway beyond, she saw a horse struggling with a more than ample load, and a carter of the sort that seems to bear a sullen hatred against the animal that helps him to earn a living. Lady Carlotta promptly betook her to the roadway, and put rather a different complexion on the struggle. Certain of her acquaintances were wont to give her plentiful admonition as to the undesirability of interfering on behalf of a distressed animal, such interference being "none of her business". Only once had she put the doctrine of non-interference into practice, when one of its most eloquent exponents had been besieged for nearly three hours in a small and extremely uncomfortable may-tree by an angry boar-pig, while Lady Carlotta, on the other side of the fence, had proceeded with the water-colour sketch she was engaged on, and refused to interfere between the boar and his prisoner. It is to be feared that she lost the friendship of the ultimately rescued lady. On this occasion she merely lost the train, which gave way to the first sign of impatience it had shown throughout the journey, and steamed off without her. She bore the desertion with philosophical indifference; her friends and relations were thoroughly well used to the fact of her luggage arriving without her. She wired a vague non-committal message to her destination to say that she was coming on "by another train". Before she had time to think what her next move might be she was confronted by an imposingly attired lady, who seemed to be taking a prolonged mental inventory of her clothes and looks.

"You must be Miss Hope, the governess I've come to meet," said the apparition, in a tone that admitted of very little argument.

"Very well, if I must I must," said Lady Carlotta to herself with dangerous meekness.

"I am Mrs. Quabarl," continued the lady; "and where, pray, is your luggage?"

"It's gone astray," said the alleged governess, falling in with the excellent rule of life that the absent are always to blame; the luggage had, in point of fact, behaved with perfect correctitude. "I've just telegraphed about it," she added, with a nearer approach to truth.

"How provoking," said Mrs. Quabarl; "these railway companies are so careless. However, my maid can lend you things for the night," and she led the way to her car.

During the drive to the Quabarl mansion Lady Carlotta was impressively introduced to the nature of the charge that had been thrust upon her; she learned that Claude and Wilfrid were delicate, sensitive young people, that Irene had the artistic temperament highly developed, and that Viola was something or other else of a mould equally commonplace among children of that class and type in the twentieth century.

"I wish them not only to be *taught*," said Mrs. Quabarl, "but *interested* in what they learn. In their history lessons, for instance, you must try to make them feel that they are being introduced to the life-stories of men and women who really lived, not merely committing a mass of names and dates to memory. French, of course, I shall expect you to talk at mealtimes several days in the week."

"I shall talk French four days of the week and Russian in the remaining three."

"Russian? My dear Miss Hope, no one in the house speaks or understands Russian."

"That will not embarrass me in the least," said Lady Carlotta coldly.

Mrs. Quabarl, to use a colloquial expression, was knocked off her perch. She was one of those imperfectly self-assured individuals who are magnificent and autocratic as long as they are not seriously opposed. The least show of unexpected resistance goes a long way towards rendering them cowed and apologetic. When the new governess failed to express wondering admiration of the large newly purchased and expensive car, and lightly alluded to the superior advantages of one or two makes which had just been put on the market, the discomfiture of her patroness became almost abject. Her feelings were those which might have animated a general of ancient warfaring days, on beholding his heaviest battle-elephant ignominiously driven off the field by slingers and javelin throwers.

At dinner that evening, although reinforced by her husband, who usually duplicated her opinions and lent her moral support generally, Mrs. Quabarl regained none of her lost ground. The governess not only helped herself well and truly to wine, but held forth with considerable show of critical knowledge on various vintage matters, concerning which the Quabarls were in no wise able to pose as authorities. Previous governesses had limited their conversation on the wine topic to a respectful and doubtless sincere expression of a preference for water. When this one went as far as to recommend a wine firm in whose hands you could not go very far wrong Mrs. Quabarl thought it time to turn the conversation into more usual channels.

"We got very satisfactory references about you from Canon Teep," she observed; "a very estimable man, I should think."

"Drinks like a fish and beats his wife, otherwise a very lovable character," said the governess imperturbably.

"My *dear* Miss Hope! I trust you are exaggerating," exclaimed the Quabarls in unison.

"One must in justice admit that there is some provocation," continued the romancer. "Mrs. Teep is quite the most irritating bridge-player that I have ever sat down with; her leads and declarations would condone a certain amount of brutality in her partner, but to souse her with the contents of the only soda-water syphon in the house on a Sunday afternoon, when one couldn't get another, argues an indifference to the comfort of others which I cannot altogether overlook. You may think me hasty in my judgments, but it was practically on account of the syphon incident that I left."

"We will talk of this some other time," said Mrs. Quabarl hastily.

"I shall never allude to it again," said the governess with decision.

Mr. Quabarl made a welcome diversion by asking what studies the new instructress proposed to inaugurate on the morrow.

"History to begin with," she informed him.

"Ah, history," he observed sagely; "now in teaching them history you must take care to interest them in what they learn. You must make them feel that they are being introduced to the life-stories of men and women who really lived—"

"I've told her all that," interposed Mrs. Quabarl.

"I teach history on the Schartz–Metterklume method," said the governess loftily.

"Ah, yes," said her listeners, thinking it expedient to assume an acquaintance at least with the name.

"What are you children doing out here?" demanded Mrs. Quabarl the next morning, on finding Irene sitting rather glumly at the head of the stairs, while her sister was perched in an attitude of depressed discomfort on the window-seat behind her, with a wolf-skin rug almost covering her.

"We are having a history lesson," came the unexpected reply. "I am supposed to be Rome, and Viola up there is the she-wolf; not a real wolf, but the figure of one that the Romans used to set store by— I forget why. Claude and Wilfrid have gone to fetch the shabby women."

"The shabby women?"

"Yes, they've got to carry them off. They didn't want to, but Miss Hope got one of father's fives-bats and said she'd give them a number nine spanking if they didn't, so they've gone to do it."

A loud, angry screaming from the direction of the lawn drew Mrs. Quabarl thither in hot haste, fearful lest the threatened castigation might even now be in process of infliction. The outcry, however, came principally from the two small daughters of the lodge-keeper, who were being hauled and pushed towards the house by the panting and dishevelled Claude and Wilfrid, whose task was rendered even more arduous by the incessant, if not very effectual, attacks of the captured maidens' small brother. The governess, fives-bat in hand, sat negligently on the stone balustrade, presiding over the scene with the cold impartiality of a Goddess of Battles. A furious and repeated chorus of "I'll tell muvver" rose from the lodge-children, but the lodge-mother, who was hard of hearing, was for the moment immersed in the preoccupation of her washtub. After an apprehensive glance in the direction of the lodge (the good woman was gifted with the highly militant temper which is sometimes the privilege of deafness) Mrs. Quabarl flew indignantly to the rescue of the struggling captives.

"Wilfrid! Claude! Let those children go at once. Miss Hope, what on earth is the meaning of this scene?"

"Early Roman history; the Sabine Women, don't you know? It's the Schartz-Metterklume method to make children understand history by acting it themselves; fixes it in their memory, you know. Of course, if, thanks to your interference, your boys go through life thinking that the Sabine women ultimately escaped, I really cannot be held responsible."

"You may be very clever and modern, Miss Hope,"

said Mrs. Quabarl firmly, "but I should like you to leave here by the next train. Your luggage will be sent after you as soon as it arrives."

"I'm not certain exactly where I shall be for the next few days," said the dismissed instructress of youth; "you might keep my luggage till I wire my address. There are only a couple of trunks and some golf-clubs and a leopard cub."

"A leopard cub!" gasped Mrs. Quabarl. Even in her departure this extraordinary person seemed destined to leave a trail of embarrassment behind her.

"Well, it's rather left off being a cub; it's more than half-grown, you know. A fowl every day and a rabbit on Sundays is what it usually gets. Raw beef makes it too excitable. Don't trouble about getting the car for me, I'm rather inclined for a walk."

And Lady Carlotta strode out of the Quabarl horizon.

The advent of the genuine Miss Hope, who had made a mistake as to the day on which she was due to arrive, caused a turmoil which that good lady was quite unused to inspiring. Obviously the Quabarl family had been woefully befooled, but a certain amount of relief came with the knowledge.

"How tiresome for you, dear Carlotta," said her hostess, when the overdue guest ultimately arrived; "how very tiresome losing your train and having to stop overnight in a strange place."

"Oh dear, no," said Lady Carlotta; "not at all tiresome—for me."

The Seventh Pullet

"It's not the daily grind that I complain of," said Blenkinthrope resentfully; "it's the dull grey sameness of my life outside of office hours. Nothing of interest comes my way, nothing remarkable or out of the common. Even the little things that I do try to find some interest in don't seem to interest other people. Things in my garden, for instance."

"The potato that weighed just over two pounds," said his friend Gorworth.

"Did I tell you about that?" said Blenkinthrope; "I was telling the others in the train this morning. I forgot if I'd told you."

"To be exact you told me that it weighed just under two pounds, but I took into account the fact that abnormal vegetables and freshwater fish have an after-life, in which growth is not arrested."

"You're just like the others," said Blenkinthrope sadly, "you only make fun of it."

"The fault is with the potato, not with us," said Gorworth; "we are not in the least interested in it because it is not in the least interesting. The men you go up in the train with every day are just in the same case as yourself; their lives are commonplace and not very interesting to themselves, and they certainly are not going to wax enthusiastic over the commonplace events in other men's lives. Tell them something startling, dramatic, piquant that has happened to yourself or to some one in your family, and you will capture their interest at once. They will talk about you with a certain personal pride to all their acquaintances. 'Man I know intimately, fellow called Blenkinthrope, lives down my way, had two of his fingers clawed clean off by a lobster he was carrying home to supper. Doctor says entire hand may have to come off.' Now that is conversation of a very high order. But imagine walking into a tennis club with the remark: 'I know a man who has grown a potato weighing two and a quarter pounds.'"

"But hang it all, my dear fellow," said Blenkinthrope impatiently, "haven't I just told you that nothing of a remarkable nature ever happens to me?"

"Invent something," said Gorworth. Since winning a prize for excellence in Scriptural knowledge at a preparatory school he had felt licensed to be a little more unscrupulous than the circle he moved in. Much might surely be excused to one who in early life could give a list of seventeen trees mentioned in the Old Testament.

"What sort of thing?" asked Blenkinthrope, somewhat snappishly.

"A snake got into your hen-run yesterday morning and killed six out of seven pullets, first mesmerising them with its eyes and then biting them as they stood helpless. The seventh pullet was one of that French sort, with feathers all over its eyes, so it escaped the mesmeric snare, and just flew at what it could see of the snake and pecked it to pieces."

"Thank you," said Blenkinthrope stiffly; "it's a very clever invention. If such a thing had really happened in my poultry-run I admit I should have been proud and interested to tell people about it. But I'd rather stick to fact, even if it is plain fact." All the same his mind dwelt wistfully on the story of the Seventh Pullet. He could picture himself telling it in the train amid the absorbed interest of his fellow-passengers. Unconsciously all sorts of little details and improvements began to suggest themselves.

Wistfulness was still his dominant mood when he took his seat in the railway carriage the next morning. Opposite him sat Stevenham, who had attained to a recognised brevet of importance through the fact of an uncle having dropped dead in the act of voting at a Parliamentary election. That had happened three years ago, but Stevenham was still deferred to on all questions of home and foreign politics.

"Hullo, how's the giant mushroom, or whatever it was?" was all the notice Blenkinthrope got from his fellow travellers.

Young Duckby, whom he mildly disliked, speedily monopolised the general attention by an account of a domestic bereavement.

"Had four young pigeons carried off last night by a whacking big rat. Oh, a monster he must have been; you could tell by the size of the hole he made breaking into the loft."

No moderate-sized rat ever seemed to carry out any predatory operations in these regions; they were all enormous in their enormity.

"Pretty hard lines that," continued Duckby, seeing

that he had secured the attention and respect of the company; "four squeakers carried off at one swoop. You'd find it rather hard to match that in the way of unlooked-for bad luck."

"I had six pullets out of a pen of seven killed by a snake yesterday afternoon," said Blenkinthrope, in a voice which he hardly recognised as his own.

"By a snake?" came in excited chorus.

"It fascinated them with its deadly, glittering eyes, one after the other, and struck them down while they stood helpless. A bedridden neighbour, who wasn't able to call for assistance, witnessed it all from her bedroom window."

"Well, I never!" broke in the chorus, with variations.

"The interesting part of it is about the seventh pullet, the one that didn't get killed," resumed Blenkinthrope, slowly lighting a cigarette. His diffidence had left him, and he was beginning to realise how safe and easy depravity can seem once one has the courage to begin. "The six dead birds were Minorcas; the seventh was a Houdan with a mop of feathers all over its eyes. It could hardly see the snake at all, so of course it wasn't mesmerised like the others. It just could see something wriggling on the ground, and went for it and pecked it to death."

"Well, I'm blessed!" exclaimed the chorus.

In the course of the next few days Blenkinthrope discovered how little the loss of one's self-respect affects one when one has gained the esteem of the world. His story found its way into one of the poultry papers, and was copied thence into a daily news-sheet as a matter of general interest. A lady wrote from the

North of Scotland recounting a similar episode which she had witnessed as occurring between a stoat and a blind grouse. Somehow a lie seems so much less reprehensible when one can call it a lee.

For a while the adapter of the Seventh Pullet story enjoyed to the full his altered standing as a person of consequence, one who had had some share in the strange events of his times. Then he was thrust once again into the cold grey background by the sudden blossoming into importance of Smith-Paddon, a daily fellow traveller, whose little girl had been knocked down and nearly hurt by a car belonging to a musical-comedy actress. The actress was not in the car at the time, but she was in numerous photographs which appeared in the illustrated papers of Zoto Dobreen inquiring after the well-being of Maisie, daughter of Edmund Smith-Paddon, Esq. With this new human interest to absorb them the travelling companions were almost rude when Blenkinthrope tried to explain his contrivance for keeping vipers and peregrine falcons out of his chicken-run.

Gorworth, to whom he unburdened himself in private, gave him the same counsel as theretofore.

"Invent something."

"Yes, but what?"

The ready affirmative coupled with the question betrayed a significant shifting of the ethical standpoint.

It was a few days later that Blenkinthrope revealed a chapter of family history to the customary gathering in the railway carriage.

"Curious thing happened to my aunt, the one who lives in Paris," he began. He had several aunts, but they were all geographically distributed over Greater London.

"She was sitting on a seat in the Bois the other afternoon, after lunching at the Roumanian Legation."

Whatever the story gained in picturesqueness from the dragging-in of diplomatic "atmosphere", it ceased from that moment to command any acceptance as a record of current events. Gorworth had warned his neophyte that this would be the case, but the traditional enthusiasm of the neophyte had triumphed over discretion.

"She was feeling rather drowsy, the effect probably of the champagne, which she's not in the habit of taking in the middle of the day."

A subdued murmur of admiration went round the company. Blenkinthrope's aunts were not used to taking champagne in the middle of the year, regarding it exclusively as a Christmas and New Year accessory.

"Presently a rather portly gentleman passed by her seat and paused an instant to light a cigar. At that moment a youngish man came up behind him, drew the blade from a swordstick, and stabbed him half a dozen times through and through. 'Scoundrel,' he cried to his victim, 'you do not know me. My name is Henri Leturc.' The elder man wiped away some of the blood that was spattering his clothes, turned to his assailant, and said: 'And since when has an attempted assassination been considered an introduction?' Then he finished lighting his cigar and walked away. My aunt had intended screaming for the police, but seeing the indifference with which the principal in the affair treated the matter she felt that it would be an impertinence on her part to interfere. Of course I need hardly say she put the whole thing down to the effects of a warm, drowsy afternoon and the Legation champagne. Now comes the astonishing part of my story. A fortnight later a bank manager was stabbed to death with a swordstick in that very part of the Bois. His assassin was the son of a charwoman formerly working at the bank, who had been dismissed from her job by the manager on account of chronic intemperance. His name was Henri Leturc."

From that moment Blenkinthrope was tacitly accepted as the Munchausen of the party. No effort was spared to draw him out from day to day in the exercise of testing their powers of credulity, and Blenkinthrope, in the false security of an assured and receptive audience, waxed industrious and ingenious in supplying the demand for marvels. Duckby's satirical story of a tame otter that had a tank in the garden to swim in, and whined restlessly whenever the water-rate was overdue, was scarcely an unfair parody of some of Blenkinthrope's wilder efforts. And then one day came Nemesis.

Returning to his villa one evening, Blenkinthrope found his wife sitting in front of a pack of cards, which she was scrutinising with unusual concentration.

"The same old patience-game?" he asked carelessly.

"No, dear; this is the Death's Head patience, the most difficult of them all. I've never got it to work out, and somehow I should be rather frightened if I did. Mother only got it out once in her life; she was afraid of it, too. Her great-aunt had done it once and fallen dead from excitement the next moment, and Mother always had a feeling that she would die if she ever got it out. She died the same night that she did it. She was in bad health at the time, certainly, but it was a strange coincidence."

"Don't do it if it frightens you," was Blenkinthrope's practical comment as he left the room. A few minutes later his wife called to him.

"John, it gave me such a turn, I nearly got it out. Only the five of diamonds held me up at the end. I really thought I'd done it."

"Why, you can do it," said Blenkinthrope, who had come back to the room; "if you shift the eight of clubs on to that open nine the five can be moved on to the six."

His wife made the suggested move with hasty, trembling fingers, and piled the outstanding cards on to their respective packs. Then she followed the example of her mother and great-aunt.

Blenkinthrope had been genuinely fond of his wife, but in the midst of his bereavement one dominant thought obtruded itself. Something sensational and real had at last come into his life; no longer was it a grey, colourless record. The headlines which might appropriately describe his domestic tragedy kept shaping themselves in his brain. "Inherited presentiment comes true." "The Death's Head patience: Card-game that justified its sinister name in three generations." He wrote out a full story of the fatal occurrence for the *Essex Vedette*, the editor of which was a friend of his, and to another friend he gave a condensed account, to be taken up to the office of one of the halfpenny dailies. But in both cases his reputation as a romancer stood fatally in the way of the fulfilment of his ambitions. "Not the right thing to be Munchausening in a time of sorrow," agreed his friends among themselves, and a brief note of regret at the "sudden death of the wife of our respected neighbour, Mr. John Blenkinthrope, from heart failure," appearing in the news column of the local paper was the forlorn outcome of his visions of widespread publicity.

Blenkinthrope shrank from the society of his erstwhile travelling companions and took to travelling townwards by an earlier train. He sometimes tries to enlist the sympathy and attention of a chance acquaintance in details of the whistling prowess of his best canary or the dimensions of his largest beetroot; he scarcely recognises himself as the man who was once spoken about and pointed out as the owner of the Seventh Pullet.

The Blind Spot

"You've just come back from Adelaide's funeral, haven't you?" said Sir Lulworth to his nephew; "I suppose it was very like most other funerals?"

"I'll tell you all about it at lunch," said Egbert.

"You'll do nothing of the sort. It wouldn't be respectful either to your great-aunt's memory or to the lunch. We begin with Spanish olives, then a borsch, then more olives and a bird of some kind, and a rather enticing Rhenish wine, not at all expensive as wines go in this country, but still quite laudable in its way. Now there's absolutely nothing in that menu that harmonises in the least with the subject of your great-aunt Adelaide or her funeral. She was a charming woman, and quite as intelligent as she had any need to be, but somehow she always reminded me of an English cook's idea of a Madras curry."

"She used to say you were frivolous," said Egbert. Something in his tone suggested that he rather endorsed the verdict.

"I believe I once considerably scandalised her by declaring that clear soup was a more important factor in life than a clear conscience. She had very little sense of proportion. By the way, she made you her principal heir, didn't she?"

"Yes," said Egbert, "and executor as well. It's in that connection that I particularly want to speak to you."

"Business is not my strong point at any time," said Sir Lulworth, "and certainly not when we're on the immediate threshold of lunch."

"It isn't exactly business," explained Egbert, as he followed his uncle into the dining-room. "It's something rather serious. Very serious."

"Then we can't possibly speak about it now," said Sir Lulworth; "no one could talk seriously during a borsch. A beautifully constructed borsch, such as you are going to experience presently, ought not only to banish conversation but almost to annihilate thought. Later on, when we arrive at the second stage of olives, I shall be quite ready to discuss that new book on Borrow, or, if you prefer it, the present situation in the Grand Duchy of Luxemburg. But I absolutely decline to talk anything approaching business till we have finished with the bird."

For the greater part of the meal Egbert sat in an abstracted silence, the silence of a man whose mind is focussed on one topic. When the coffee stage had been reached he launched himself suddenly athwart his uncle's reminiscences of the Court of Luxemburg.

"I think I told you that great-aunt Adelaide had made me her executor. There wasn't very much to be done in the way of legal matters, but I had to go through her papers."

"That would be a fairly heavy task in itself. I should imagine there were reams of family letters."

"Stacks of them, and most of them highly uninteresting. There was one packet, however, which I thought might repay a careful perusal. It was a bundle of correspondence from her brother Peter."

"The Canon of tragic memory," said Lulworth.

"Exactly, of tragic memory, as you say; a tragedy that has never been fathomed."

"Probably the simplest explanation was the correct one," said Sir Lulworth; "he slipped on the stone staircase and fractured his skull in falling."

Egbert shook his head. "The medical evidence all went to prove that the blow on the head was struck by some one coming up behind him. A wound caused by violent contact with the steps could not possibly have been inflicted at that angle of the skull. They experimented with a dummy figure falling in every conceivable position."

"But the motive?" exclaimed Sir Lulworth; "no one had any interest in doing away with him, and the number of people who destroy Canons of the Established Church for the mere fun of killing must be extremely limited. Of course there are individuals of weak mental balance who do that sort of thing, but they seldom conceal their handiwork; they are more generally inclined to parade it."

"His cook was under suspicion," said Egbert shortly.

"I know he was," said Sir Lulworth, "simply because he was about the only person on the premises at the time of the tragedy. But could anything be sillier than trying to fasten a charge of murder on to Sebastien? He had nothing to gain, in fact, a good deal to lose, from the death of his employer. The Canon was paying him quite as good wages as I was able to offer him when I took him over into my service. I have since raised them to something a little more in accordance with his real worth, but at the time he was glad to find a new place without troubling about an increase of wages. People were fighting rather shy of him, and he had no friends in this country. No; if any one in the world was interested in the prolonged life and unimpaired digestion of the Canon it would certainly be Sebastien."

"People don't always weigh the consequences of their rash acts," said Egbert, "otherwise there would be very few murders committed. Sebastien is a man of hot temper."

"He is a southerner," admitted Sir Lulworth; "to be geographically exact I believe he hails from the French slopes of the Pyrenees. I took that into consideration when he nearly killed the gardener's boy the other day for bringing him a spurious substitute for sorrel. One must always make allowances for origin and locality and early environment; 'Tell me your longitude and I'll know what latitude to allow you,' is my motto."

"There, you see," said Egbert, "he nearly killed the gardener's boy."

"My dear Egbert, between nearly killing a gardener's boy and altogether killing a Canon there is a wide difference. No doubt you have often felt a temporary desire to kill a gardener's boy; you have never given way to it, and I respect you for your self-control. But I don't suppose you have ever wanted to kill an octogenarian Canon. Besides, as far as we know, there had never been any quarrel or disagreement between the two men. The evidence at the inquest brought that out very clearly."

"Ah!" said Egbert, with the air of a man coming at last into a deferred inheritance of conversational importance, "that is precisely what I want to speak to you about."

He pushed away his coffee cup and drew a pocket-book from his inner breast-pocket. From the depths of the pocket-book he produced an envelope, and from the envelope he extracted a letter, closely written in a small, neat handwriting.

"One of the Canon's numerous letters to Aunt Adelaide," he explained, "written a few days before his death. Her memory was already failing when she received it, and I dare say she forgot the contents as soon as she had read it; otherwise, in the light of what subsequently happened, we should have heard something of this letter before now. If it had been produced at the inquest I fancy it would have made some difference in the course of affairs. The evidence, as you remarked just now, choked off suspicion against Sebastien by disclosing an utter absence of anything that could be considered a motive or provocation for the crime, if crime there was."

"Oh, read the letter," said Sir Lulworth impatiently.

"It's a long rambling affair, like most of his letters in his later years," said Egbert. "I'll read the part that bears immediately on the mystery.

"'I very much fear I shall have to get rid of Sebastien. He cooks divinely, but he has the temper of a fiend or an anthropoid ape, and I am really in bodily fear of him. We had a dispute the other day as to the correct sort of lunch to be served on Ash Wednesday, and I got so irritated and annoyed at his conceit and obstinacy that at last I threw a cupful of coffee in his face and called him at the same time an impudent jackanapes. Very little of the coffee went actually in his face, but I have never seen a human being show such deplorable lack of self-control. I laughed at the threat of killing me that he spluttered out in his rage, and thought the whole thing would blow over, but I have several times since caught him scowling and muttering in a highly unpleasant fashion, and lately I have fancied that he was dogging my footsteps about the grounds, particularly when I walk of an evening in the Italian Garden.'

"It was on the steps in the Italian Garden that the body was found," commented Egbert, and resumed reading.

" 'I dare say the danger is imaginary; but I shall feel more at ease when he has quitted my service.' "

Egbert paused for a moment at the conclusion of the extract; then, as his uncle made no remark, he added: "If lack of motive was the only factor that saved Sebastien from prosecution I fancy this letter will put a different complexion on matters."

"Have you shown it to any one else?" asked Sir Lulworth, reaching out his hand for the incriminating piece of paper.

"No," said Egbert, handing it across the table, "I thought I would tell you about it first. Heavens, what are you doing?"

Egbert's voice rose almost to a scream. Sir Lulworth had flung the paper well and truly into the glowing centre of the grate. The small, neat handwriting shrivelled into black flaky nothingness.

"What on earth did you do that for?" gasped Egbert. "That letter was our one piece of evidence to connect Sebastien with the crime."

"That is why I destroyed it," said Sir Lulworth.

"But why should you want to shield him?" cried Egbert; "the man is a common murderer."

"A common murderer, possibly, but a very uncommon cook."

A Touch of Realism

"I hope you've come full of suggestions for Christmas," said Lady Blonze to her latest arrived guest; "the old-fashioned Christmas and the up-to-date Christmas are both so played out. I want to have something really original this year."

"I was staying with the Mathesons last month," said Blanche Boveal eagerly, "and we had such a good idea. Every one in the house-party had to be a character and behave consistently all the time, and at the end of the visit one had to guess what every one's character was. The one who was voted to have acted his or her character best got a prize."

"It sounds amusing," said Lady Blonze.

"I was St. Francis of Assisi," continued Blanche; "we hadn't got to keep to our right sexes. I kept getting up in the middle of a meal, and throwing out food to the birds; you see, the chief thing that one remembers of St. Francis is that he was fond of the birds. Every one was so stupid about it, and thought that I was the old man who feeds the sparrows in the Tuileries Gardens. Then Colonel Pentley was the Jolly Miller on the banks of Dee."

"How on earth did he do that?" asked Bertie van Tahn.

"'He laughed and sang from morn till night,'" explained Blanche.

"How dreadful for the rest of you," said Bertie; "and anyway he wasn't on the banks of Dee."

"One had to imagine that," said Blanche.

"If you could imagine all that you might as well imagine cattle on the further bank and keep on calling them home, Mary-fashion, across the sands of Dee. Or you might change the river to the Yarrow and imagine it was on the top of you, and say you were Willie, or whoever it was, drowned in Yarrow."

"Of course it's easy to make fun of it," said Blanche sharply, "but it was extremely interesting and amusing. The prize was rather a fiasco, though. You see, Millie Matheson said her character was Lady Bountiful, and as she was our hostess of course we all had to vote that she had carried out her character better than any one. Otherwise I ought to have got the prize."

"It's quite an idea for a Christmas party," said Lady Blonze; "we must certainly do it here."

Sir Nicholas was not so enthusiastic. "Are you quite sure, my dear, that you're wise in doing this thing?" he said to his wife when they were alone together. "It might do very well at the Mathesons, where they had rather a staid, elderly house-party, but here it will be a different matter. There is the Durmot flapper, for instance, who simply stops at nothing, and you know what Van Tahn is like. Then there is Cyril Skatterly; he has madness on one side of his family and a Hungarian grandmother on the other."

"I don't see what they could do that would matter," said Lady Blonze.

"It's the unknown that is to be dreaded," said Sir Nicholas. "If Skatterly took it into his head to represent a Bull of Bashan, well, I'd rather not be here."

"Of course we shan't allow any Bible characters. Besides, I don't know what the Bulls of Bashan really did that was so very dreadful; they just came round and gaped, as far as I remember."

"My dear, you don't know what Skatterly's Hungarian imagination mightn't read into the part; it would be small satisfaction to say to him afterwards: 'You've behaved as no Bull of Bashan would have behaved.' "

"Oh, you're an alarmist," said Lady Blonze; "I particularly want to have this idea carried out. It will be sure to be talked about a lot."

"That is quite possible," said Sir Nicholas.

Dinner that evening was not a particularly lively affair; the strain of trying to impersonate a self-imposed character or to glean hints of identity from other people's conduct acted as a check on the natural festivity of such a gathering. There was a general feeling of gratitude and acquiescence when good-natured Rachel Klammerstein suggested that there should be an hour or two's respite from "the game" while they all listened to a little piano-playing after dinner. Rachel's love of piano music was not indiscriminate, and concentrated itself chiefly on selections rendered by her idolised offspring, Moritz and Augusta, who, to do them justice, played remarkably well.

The Klammersteins were deservedly popular as Christmas guests; they gave expensive gifts lavishly on Christmas Day and New Year, and Mrs. Klammerstein had already dropped hints of her intention to present the prize for the best enacted character in the game competition. Every one had brightened at this prospect; if it had fallen to Lady Blonze, as hostess, to provide the prize, she would have considered that a little souvenir of some twenty or twenty-five shillings' value would meet the case, whereas coming from a Klammerstein source it would certainly run to several guineas.

The close time for impersonation efforts came to an end with the final withdrawal of Moritz and Augusta from the piano. Blanche Boveal retired early, leaving the room in a series of laboured leaps that she hoped might be recognised as a tolerable imitation of Pavlova. Vera Durmot, the sixteen-year-old flapper, expressed her confident opinion that the performance was intended to typify Mark Twain's famous jumping frog, and her diagnosis of the case found general acceptance. Another guest to set an example of early bed-going was Waldo Plubley, who conducted his life on a minutely regulated system of time-tables and hygienic routine. Waldo was a plump, indolent young man of seven-and-twenty, whose mother had early in his life decided for him that he was unusually delicate, and by dint of much coddling and homekeeping had succeeded in making him physically soft and mentally peevish. Nine hours' unbroken sleep, preceded by elaborate breathing exercises and other hygienic ritual, was among the indispensable regulations which Waldo imposed on himself, and there were innumerable small observances which he exacted from those who were in any way obliged to minister to his requirements; a special teapot for the decoction of his early tea was always solemnly handed over to the bedroom staff of any house in which he happened to be staying. No one had ever quite mastered the mechanism of this precious vessel, but Bertie van Tahn was responsible for the legend that its spout had to be kept facing north during the process of infusion.

On this particular night the irreducible nine hours were severely mutilated by the sudden and by no means noiseless incursion of a pyjama-clad figure into Waldo's room at an hour midway between midnight and dawn.

"What is the matter? What are you looking for?" asked the awakened and astonished Waldo, slowly recognising Van Tahn, who appeared to be searching hastily for something he had lost.

"Looking for sheep," was the reply.

"Sheep?" exclaimed Waldo.

"Yes, sheep. You don't suppose I'm looking for giraffes, do you?"

"I don't see why you should expect to find either in my room," retorted Waldo furiously.

"I can't argue the matter at this hour of the night," said Bertie, and began hastily rummaging in the chest of drawers. Shirts and underwear went flying on to the floor.

"There are no sheep here, I tell you," screamed Waldo.

"I've only got your word for it," said Bertie, whisking most of the bedclothes on to the floor; "if you weren't concealing something you wouldn't be so agitated."

Waldo was by this time convinced that Van Tahn was raving mad, and made an anxious effort to humour him.

"Go back to bed like a dear fellow," he pleaded, "and your sheep will turn up all right in the morning."

"I dare say," said Bertie gloomily, "without their

tails. Nice fool I shall look with a lot of Manx sheep."

And by way of emphasising his annoyance at the prospect he sent Waldo's pillows flying to the top of the wardrobe.

"But *why* no tails?" asked Waldo, whose teeth were chattering with fear and rage and lowered temperature.

"My dear boy, have you never heard the ballad of Little Bo-Peep?" said Bertie with a chuckle. "It's my character in the Game, you know. If I didn't go hunting about for my lost sheep no one would be able to guess who I was; and now go to sleepy weeps like a good child or I shall be cross with you."

"I leave you to imagine," wrote Waldo in the course of a long letter to his mother, "how much sleep I was able to recover that night, and you know how essential nine uninterrupted hours of slumber are to my health."

On the other hand he was able to devote some wakeful hours to exercises in breathing wrath and fury against Bertie van Tahn.

Breakfast at Blonzecourt was a scattered meal, on the "come when you please" principle, but the house-party was supposed to gather in full strength at lunch. On the day after the "Game" had been started there were, however, some notable absentees. Waldo Plubley, for instance, was reported to be nursing a headache. A large breakfast and an "A.B.C." had been taken up to his room, but he had made no appearance in the flesh.

"I expect he's playing up to some character," said Vera Durmot; "isn't there a thing of Moliere's, '*Le Malade Imaginaire*'? I expect he's that."

Eight or nine lists came out, and were duly pencilled

with the suggestion.

"And where are the Klammersteins?" asked Lady Blonze; "they're usually so punctual."

"Another character pose, perhaps," said Bertie van Tahn; "'the Lost Ten Tribes'."

"But there are only three of them. Besides, they'll want their lunch. Hasn't any one seen anything of them?"

"Didn't you take them out in your car?" asked Blanche Boveal, addressing herself to Cyril Skatterly.

"Yes, took them out to Slogberry Moor immediately after breakfast. Miss Durmot came too."

"I saw you and Vera come back," said Lady Blonze, "but I didn't see the Klammersteins. Did you put them down in the village?"

"No," said Skatterly shortly.

"But where are they? Where did you leave them?"

"We left them on Slogberry Moor," said Vera calmly.

"On Slogberry Moor? Why, it's more than thirty miles away! How are they going to get back?"

"We didn't stop to consider that," said Skatterly; "we asked them to get out for a moment, on the pretence that the car had stuck, and then we dashed off full speed and left them there."

"But how dare you do such a thing? It's most inhuman! Why, it's been snowing for the last hour."

"I expect there'll be a cottage or farmhouse somewhere if they walk a mile or two."

"But why on earth have you done it?"

The question came in a chorus of indignant bewilderment.

"*That* would be telling what our characters are meant to be," said Vera.

"Didn't I warn you?" said Sir Nicholas tragically to his wife.

"It's something to do with Spanish history; we don't mind giving you that clue," said Skatterly, helping himself cheerfully to salad, and then Bertie van Tahn broke forth into peals of joyous laughter.

"I've got it! Ferdinand and Isabella deporting the Jews! Oh, lovely! Those two have certainly won the prize; we shan't get anything to beat that for thoroughness."

Lady Blonze's Christmas party was talked about and written about to an extent that she had not anticipated in her most ambitious moments. The letters from Waldo's mother would alone have made it memorable.

The Byzantine Omelette

Sophie Chattel-Monkheim was a Socialist by conviction and a Chattel-Monkheim by marriage. The particular member of that wealthy family whom she had married was rich, even as his relatives counted riches. Sophie had very advanced and decided views as to the distribution of money: it was a pleasing and fortunate circumstance that she also had the money. When she inveighed eloquently against the evils of capitalism at drawing-room meetings and Fabian conferences she was conscious of a comfortable feeling that the system, with all its inequalities and iniquities, would probably last her time. It is one of the consolations of middle-aged reformers that the good they inculcate must live after them if it is to live at all.

On a certain spring evening, somewhere towards the dinner-hour, Sophie sat tranquilly between her mirror and her maid, undergoing the process of having her hair built into an elaborate reflection of the prevailing fashion. She was hedged round with a great peace, the peace of one who has attained a desired end with much effort and perseverance, and who has found it still eminently desirable in its attainment. The Duke of Syria had consented to come beneath her roof as a guest, was even now installed beneath her roof, and would shortly be sitting at her dining-table. As a good Socialist, Sophie disapproved of social distinctions, and derided the idea of a princely caste, but if there were to be these artificial gradations of rank and dignity she was pleased and anxious to have an exalted specimen of an exalted order included in her house-party. She was broad-minded enough to love the sinner while hating the sin—not that she entertained any warm feeling of personal affection for the Duke of Syria, who was a comparative stranger, but still, as Duke of Syria, he was very, very welcome beneath her roof. She could not have explained why, but no one was likely to ask her for an explanation, and most hostesses envied her.

"You must surpass yourself tonight, Richardson," she said complacently to her maid; "I must be looking my very best. We must all surpass ourselves."

The maid said nothing, but from the concentrated look in her eyes and the deft play of her fingers it was evident that she was beset with the ambition to surpass herself.

A knock came at the door, a quiet but peremptory knock, as of some one who would not be denied.

"Go and see who it is," said Sophie; "it may be something about the wine."

Richardson held a hurried conference with an invisible messenger at the door; when she returned there was noticeable a curious listlessness in place of her hitherto alert manner.

"What is it?" asked Sophie.

"The household servants have 'downed tools', madame," said Richardson.

"Downed tools!" exclaimed Sophie; "do you mean to

say they've gone on strike?"

"Yes, madame," said Richardson, adding the information: "It's Gaspare that the trouble is about."

"Gaspare?" said Sophie wonderingly; "the emergency chef! The omelette specialist!"

"Yes, madame. Before he became an omelette specialist he was a valet, and he was one of the strike-breakers in the great strike at Lord Grimford's two years ago. As soon as the household staff here learned that you had engaged him they resolved to 'down tools' as a protest. They haven't got any grievance against you personally, but they demand that Gaspare should be immediately dismissed."

"But," protested Sophie, "he is the only man in England who understands how to make a Byzantine omelette. I engaged him specially for the Duke of Syria's visit, and it would be impossible to replace him at short notice. I should have to send to Paris, and the Duke loves Byzantine omelettes. It was the one thing we talked about coming from the station."

"He was one of the strike-breakers at Lord Grimford's," reiterated Richardson.

"This is too awful," said Sophie; "a strike of servants at a moment like this, with the Duke of Syria staying in the house. Something must be done immediately. Quick, finish my hair and I'll go and see what I can do to bring them round."

"I can't finish your hair, madame," said Richardson quietly, but with immense decision. "I belong to the union and I can't do another half-minute's work till the strike is settled. I'm sorry to be disobliging."

"But this is inhuman!" exclaimed Sophie tragically;

"I've always been a model mistress and I've refused to employ any but union servants, and this is the result. I can't finish my hair myself; I don't know how to. What am I to do? It's wicked!"

"Wicked is the word," said Richardson; "I'm a good Conservative and I've no patience with this Socialist foolery, asking your pardon. It's tyranny, that's what it is, all along the line, but I've my living to make, same as other people, and I've got to belong to the union. I couldn't touch another hairpin without a strike permit, not if you was to double my wages."

The door burst open and Catherine Malsom raged into the room.

"Here's a nice affair," she screamed, "a strike of household servants without a moment's warning, and I'm left like this! I can't appear in public in this condition."

After a very hasty scrutiny Sophie assured her that she could not.

"Have they *all* struck?" she asked her maid.

"Not the kitchen staff," said Richardson, "they belong to a different union."

"Dinner at least will be assured," said Sophie, "that is something to be thankful for."

"Dinner!" snorted Catherine, "what on earth is the good of dinner when none of us will be able to appear at it? Look at your hair—and look at me! or rather, don't."

"I know it's difficult to manage without a maid; can't your husband be any help to you?" asked Sophie despairingly.

"Henry? He's in worse case than any of us. His man is the only person who really understands that ridiculous new-fangled Turkish bath that he insists on taking with him everywhere."

"Surely he could do without a Turkish bath for one evening," said Sophie; "I can't appear without hair, but a Turkish bath is a luxury."

"My good woman," said Catherine, speaking with a fearful intensity, "Henry was *in* the bath when the strike started. *In* it, do you understand? He's there now."

"Can't he get out?"

"He doesn't know how to. Every time he pulls the lever marked 'release' he only releases hot steam. There are two kinds of steam in the bath, 'bearable' and 'scarcely bearable'; he has released them both. By this time I'm probably a widow."

"I simply can't send away Gaspare," wailed Sophie; "I should never be able to secure another omelette specialist."

"Any difficulty that I may experience in securing another husband is of course a trifle beneath any one's consideration," said Catherine bitterly.

Sophie capitulated. "Go," she said to Richardson, "and tell the Strike Committee, or whoever are directing this affair, that Gaspare is herewith dismissed. And ask Gaspare to see me presently in the library, when I will pay him what is due to him and make what excuses I can; and then fly back and finish my hair."

Some half an hour later Sophie marshalled her guests in the Grand Salon preparatory to the formal march to the dining-room. Except that Henry Malsom was of the ripe raspberry tint that one sometimes sees at private theatricals representing the human complexion, there was little outward sign among those assembled of the crisis that had just been encountered and surmounted. But the tension had been too stupefying while it lasted not to leave some mental effects behind it. Sophie talked at random to her illustrious guest, and found her eyes straying with increasing frequency towards the great doors through which would presently come the blessed announcement that dinner was served. Now and again she glanced mirror-ward at the reflection of her wonderfully coiffed hair, as an insurance underwriter might gaze thankfully at an overdue vessel that had ridden safely into harbour in the wake of a devastating hurricane. Then the doors opened and the welcome figure of the butler entered the room. But he made no general announcement of a banquet in readiness, and the doors closed behind him; his message was for Sophie alone.

"There is no dinner, madame," he said gravely; "the kitchen staff have 'downed tools'. Gaspare belongs to the Union of Cooks and Kitchen Employés, and as soon as they heard of his summary dismissal at a moment's notice they struck work. They demand his instant reinstatement and an apology to the union. I may add, madame, that they are very firm; I've been obliged even to hand back the dinner rolls that were already on the table."

After the lapse of eighteen months Sophie Chattel-Monkheim is beginning to go about again among her old haunts and associates, but she still has to be very careful. The doctors will not let her attend anything at all exciting, such as a drawing-room meeting or a Fabian conference; it is doubtful, indeed, whether she wants to.

The Feast of Nemesis

"It's a good thing that Saint Valentine's Day has dropped out of vogue," said Mrs. Thackenbury; "what with Christmas and New Year and Easter, not to speak of birthdays, there are quite enough remembrance days as it is. I tried to save myself trouble at Christmas by just sending flowers to all my friends, but it wouldn't work; Gertrude has eleven hot-houses and about thirty gardeners, so it would have been ridiculous to send flowers to her, and Milly has just started a florist's shop, so it was equally out of the question there. The stress of having to decide in a hurry what to give to Gertrude and Milly just when I thought I'd got the whole question nicely off my mind completely ruined my Christmas, and then the awful monotony of the letters of thanks: 'Thank you so much for your lovely flowers. It was so good of you to think of me.' Of course in the majority of cases I hadn't thought about the recipients at all; their names were down in my list of 'people who must not be left out'. If I trusted to remembering them there would be some awful sins of omission."

"The trouble is," said Clovis to his aunt, "all these days of intrusive remembrance harp so persistently on one aspect of human nature and entirely ignore the other; that is why they become so perfunctory and artificial. At Christmas and New Year you are emboldened and encouraged by convention to send gushing messages of optimistic goodwill and servile affection to people whom you would scarcely ask to lunch unless some one else had failed you at the last moment; if you are supping at a restaurant on New Year's Eve you are permitted and expected to join hands and sing 'For Auld Lang Syne' with strangers whom you have never seen before and never want to see again. But no licence is allowed in the opposite direction."

"Opposite direction; what opposite direction?" queried Mrs. Thackenbury.

"There is no outlet for demonstrating your feelings towards people whom you simply loathe. That is really the crying need of our modern civilisation. Just think how jolly it would be if a recognised day were set apart for the paying off of old scores and grudges, a day when one could lay oneself out to be gracefully vindictive to a carefully treasured list of 'people who must not be let off'. I remember when I was at a private school we had one day, the last Monday of the term I think it was, consecrated to the settlement of feuds and grudges; of course we did not appreciate it as much as it deserved, because after all, any day of the term could be used for that purpose. Still, if one had chastised a smaller boy for being cheeky weeks before, one was always permitted on that day to recall the episode to his memory by chastising him again. That is what the French call reconstructing the crime."

"I should call it reconstructing the punishment," said Mrs. Thackenbury; "and, anyhow, I don't see how you could introduce a system of primitive school-boy vengeance into civilised adult life. We haven't outgrown our passions, but we are supposed to have learned how to keep them within strictly decorous limits."

"Of course the thing would have to be done furtively and politely," said Clovis; "the charm of it would be that it would never be perfunctory like the other thing. Now, for instance, you say to yourself: 'I must show the Webleys some attention at Christmas, they were kind to dear Bertie at Bournemouth,' and you send them a calendar, and daily for six days after Christmas the male Webley asks the female Webley if she has remembered to thank you for the calendar you sent them. Well, transplant that idea to the other and more human side of your nature, and say to yourself: 'Next Thursday is Nemesis Day; what on earth can I do to those odious people next door who made such an absurd fuss when Ping Yang bit their youngest child?' Then you'd get up awfully early on the allotted day and climb over into their garden and dig for truffles on their tennis court with a good gardening fork, choosing, of course, that part of the court that was screened from observation by the laurel bushes. You wouldn't find any truffles but you would find a great peace, such as no amount of present-giving could ever bestow."

"I shouldn't," said Mrs. Thackenbury, though her air of protest sounded a bit forced, "I should feel rather a worm for doing such a thing."

"You exaggerate the power of upheaval which a worm would be able to bring into play in the limited time available," said Clovis; "if you put in a strenuous ten minutes with a really useful fork, the result ought to suggest the operations of an unusually masterful mole or a badger in a hurry."

"They might guess I had done it," said Mrs. Thackenbury.

"Of course they would," said Clovis; "that would be half the satisfaction of the thing, just as you like people at Christmas to know what presents or cards you've sent them. The thing would be much easier to manage, of course, when you were on outwardly friendly terms with the object of your dislike. That greedy little Agnes Blaik, for instance, who thinks of nothing but her food, it would be quite simple to ask her to a picnic in some wild woodland spot and lose her just before lunch was served; when you found her again every morsel of food could have been eaten up."

"It would require no ordinary human strategy to lose Agnes Blaik when luncheon was imminent: in fact, I don't believe it could be done."

"Then have all the other guests, people whom you dislike, and lose the luncheon. It could have been sent by accident in the wrong direction."

"It would be a ghastly picnic," said Mrs. Thackenbury.

"For them, but not for you," said Clovis; "you would have had an early and comforting lunch before you started, and you could improve the occasion by mentioning in detail the items of the missing banquet —the lobster Newburg and the egg mayonnaise, and the curry that was to have been heated in a chafing-dish. Agnes Blaik would be delirious long before you got to the list of wines, and in the long interval of waiting, before they had quite abandoned hope of the

214

lunch turning up, you could induce them to play silly games, such as that idiotic one of 'the Lord Mayor's dinner-party', in which every one has to choose the name of a dish and do something futile when it is called out. In this case they would probably burst into tears when their dish is mentioned. It would be a heavenly picnic."

Mrs. Thackenbury was silent for a moment; she was probably making a mental list of the people she would like to invite to the Duke Humphrey picnic. Presently she asked: "And that odious young man, Waldo Plubley, who is always coddling himself—have you thought of anything that one could do to him?" Evidently she was beginning to see the possibilities of Nemesis Day.

"If there was anything like a general observance of the festival," said Clovis, "Waldo would be in such demand that you would have to bespeak him weeks beforehand, and even then, if there were an east wind blowing or a cloud or two in the sky he might be too careful of his precious self to come out. It would be rather jolly if you could lure him into a hammock in the orchard, just near the spot where there is a wasps' nest every summer. A comfortable hammock on a warm afternoon would appeal to his indolent tastes, and then, when he was getting drowsy, a lighted fusee thrown into the nest would bring the wasps out in an indignant mass, and they would soon find a 'home away from home' on Waldo's fat body. It takes some doing to get out of a hammock in a hurry."

"They might sting him to death," protested Mrs. Thackenbury.

"Waldo is one of those people who would be

215

enormously improved by death," said Clovis; "but if you didn't want to go as far as that, you could have some wet straw ready to hand, and set it alight under the hammock at the same time that the fusee was thrown into the nest; the smoke would keep all but the most militant of the wasps just outside the stinging line, and as long as Waldo remained within its protection he would escape serious damage, and could be eventually restored to his mother, kippered all over and swollen in places, but still perfectly recognisable."

"His mother would be my enemy for life," said Mrs. Thackenbury.

"That would be one greeting less to exchange at Christmas," said Clovis.

The Dreamer

It was the season of sales. The august establishment of Walpurgis and Nettlepink had lowered its prices for an entire week as a concession to trade observances, much as an Archduchess might protestingly contract an attack of influenza for the unsatisfactory reason that influenza was locally prevalent. Adela Chemping, who considered herself in some measure superior to the allurements of an ordinary bargain sale, made a point of attending the reduction week at Walpurgis and Nettlepink's.

"I'm not a bargain hunter," she said, "but I like to go where bargains are."

Which showed that beneath her surface strength of character there flowed a gracious undercurrent of human weakness.

With a view to providing herself with a male escort Mrs. Chemping had invited her youngest nephew to accompany her on the first day of the shopping expedition, throwing in the additional allurement of a cinematograph theatre and the prospect of light refreshment. As Cyprian was not yet eighteen, she hoped he might not have reached that stage in masculine development when parcel-carrying is looked on as a thing abhorrent.

"Meet me just outside the floral department," she

wrote to him, "and don't be a moment later than eleven."

Cyprian was a boy who carried with him through early life the wondering look of a dreamer, the eyes of one who sees things that are not visible to ordinary mortals, and invests the commonplace things of this world with qualities unsuspected by plainer folk—the eyes of a poet or a house agent. He was quietly dressed —that sartorial quietude which frequently accompanies early adolescence, and is usually attributed by novel-writers to the influence of a widowed mother. His hair was brushed back in a smoothness as of ribbon seaweed and seamed with a narrow furrow that scarcely aimed at being a parting. His aunt particularly noted this item of his toilet when they met at the appointed rendezvous, because he was standing waiting for her bareheaded.

"Where is your hat?" she asked.

"I didn't bring one with me," he replied.

Adela Chemping was slightly scandalised.

"You are not going to be what they call a Nut, are you?" she inquired with some anxiety, partly with the idea that a Nut would be an extravagance which her sister's small household would scarcely be justified in incurring, partly, perhaps, with the instinctive apprehension that a Nut, even in its embryo stage, would refuse to carry parcels.

Cyprian looked at her with his wondering, dreamy eyes.

"I didn't bring a hat," he said, "because it is such a nuisance when one is shopping; I mean it is so awkward if one meets any one one knows and has to take one's hat off when one's hands are full of parcels. If one hasn't got a hat on one can't take it off."

Mrs. Chemping sighed with great relief; her worst fear had been laid at rest.

"It is more orthodox to wear a hat," she observed, and then turned her attention briskly to the business in hand.

"We will go first to the table-linen counter," she said, leading the way in that direction; "I should like to look at some napkins."

The wondering look deepened in Cyprian's eyes as he followed his aunt; he belonged to a generation that is supposed to be over-fond of the rôle of mere spectator, but looking at napkins that one did not mean to buy was a pleasure beyond his comprehension. Mrs. Chemping held one or two napkins up to the light and stared fixedly at them, as though she half expected to find some revolutionary cypher written on them in scarcely visible ink; then she suddenly broke away in the direction of the glassware department.

"Millicent asked me to get her a couple of decanters if there were any going really cheap," she explained on the way, "and I really do want a salad bowl. I can come back to the napkins later on."

She handled and scrutinised a large number of decanters and a long series of salad bowls, and finally bought seven chrysanthemum vases.

"No one uses that kind of vase nowadays," she informed Cyprian, "but they will do for presents next Christmas."

Two sunshades that were marked down to a price that Mrs. Chemping considered absurdly cheap were added to her purchases.

"One of them will do for Ruth Colson; she is going

out to the Malay States, and a sunshade will always be useful there. And I must get her some thin writing paper. It takes up no room in one's baggage."

Mrs. Chemping bought stacks of writing paper; it was so cheap, and it went so flat in a trunk or portmanteau. She also bought a few envelopes— envelopes somehow seemed rather an extragavance compared with notepaper.

"Do you think Ruth will like blue or grey paper?" she asked Cyprian.

"Grey," said Cyprian, who had never met the lady in question.

"Have you any mauve notepaper of this quality?" Adela asked the assistant.

"We haven't any mauve," said the assistant, "but we've two shades of green and a darker shade of grey."

Mrs. Chemping inspected the greens and the darker grey, and chose the blue.

"Now we can have some lunch," she said.

Cyprian behaved in an exemplary fashion in the refreshment department, and cheerfully accepted a fish cake and a mince pie and a small cup of coffee as adequate restoratives after two hours of concentrated shopping. He was adamant, however, in resisting his aunt's suggestion that a hat should be bought for him at the counter where men's head-wear was being disposed of at temptingly reduced prices.

"I've got as many hats as I want at home," he said, "and besides, it rumples one's hair so, trying them on."

Perhaps he was going to develop into a Nut after all. It was a disquieting symptom that he left all the parcels in charge of the cloak-room attendant.

"We shall be getting more parcels presently," he said, "so we need not collect these till we have finished our shopping."

His aunt was doubtfully appeased; some of the pleasure and excitement of a shopping expedition seemed to evaporate when one was deprived of immediate personal contact with one's purchases.

"I'm going to look at those napkins again," she said, as they descended the stairs to the ground floor. "You need not come," she added, as the dreaming look in the boy's eyes changed for a moment into one of mute protest, "you can meet me afterwards in the cutlery department; I've just remembered that I haven't a corkscrew in the house that can be depended on."

Cyprian was not to be found in the cutlery department when his aunt in due course arrived there, but in the crush and bustle of anxious shoppers and busy attendants it was an easy matter to miss any one. It was in the leather goods department some quarter of an hour later that Adela Chemping caught sight of her nephew, separated from her by a rampart of suitcases and portmanteaux and hemmed in by the jostling crush of human beings that now invaded every corner of the great shopping emporium. She was just in time to witness a pardonable but rather embarrassing mistake on the part of a lady who had wriggled her way with unstayable determination towards the bareheaded Cyprian, and was now breathlessly demanding the sale price of a handbag which had taken her fancy.

"There now," exclaimed Adela to herself, "she takes him for one of the shop assistants because he hasn't got a hat on. I wonder it hasn't happened before."

Perhaps it had. Cyprian, at any rate, seemed neither startled nor embarrassed by the error into which the good lady had fallen. Examining the ticket on the bag, he announced in a clear, dispassionate voice:

"Black seal, thirty-four shillings, marked down to twenty-eight. As a matter of fact, we are clearing them out at a special reduction price of twenty-six shillings. They are going off rather fast."

"I'll take it," said the lady, eagerly digging some coins out of her purse.

"Will you take it as it is?" asked Cyprian; "it will be a matter of a few minutes to get it wrapped up, there is such a crush."

"Never mind, I'll take it as it is," said the purchaser, clutching her treasure and counting the money into Cyprian's palm.

Several kind strangers helped Adela into the open air.

"It's the crush and the heat," said one sympathiser to another; "it's enough to turn any one giddy."

When she next came across Cyprian he was standing in the crowd that pushed and jostled around the counters of the book department. The dream look was deeper than ever in his eyes. He had just sold two books of devotion to an elderly Canon.

The Forbidden Buzzards

"Is match-making at all in your line?"

Hugo Peterby asked the question with a certain amount of personal interest.

"I don't specialise in it," said Clovis; "it's all right while you're doing it, but the after-effects are sometimes so disconcerting—the mute reproachful looks of the people you've aided and abetted in matrimonial experiments. It's as bad as selling a man a horse with half a dozen latent vices and watching him discover them piecemeal in the course of the hunting season. I suppose you're thinking of the Coulterneb girl. She's certainly jolly, and quite all right as far as looks go, and I believe a certain amount of money adheres to her. What I don't see is how you will ever manage to propose to her. In all the time I've known her I don't remember her to have stopped talking for three consecutive minutes. You'll have to race her six times round the grass paddock for a bet, and then blurt your proposal out before she's got her wind back. The paddock is laid up for hay, but if you're really in love with her you won't let a consideration of that sort stop you, especially as it's not your hay."

"I think I could manage the proposing part right enough," said Hugo, "if I could count on being left alone with her for four or five hours. The trouble is that I'm not likely to get anything like that amount of grace. That fellow Lanner is showing signs of interesting himself in the same quarter. He's quite heartbreakingly rich and is rather a swell in his way; in fact, our hostess is obviously a bit flattered at having him here. If she gets wind of the fact that he's inclined to be attracted by Betty Coulterneb she'll think it a splendid match and throw them into each other's arms all day long, and then where will my opportunities come in? My one anxiety is to keep him out of the girl's way as much as possible, and if you could help me—"

"If you want me to trot Lanner round the country-side, inspecting alleged Roman remains and studying local methods of bee culture and crop raising, I'm afraid I can't oblige you," said Clovis. "You see, he's taken something like an aversion to me since the other night in the smoking-room."

"What happened in the smoking-room?"

"He trotted out some well-worn chestnut as the latest thing in good stories, and I remarked, quite innocently, that I never could remember whether it was George II or James II who was so fond of that particular story, and now he regards me with politely draped dislike. I'll do my best for you, if the opportunity arises, but it will have to be in a roundabout, impersonal manner."

"It's so nice having Mr. Lanner here," confided Mrs. Olston to Clovis the next afternoon; "he's always been engaged when I've asked him before. Such a nice man; he really ought to be married to some nice girl. Between you and me, I have an idea that he came down here for a certain reason."

"I've had much the same idea," said Clovis, lowering his voice; "in fact, I'm almost certain of it."

"You mean he's attracted by—" began Mrs. Olston eagerly.

"I mean he's here for what he can get," said Clovis.

"For what he can *get*?" said the hostess with a touch of indignation in her voice; "what do you mean? He's a very rich man. What should he want to get here?"

"He has one ruling passion," said Clovis, "and there's something he can get here that is not to be had for love nor for money anywhere else in the country, as far as I know."

"But what? Whatever do you mean? What is his ruling passion?"

"Egg-collecting," said Clovis. "He has agents all over the world getting rare eggs for him, and his collection is one of the finest in Europe; but his great ambition is to collect his treasures personally. He stops at no expense nor trouble to achieve that end."

"Good heavens! The buzzards, the rough-legged buzzards!" exclaimed Mrs. Olston; "you don't think he's going to raid their nest?"

"What do you think yourself?" asked Clovis; "the only pair of rough-legged buzzards known to breed in this country are nesting in your woods. Very few people know about them, but as a member of the league for protecting rare birds that information would be at his disposal. I came down in the train with him, and I noticed that a bulky volume of Dresser's *Birds of Europe* was one of the requisites that he had packed in his travelling-kit. It was the volume dealing with short-winged hawks and buzzards."

Clovis believed that if a lie was worth telling it was worth telling well.

"This is appalling," said Mrs. Olston; "my husband would never forgive me if anything happened to those birds. They've been seen about the woods for the last year or two, but this is the first time they've nested. As you say, they are almost the only pair known to be breeding in the whole of Great Britain; and now their nest is going to be harried by a guest staying under my roof. I must do something to stop it. Do you think if I appealed to him—?"

Clovis laughed.

"There is a story going about, which I fancy is true in most of its details, of something that happened not long ago somewhere on the coast of the Sea of Marmora, in which our friend had a hand. A Syrian night-jar, or some such bird, was known to be breeding in the olive gardens of a rich Armenian, who for some reason or other wouldn't allow Lanner to go in and take the eggs though he offered cash down for the permission. The Armenian was found beaten nearly to death a day or two later, and his fences levelled. It was assumed to be a case of Mussulman aggression, and noted as such in all the Consular reports, but the eggs are in the Lanner collection. No, I don't think I should appeal to his better feelings if I were you."

"I must do something," said Mrs. Olston tearfully; "my husband's parting words when he went off to Norway were an injunction to see that those birds were not disturbed, and he's asked about them every time he's written. Do suggest something."

"I was going to suggest picketing," said Clovis.

"Picketing! You mean setting guards round the birds?"

"No; round Lanner. He can't find his way through those woods by night, and you could arrange that you or Evelyn or Jack or the German governess should be by his side in relays all day long. A fellow guest he could get rid of, but he couldn't very well shake off members of the household, and even the most determined collector would hardly go climbing after forbidden buzzards' eggs with a German governess hanging round his neck, so to speak."

Lanner, who had been lazily watching for an opportunity for prosecuting his courtship of the Coulterneb girl, found presently that his chances of getting her to himself for ten minutes even were non-existent. If the girl was ever alone he never was. His hostess had changed suddenly, as far as he was concerned, from the desirable type that lets her guests do nothing in the way that best pleases them, to the sort that drags them over the ground like so many harrows. She showed him the herb garden and the greenhouses, the village church, some water-colour sketches that her sister had done in Corsica, and the place where it was hoped that celery would grow later in the year. He was shown all the Aylesbury ducklings and the row of wooden hives where there would have been bees if there had not been bee disease. He was also taken to the end of a long lane and shown a distant mound whereon local tradition reported that the Danes had once pitched a camp. And when his hostess had to desert him temporarily for other duties he would find Evelyn walking solemnly by his side. Evelyn was fourteen and talked chiefly about good and evil, and of how much one might accomplish in the way of regenerating the world if one was thoroughly determined to do one's utmost. It was generally rather a relief when she was displaced by Jack, who was nine years old, and talked exclusively about the Balkan War without throwing any fresh light on its political or military history. The German governess told Lanner more about Schiller than he had ever heard in his life about any one person; it was perhaps his own fault for having told her that he was not interested in Goethe. When the governess went off picket duty the hostess was again on hand with a not-to-be-gainsaid invitation to visit the cottage of an old woman who remembered Charles James Fox; the woman had been dead for two or three years, but the cottage was still there. Lanner was called back to town earlier than he had originally intended.

Hugo did not bring off his affair with Betty Coulterneb. Whether she refused him or whether, as was more generally supposed, he did not get a chance of saying three consecutive words, has never been exactly ascertained. Anyhow, she is still the jolly Coulterneb girl.

The buzzards successfully reared two young ones, which were shot by a local hairdresser.

A Defensive Diamond

Treddleford sat in an easeful arm-chair in front of a slumberous fire, with a volume of verse in his hand and the comfortable consciousness that outside the club windows the rain was dripping and pattering with persistent purpose. A chill, wet October afternoon was merging into a bleak, wet October evening, and the club smoking-room seemed warmer and cosier by contrast. It was an afternoon on which to be wafted away from one's climatic surroundings, and *The Golden Journey to Samarkand* promised to bear Treddleford well and bravely into other lands and under other skies. He had already migrated from London the rain-swept to Bagdad the Beautiful, and stood by the Sun Gate "in the olden time" when an icy breath of imminent annoyance seemed to creep between the book and himself. Amblecope, the man with the rest-less, prominent eyes and the mouth ready mobilised for conversational openings, had planted himself in a neighbouring arm-chair. For a twelvemonth and some odd weeks Treddleford had skilfully avoided making the acquaintance of his voluble fellow-clubman; he had marvellously escaped from the infliction of his relentless record of tedious personal achievements, or alleged achievements, on golf links, turf, and gaming table, by flood and field and covert-side. Now his season of immunity was coming to an end. There was no escape; in another moment he would be numbered among those who knew Amblecope to speak to—or rather, to suffer being spoken to.

The intruder was armed with a copy of *Country Life*, not for purposes of reading, but as an aid to conversational ice-breaking.

"Rather a good portrait of Throstlewing," he remarked explosively, turning his large challenging eyes on Treddleford; "somehow it reminds me very much of Yellowstep, who was supposed to be such a good thing for the Grand Prix in 1903. Curious race that was; I suppose I've seen every race for the Grand Prix for the last—"

"Be kind enough never to mention the Grand Prix in my hearing," said Treddleford desperately; "it awakens acutely distressing memories. I can't explain why without going into a long and complicated story."

"Oh, certainly, certainly," said Amblecope hastily; long and complicated stories that were not told by himself were abominable in his eyes. He turned the pages of *Country Life* and became spuriously interested in the picture of a Mongolian pheasant.

"Not a bad representation of the Mongolian variety," he exclaimed, holding it up for his neighbour's inspection. "They do very well in some covers. Take some stopping too, once they're fairly on the wing. I suppose the biggest bag I ever made in two successive days—"

"My aunt, who owns the greater part of Lincolnshire," broke in Treddleford, with dramatic abruptness, "possesses perhaps the most remarkable record in the way of a pheasant bag that has ever been achieved. She is seventy-five and can't hit a thing, but she always goes out with the guns. When I say she can't hit a thing, I don't mean to say that she doesn't occasionally endanger the lives of her fellow-guns, because that wouldn't be true. In fact, the chief Government Whip won't allow Ministerial M.P.'s to go out with her; 'We don't want to incur by-elections needlessly,' he quite reasonably observed. Well, the other day she winged a pheasant, and brought it to earth with a feather or two knocked out of it; it was a runner, and my aunt saw herself in danger of being done out of about the only bird she'd hit during the present reign. Of course she wasn't going to stand that; she followed it through bracken and brushwood, and when it took to the open country and started across a ploughed field she jumped on to the shooting pony and went after it. The chase was a long one, and when my aunt at last ran the bird to a standstill she was nearer home than she was to the shooting party; she had left that some five miles behind her."

"Rather a long run for a wounded pheasant," snapped Amblecope.

"The story rests on my aunt's authority," said Treddleford coldly, "and she is local vice-president of the Young Women's Christian Association. She trotted three miles or so to her home, and it was not till the middle of the afternoon that it was discovered that the lunch for the entire shooting party was in a pannier attached to the pony's saddle. Anyway, she got her bird."

"Some birds, of course, take a lot of killing," said Amblecope; "so do some fish. I remember once I was fishing in the Exe, lovely trout stream, lots of fish, though they don't run to any great size—"

"One of them did," announced Treddleford, with emphasis. "My uncle, the Bishop of Southmolton, came across a giant trout in a pool just off the main stream of the Exe near Ugworthy; he tried it with every kind of fly and worm every day for three weeks without an atom of success, and then Fate intervened on his behalf. There was a low stone bridge just over this pool, and on the last day of his fishing holiday a motor van ran violently into the parapet and turned completely over; no one was hurt, but part of the parapet was knocked away, and the entire load that the van was carrying was pitched over and fell a little way into the pool. In a couple of minutes the giant trout was flapping and twisting on bare mud at the bottom of a waterless pool, and my uncle was able to walk down to him and fold him to his breast. The van-load consisted of blotting-paper, and every drop of water in that pool had been sucked up into the mass of spilt cargo."

There was silence for nearly half a minute in the smoking-room, and Treddleford began to let his mind steal back towards the golden road that led to Samarkand. Amblecope, however, rallied, and remarked in a rather tired and dispirited voice:

"Talking of motor accidents, the narrowest squeak I ever had was the other day, motoring with old Tommy Yarby in North Wales. Awfully good sort, old Yarby, thorough good sportsman, and the best—"

"It was in North Wales," said Treddleford, "that my sister met with her sensational carriage accident last year. She was on her way to a garden-party at Lady Nineveh's, about the only garden-party that ever comes

232

to pass in those parts in the course of the year, and therefore a thing that she would have been very sorry to miss. She was driving a young horse that she'd only bought a week or two previously, warranted to be perfectly steady with motor traffic, bicycles, and other common objects of the roadside. The animal lived up to its reputation, and passed the most explosive of motor-bikes with an indifference that almost amounted to apathy. However, I suppose we all draw the line some-where, and this particular cob drew it at travelling wild beast shows. Of course my sister didn't know that, but she knew it very distinctly when she turned a sharp corner and found herself in a mixed company of camels, piebald horses, and canary-coloured vans. The dog-cart was overturned in a ditch and kicked to splinters, and the cob went home across country. Neither my sister nor the groom was hurt, but the problem of how to get to the Nineveh garden party, some three miles distant, seemed rather difficult to solve; once there, of course, my sister would easily find some one to drive her home. 'I suppose you wouldn't care for the loan of a couple of my camels?' the showman suggested, in humorous sympathy. ' I would,' said my sister, who had ridden camel-back in Egypt, and she overruled the objections of the groom, who hadn't. She picked out two of the most presentable-looking of the beasts and had them dusted and made as tidy as was possible at short notice, and set out for the Nineveh mansion. You may imagine the sensation that her small but imposing caravan created when she arrived at the hall door. The entire garden party flocked up to gape. My sister was rather glad to slip down from her camel, and the groom was thankful to scramble down from his. Then young Billy Doulton, of the Dragoon Guards, who has been a lot at Aden and thinks he knows camel-language backwards, thought he would show off by making the beasts kneel down in orthodox fashion. Unfortunately camel words-of-command are not the same all the world over; these were magnificent Turkestan camels, accustomed to stride up the stony terraces of mountain passes, and when Doulton shouted at them they went side by side up the front steps, into the entrance hall, and up the grand staircase. The German governess met them just at the turn of the corridor. The Ninevehs nursed her with devoted attention for weeks, and when I last heard from them she was well enough to go about her duties again, but the doctor says she will always suffer from Hagenbeck heart."

Amblecope got up from his chair and moved to another part of the room. Treddleford reopened his book and betook himself once more across

The dragon-green, the luminous, the dark, the serpent-haunted sea.

For a blessed half-hour he disported himself in imagination by the "gay Aleppo-Gate", and listened to the bird-voiced singing-man. Then the world of today called him back; a page summoned him to speak with a friend on the telephone.

As Treddleford was about to pass out of the room he encountered Amblecope, also passing out, on his way to the billiard-room, where, perchance, some luckless wight might be secured and held fast to listen to the number of his attendances at the Grand Prix, with subsequent remarks on Newmarket and the Cambridgeshire. Amblecope made as if to pass out first, but a new-born pride was surging in Treddleford's breast and he waved him back.

"I believe I take precedence," he said coldly; "you are merely the club Bore; I am the club Liar."

The Disappearance of Crispina Umberleigh

In a first-class carriage of a train speeding Balkanward across the flat, green Hungarian plain two Britons sat in friendly, fitful converse. They had first foregathered in the cold grey dawn at the frontier line, where the presiding eagle takes on an extra head and Teuton lands pass from Hohenzollern to Habsburg keeping—and where a probing official beak requires to delve in polite and perhaps perfunctory, but always tiresome, manner into the baggage of sleep-hungry passengers. After a day's break of their journey at Vienna the travellers had again foregathered at the trainside and paid one another the compliment of settling instinctively into the same carriage. The elder of the two had the appearance and manner of a diplomat; in point of fact he was the well-connected foster-brother of a wine business. The other was certainly a journalist. Neither man was talkative and each was grateful to the other for not being talkative. That is why from time to time they talked.

One topic of conversation naturally thrust itself forward in front of all others. In Vienna the previous day they had learned of the mysterious vanishing of a world-famous picture from the walls of the Louvre.

"A dramatic disappearance of that sort is sure to produce a crop of imitations," said the Journalist.

"It has had a lot of anticipations, for the matter of that," said the Wine-brother.

"Oh, of course there have been thefts from the Louvre before."

"I was thinking of the spiriting away of human beings rather than pictures. In particular I was thinking of the case of my aunt, Crispina Umberleigh."

"I remember hearing something of the affair," said the Journalist, "but I was away from England at the time. I never quite knew what was supposed to have happened."

"You may hear what really happened if you will respect it as a confidence," said the Wine Merchant. "In the first place I may say that the disappearance of Mrs. Umberleigh was not regarded by the family entirely as a bereavement. My uncle, Edward Umberleigh, was not by any means a weak-kneed individual, in fact in the world of politics he had to be reckoned with more or less as a strong man, but he was unmistakably dominated by Crispina; indeed I never met any human being who was not frozen into subjection when brought into prolonged contact with her. Some people are born to command; Crispina Mrs. Umberleigh was born to legislate, codify, administrate, censor, license, ban, execute, and sit in judgment generally. If she was not born with that destiny she adopted it at an early age. From the kitchen regions upwards every one in the household came under her despotic sway and stayed there with the submissiveness of molluscs involved in a glacial epoch. As a nephew on a footing of only occasional visits she affected me merely as an epidemic, disagreeable while it lasted, but without any permanent effect; but her own sons and daughters stood

237

in mortal awe of her; their studies, friendships, diet, amusements, religious observances, and way of doing their hair were all regulated and ordained according to the august lady's will and pleasure. This will help you to understand the sensation of stupefaction which was caused in the family when she unobtrusively and inexplicably vanished. It was as though St. Paul's Cathedral or the Piccadilly Hotel had disappeared in the night, leaving nothing but an open space to mark where it had stood. As far as was known nothing was troubling her; in fact there was much before her to make life particularly well worth living. The youngest boy had come back from school with an unsatisfactory report, and she was to have sat in judgment on him the very afternoon of the day she disappeared—if it had been he who had vanished in a hurry one could have supplied the motive. Then she was in the middle of a newspaper correspondence with a rural dean in which she had already proved him guilty of heresy, inconsistency, and unworthy quibbling, and no ordinary consideration would have induced her to discontinue the controversy. Of course the matter was put in the hands of the police, but as far as possible it was kept out of the papers, and the generally accepted explanation of her withdrawal from her social circle was that she had gone into a nursing home."

"And what was the immediate effect on the home circle?" asked the Journalist.

"All the girls bought themselves bicycles; the feminine cycling craze was still in existence, and Crispina had rigidly vetoed any participation in it among the members of her household. The youngest boy let himself go to such an extent during his next term that it had to be his last as far as that particular establishment was concerned. The elder boys propounded a theory that their mother might be wandering somewhere abroad, and searched for her assiduously, chiefly, it must be admitted, in a class of Montmartre resort where it was extremely improbable that she would be found."

"And all this while couldn't your uncle get hold of the least clue?"

"As a matter of fact he had received some information, though of course I did not know of it at the time. He got a message one day telling him that his wife had been kidnapped and smuggled out of the country; she was said to be hidden away, in one of the islands off the coast of Norway I think it was, in comfortable surroundings and well cared for. And with the information came a demand for money; a lump sum of £2000 was to be paid yearly. Failing this she would be immediately restored to her family."

The Journalist was silent for a moment, and then began to laugh quietly.

"It was certainly an inverted form of holding to ransom," he said.

"If you had known my aunt," said the Wine Merchant, "you would have wondered that they didn't put the figure higher."

"I realise the temptation. Did your uncle succumb to it?"

"Well, you see, he had to think of others as well as himself. For the family to have gone back into the Crispina thraldom after having tasted the delights of liberty would have been a tragedy, and there were even wider considerations to be taken into account. Since his bereavement he had unconsciously taken up a far bolder and more initiatory line in public affairs, and his popularity and influence had increased correspondingly. From being merely a strong man in the political world he began to be spoken of as *the* strong man. All this he knew would be jeopardised if he once more dropped into the social position of the husband of Mrs. Umberleigh. He was a rich man, and the £2000 a year, though not exactly a fleabite, did not seem an extravagant price to pay for the boarding-out of Crispina. Of course, he had severe qualms of conscience about the arrangement. Later on, when he took me into his confidence, he told me that in paying the ransom, or hush-money as I should have called it, he was partly influenced by the fear that if he refused it the kidnappers might have vented their rage and disappointment on their captive. It was better, he said, to think of her being well cared for as a highly valued paying-guest in one of the Lofoden Islands than to have her struggling miserably home in a maimed and mutilated condition. Anyway he paid the yearly instalment as punctually as one pays a fire insurance, and with equal promptitude there would come an acknowledgment of the money and a brief statement to the effect that Crispina was in good health and fairly cheerful spirits. One report even mentioned that she was busying herself with a scheme for proposed reforms in Church management to be pressed on the local pastorate. Another spoke of a rheumatic attack and a journey to a 'cure' on the mainland, and on that occasion an additional £80 was demanded and conceded. Of course it was to the interest of the kidnappers to keep their charge in good health, but the secrecy with which they managed to shroud their arrangements argued a really wonderful organisation. If my uncle was paying a rather high price, at least he could console himself with the reflection that he was paying specialists' fees."

"Meanwhile had the police given up all attempts to track the missing lady?" asked the Journalist.

"Not entirely; they came to my uncle from time to time to report on clues which they thought might yield some elucidation as to her fate or whereabouts, but I think they had their suspicions that he was possessed of more information than he had put at their disposal. And then, after a disappearance of more than eight years, Crispina returned with dramatic suddenness to the home she had left so mysteriously."

"She had given her captors the slip?"

"She had never been captured. Her wandering away had been caused by a sudden and complete loss of memory. She usually dressed rather in the style of a superior kind of charwoman, and it was not so very surprising that she should have imagined that she was one; and still less that people should accept her statement and help her to get work. She had wandered as far afield as Birmingham, and found fairly steady employment there, her energy and enthusiasm in putting people's rooms in order counter-balancing her obstinate and domineering characteristics. It was the shock of being patronisingly addressed as 'my good woman' by a curate, who was disputing with her where the stove should be placed in a parish concert hall that led to the sudden restoration of her memory. 'I think you forget who you are speaking to,' she observed crushingly, which was rather unduly severe, considering she had only just remembered it herself."

"But," exclaimed the Journalist, "the Lofoden Island people! Who had they got hold of?"

"A purely mythical prisoner. It was an attempt in the first place by some one who knew something of the domestic situation, probably a discharged valet, to bluff a lump sum out of Edward Umberleigh before the missing woman turned up; the subsequent yearly instalments were an unlooked-for increment to the original haul.

"Crispina found that the eight years' interregnum had materially weakened her ascendancy over her now grown-up offspring. Her husband, however, never accomplished anything great in the political world after her return; the strain of trying to account satisfactorily for an unspecified expenditure of £16,000 spread over eight years sufficiently occupied his mental energies. Here is Belgrad and another custom house."

Bertie's Christmas Eve

It was Christmas Eve, and the family circle of Luke Steffink, Esq., was aglow with the amiability and random mirth which the occasion demanded. A long and lavish dinner had been partaken of, waits had been round and sung carols; the house-party had regaled itself with more caroling on its own account, and there had been romping which, even in a pulpit reference, could not have been condemned as ragging. In the midst of the general glow, however, there was one black unkindled cinder.

Bertie Steffink, nephew of the aforementioned Luke, had early in life adopted the profession of ne'er-do-weel; his father had been something of the kind before him. At the age of eighteen Bertie had commenced that round of visits to our Colonial possessions, so seemly and desirable in the case of a Prince of the Blood, so suggestive of insincerity in a young man of the middle class. He had gone to grow tea in Ceylon and fruit in British Columbia, and to help sheep to grow wool in Australia. At the age of twenty he had just returned from some similar errand in Canada, from which it may be gathered that the trial he gave to these various experiments was of the summary drum-head nature. Luke Steffink, who fulfilled the troubled role of guardian and deputy-parent to Bertie, deplored the persistent manifestation of the homing instinct on his nephew's part, and his solemn thanks earlier in the day for the blessing of reporting a united family had no reference to Bertie's return.

Arrangements had been promptly made for packing the youth off to a distant corner of Rhodesia, whence return would be a difficult matter; the journey to this uninviting destination was imminent, in fact a more careful and willing traveller would have already begun to think about his packing. Hence Bertie was in no mood to share in the festive spirit which displayed itself around him, and resentment smouldered within him at the eager, self-absorbed discussion of social plans for the coming months which he heard on all sides. Beyond depressing his uncle and the family circle generally by singing "Say au revoir, and not good-bye", he had taken no part in the evening's conviviality.

Eleven o'clock had struck some half-hour ago, and the elder Steffinks began to throw out suggestions leading up to that process which they called retiring for the night.

"Come, Teddie, it's time you were in your little bed, you know," said Luke Steffink to his thirteen-year-old son.

"That's where we all ought to be," said Mrs. Steffink.

"There wouldn't be room," said Bertie.

The remark was considered to border on the scandalous; everybody ate raisins and almonds with the nervous industry of sheep feeding during threatening weather.

"In Russia," said Horace Bordenby, who was staying in the house as a Christmas guest, "I've read that the

244

peasants believe that if you go into a cow-house or stable at midnight on Christmas Eve you will hear the animals talk. They're supposed to have the gift of speech at that one moment of the year."

"Oh, *do* let's *all* go down to the cow-house and listen to what they've got to say!" exclaimed Beryl, to whom anything was thrilling and amusing if you did it in a troop.

Mrs. Steffink made a laughing protest, but gave a virtual consent by saying, "We must all wrap up well, then." The idea seemed a scatterbrained one to her, and almost heathenish, but if afforded an opportunity for "throwing the young people together", and as such she welcomed it. Mr. Horace Bordenby was a young man with quite substantial prospects, and he had danced with Beryl at a local subscription ball a sufficient number of times to warrant the authorised inquiry on the part of the neighbours whether "there was anything in it". Though Mrs. Steffink would not have put it in so many words, she shared the idea of the Russian peasantry that on this night the beast might speak.

The cow-house stood at the junction of the garden with a small paddock, an isolated survival, in a suburban neighbourhood, of what had once been a small farm. Luke Steffink was complacently proud of his cow-house and his two cows; he felt that they gave him a stamp of solidity which no number of Wyandottes or Orpingtons could impart. They even seemed to link him in a sort of inconsequent way with those patriarchs who derived importance from their floating capital of flocks and herbs, he-asses and she-asses. It had been an anxious and momentous occasion when he had had to decide definitely between "the

Byre" and "the Ranch" for the naming of his villa residence. A December midnight was hardly the moment he would have chosen for showing his farm-building to visitors, but since it was a fine night, and the young people were anxious for an excuse for a mild frolic, Luke consented to chaperon the expedition. The servants had long since gone to bed, so the house was left in charge of Bertie, who scornfully declined to stir out on the pretext of listening to bovine conversation.

"We must go quietly," said Luke, as he headed the procession of giggling young folk, brought up in the rear by the shawled and hooded figure of Mrs. Steffink; "I've always laid stress on keeping this a quiet and orderly neighbourhood."

It was a few minutes to midnight when the party reached the cow-house and made its way in by the light of Luke's stable lantern. For a moment every one stood in silence, almost with a feeling of being in church.

"Daisy—the one lying down—is by a shorthorn bull out of a Guernsey cow," announced Luke in a hushed voice, which was in keeping with the foregoing impression.

"Is she?" said Bordenby, rather as if he had expected her to be by Rembrandt.

"Myrtle is—"

Myrtle's family history was cut short by a little scream from the women of the party.

The cow-house door had closed noiselessly behind them and the key had turned gratingly in the lock; then they heard Bertie's voice pleasantly wishing them good-night and his footsteps retreating along the garden path.

Luke Steffink strode to the window; it was a small

square opening of the old-fashioned sort, with iron bars let into the stonework.

"Unlock the door this instant," he shouted, with as much air of menacing authority as a hen might assume when screaming through the bars of a coop at a marauding hawk. In reply to his summons the hall door closed with a defiant bang.

A neighbouring clock struck the hour of midnight. If the cows had received the gift of human speech at that moment they would not have been able to make themselves heard. Seven or eight other voices were engaged in describing Bertie's present conduct and his general character at a high pressure of excitement and indignation.

In the course of half an hour or so everything that it was permissible to say about Bertie had been said some dozens of times, and other topics began to come to the front—the extreme mustiness of the cow-house, the possibility of it catching fire, and the probability of it being a Rowton House for the vagrant rats of the neighbourhood. And still no sign of deliverance came to the unwilling vigil-keepers.

Towards one o'clock the sound of rather boisterous and undisciplined carol-singing approached rapidly, and came to a sudden anchorage, apparently just outside the garden-gate. A motor-load of youthful "bloods", in a high state of conviviality, had made a temporary halt for repairs; the stoppage, however, did not extend to the vocal efforts of the party, and the watchers in the cow-shed were treated to a highly unauthorised rendering of "Good King Wenceslas", in which the adjective "good" appeared to be very carelessly applied.

The noise had the effect of bringing Bertie out into the garden, but he utterly ignored the pale, angry faces peering out at the cow-house window, and concentrated his attention on the revellers outside the gate.

"Wassail, you chaps!" he shouted.

"Wassail, old sport!" they shouted back; "we'd jolly well drink y'r health, only we've nothing to drink it in."

"Come and wassail inside," said Bertie hospitably; "I'm all alone, and there's heap's of 'wet'."

They were total strangers, but his touch of kindness made them instantly his kin. In another moment the unauthorised version of King Wenceslas, which, like many other scandals, grew worse on repetition, went echoing up the garden path; two of the revellers gave an impromptu performance on the way by executing the staircase waltz up the terraces of what Luke Steffink, hitherto with some justification, called his rock-garden. The rock part of it was still there when the waltz had been accorded its third encore. Luke, more than ever like a cooped hen behind the cow-house bars, was in a position to realise the feelings of concert-goers unable to countermand the call for an encore which they neither desire or deserve.

The hall door closed with a bang on Bertie's guests, and the sounds of merriment became faint and muffled to the weary watchers at the other end of the garden. Presently two ominous pops, in quick succession, made themselves distinctly heard.

"They've got at the champagne!" exclaimed Mrs. Steffink.

"Perhaps it's the sparkling Moselle," said Luke hopefully.

Three or four more pops were heard.

"The champagne and the sparkling Moselle," said Mrs. Steffink.

Luke uncorked an expletive which, like brandy in a temperance household, was only used on rare emergencies. Mr. Horace Bordenby had been making use of similar expressions under his breath for a considerable time past. The experiment of "throwing the young people together" had been prolonged beyond a point when it was likely to produce any romantic result.

Some forty minutes later the hall door opened and disgorged a crowd that had thrown off any restraint of shyness that might have influenced its earlier actions. Its vocal efforts in the direction of carol-singing were now supplemented by instrumental music; a Christmas-tree that had been prepared for the children of the gardener and other household retainers had yielded a rich spoil of tin trumpets, rattles, and drums. The life-story of King Wenceslas had been dropped, Luke was thankful to notice, but it was intensely irritating for the chilled prisoners in the cow-house to be told that it was "a hot time in the old town tonight", together with some accurate but entirely superfluous information as to the imminence of Christmas morning. Judging by the protests which began to be shouted from the upper windows of neighbouring houses the sentiments prevailing in the cow-house were heartily echoed in other quarters.

The revellers found their car, and, what was more remarkable, managed to drive off in it, with a parting fanfare of tin trumpets. The lively beat of a drum disclosed the fact that the master of the revels remained on the scene.

"Bertie!" came in an angry, imploring chorus of shouts and screams from the cow-house window.

"Hullo," cried the owner of the name, turning his rather errant steps in the direction of the summons; "are you people still there? Must have heard everything cows got to say by this time. If you haven't, no use waiting. After all, it's a Russian legend, and Russian Chrismush Eve not due for 'nother fortnight. Better come out."

After one or two ineffectual attempts he managed to pitch the key of the cow-house door in through the window. Then, lifting his voice in the strains of "I'm afraid to go home in the dark", with a lusty drum accompaniment, he led the way back to the house. The hurried procession of the released that followed in his steps came in for a good deal of the adverse comment that his exuberant display had evoked.

It was the happiest Christmas Eve he had ever spent. To quote his own words, he had a rotten Christmas.

Forewarned

Alethia Debchance sat in a corner of an otherwise empty railway carriage, more or less at ease as regarded body, but in some trepidation as to mind. She had embarked on a social adventure of no little magnitude as compared with the accustomed seclusion and stagnation of her past life. At the age of twenty-eight she could look back on nothing more eventful than the daily round of her existence in her aunt's house at Webblehinton, a hamlet four and a half miles distant from a country town and about a quarter of a century removed from modern times. Their neighbours had been elderly and few, not much given to social intercourse, but helpful or politely sympathetic in times of illness. Newspapers of the ordinary kind were a rarity; those that Alethia saw regularly were devoted exclusively either to religion or to poultry, and the world of politics was to her an unheeded unexplored region. Her ideas on life in general had been acquired through the medium of popular respectable novel-writers, and modified or emphasised by such knowledge as her aunt, the vicar, and her aunt's housekeeper had put at her disposal. And now, in her twenty-ninth year, her aunt's death had left her, well provided for as regards income, but somewhat isolated in the matter of kith and kin and human companionship. She had some cousins who were on terms of friendly, though infrequent, correspondence with her, but as they lived permanently in Ceylon, a locality about which she knew little, beyond the assurance contained in the missionary hymn that the human element there was vile, they were not of much immediate use to her. Other cousins she also possessed, more distant as regards relationship, but not quite so geographically remote, seeing that they lived somewhere in the Midlands. She could hardly remember ever having met them, but once or twice in the course of the last three or four years they had expressed a polite wish that she should pay them a visit; they had probably not been unduly depressed by the fact that her aunt's failing health had prevented her from accepting their invitation. The note of condolence that had arrived on the occasion of her aunt's death had included a vague hope that Alethia would find time in the near future to spend a few days with her cousins, and after much deliberation and many hesitations she had written to propose herself as a guest for a definite date some weeks ahead. The family, she reflected with relief, was not a large one; the two daughters were married and away, there was only old Mrs. Bludward and her son Robert at home. Mrs. Bludward was something of an invalid, and Robert was a young man who had been at Oxford and was going into Parliament. Further than that Alethia's information did not go; her imagination, founded on her extensive knowledge of the people one met in novels, had to supply the gaps. The mother was not difficult to place; she would either be an ultra-amiable old lady, bearing her feeble health with uncomplaining fortitude, and having a kind word for the gardener's boy and a sunny smile for the chance visitor, or else she would be cold and peevish, with eyes that pierced you like a gimlet, and a unreasoning idolatry of her son. Alethia's imagination rather inclined her to the latter view. Robert was more of a problem. There were three dominant types of manhood to be taken into consideration in working out his class-ification; there was Hugo, who was strong, good, and beautiful, a rare type and not very often met with; there was Sir Jasper, who was utterly vile and absolutely unscrupulous, and there was Nevil, who was not really bad at heart, but had a weak mouth and usually required the life-work of two good women to keep him from ultimate disaster. It was probable, Alethia con-sidered, that Robert came into the last category, in which case she was certain to enjoy the companionship of one or two excellent women, and might possibly catch glimpses of undesirable adventuresses or come face to face with reckless admiration-seeking married women. It was altogether an exciting prospect, this sudden venture into an unexplored world of unknown human beings, and Alethia rather wished that she could have taken the vicar with her; she was not, however, rich or important enough to travel with a chaplain, as the Marquis of Moystoncleugh always did in the novel she had just been reading, so she recognised that such a proceeding was out of the question.

The train which carried Alethia towards her destination was a local one, with the wayside station habit strongly developed. At most of the stations no one seemed to want to get into the train or to leave it, but at one there were several market folk on the platform, and two men, of the farmer or small cattle-dealer class, entered Alethia's carriage. Apparently they had just foregathered, after a day's business, and their conversation consisted of a rapid exchange of short friendly inquiries as to health, family, stock, and so forth, and some grumbling remarks on the weather. Suddenly, however, their talk took a dramatically interesting turn, and Alethia listened with wide-eyed attention.

"What do you think of Mister Robert Bludward, eh?"

There was a certain scornful ring in his question.

"Robert Bludward? An out-an'-out rotter, that's what he is. Ought to be ashamed to look any decent man in the face. Send him to Parliament to represent us—not much! He'd rob a poor man of his last shilling, he would."

"Ah, that he would. Tells a pack of lies to get our votes, that's all that he's after, damn him. Did you see the way the *Argus* showed him up this week? Properly exposed him, hip and thigh, I tell you."

And so on they ran, in their withering indictment. There could be no doubt that it was Alethia's cousin and prospective host to whom they were referring; the allusion to a Parliamentary candidature settled that. What could Robert Bludward have done, what manner of man could he be, that people should speak of him with such obvious reprobation?

"He was hissed down at Shoalford yesterday," said one of the speakers.

Hissed! Had it come to that? There was something dramatically biblical in the idea of Robert Bludward's neighbours and acquaintances hissing him for very scorn. Lord Hereward Stranglath had been hissed, now

Alethia came to think of it, in the eighth chapter of *Matterby Towers*, while in the act of opening a Wesleyan bazaar, because he was suspected (unjustly as it turned out afterwards) of having beaten the German governess to death. And in *Tainted Guineas* Roper Squenderby had been deservedly hissed, on the steps of the Jockey Club, for having handed a rival owner a forged telegram, containing false news of his mother's death, just before the start for an important race, thereby ensuring the withdrawal of his rival's horse. In placid Saxon–blooded England people did not demonstrate their feelings lightly and without some strong compelling cause. What manner of evildoer was Robert Bludward?

The train stopped at another small station, and the two men got out. One of them left behind him a copy of the *Argus*, the local paper to which he had made reference. Alethia pounced on it, in the expectation of finding a cultured literary endorsement of the censure which these rough farming men had expressed in their homely, honest way. She had not far to look; "Mr. Robert Bludward, Swanker", was the title of one of the principal articles in the paper. She did not exactly know what a swanker was, probably it referred to some unspeakable form of cruelty, but she read enough in the first few sentences of the article to discover that her cousin Robert, the man at whose house she was about to stay, was an unscrupulous, unprincipled character, of a low order of intelligence, yet cunning withal, and that he and his associates were responsible for most of the misery, disease, poverty, and ignorance with which the country was afflicted; never, except in one or two of the denunciatory Psalms, which she had always supposed to have be written in a spirit of exaggerated Oriental imagery, had she read such an indictment of a human being. And this monster was going to meet her at Derrelton Station in a few short minutes. She would know him at once; he would have the dark beetling brows, the quick, furtive glance, the sneering, unsavoury smile that always characterised the Sir Jaspers of this world. It was too late to escape; she must force herself to meet him with outward calm.

It was a considerable shock to her to find that Robert was fair, with a snub nose, merry eye, and rather a schoolboy manner. "A serpent in duckling's plumage," was her private comment; merciful chance had revealed him to her in his true colours.

As they drove away from the station a dissipated-looking man of the labouring class waved his hat in friendly salute. "Good luck to you, Mr. Bludward," he shouted; "you'll come out on top! We'll break old Chobham's neck for him."

"Who was that man?" asked Alethia quickly.

"Oh, one of my supporters," laughed Robert; "a bit of a poacher and a bit of a pub-loafer, but he's on the right side."

So these were the sort of associates that Robert Bludward consorted with, thought Alethia.

"Who is the person he referred to as old Chobham?" she asked.

"Sir John Chobham, the man who is opposing me," answered Robert; "that is his house away there among the trees on the right."

So there was an upright man, possibly a very Hugo in character, who was thwarting and defying the evildoer in his nefarious career, and there was a dastardly plot afoot to break his neck! Possibly the attempt would be made within the next few hours. He must certainly be warned. Alethia remembered how Lady Sylvia Broom-gate, in *Nightshade Court*, had pretended to be bolted with by her horse up to the front door of a threatened county magnate, and had whispered a warning in his ear which saved him from being the victim of foul murder. She wondered if there was a quiet pony in the stables on which she would be allowed to ride out alone. The chances were that she would be watched. Robert would come spurring after her and seize her bridle just as she was turning in at Sir John's gates.

A group of men that they passed in a village street gave them no very friendly looks, and Alethia thought she heard a furtive hiss; a moment later they came upon an errand-boy riding a bicycle. He had the frank open countenance, neatly brushed hair and tidy clothes that betoken a clear conscience and a good mother. He stared straight at the occupants of the car, and, after he had passed them, sang in his clear, boyish voice:

"We'll hang Bobby Bludward on the sour apple tree."

Robert merely laughed. That was how he took the scorn and condemnation of his fellow-men. He had goaded them to desperation with his shameless depravity till they spoke openly of putting him to a violent death, and he laughed.

Mrs. Bludward proved to be of the type that Alethia had suspected, thin-lipped, cold-eyed, and obviously devoted to her worthless son. From her no help was to be expected. Alethia locked her door that night, and placed such ramparts of furniture against it that the maid had great difficulty in breaking in with the early tea in the morning.

After breakfast Alethia, on the pretext of going to look at an outlying rose-garden, slipped away to the village through which they had passed on the previous evening. She remembered that Robert had pointed out to her a public reading-room, and here she considered it possible that she might meet Sir John Chobham, or some one who knew him well and would carry a message to him. The room was empty when she entered it; a *Graphic*, twelve days old, a yet older copy of *Punch*, and one or two local papers lay upon the central table; the other tables were stacked for the most part with chess and draughts-boards, and wooden boxes of chessmen and dominoes. Listlessly she picked up one of the papers, the *Sentinel*, and glanced at its contents. Suddenly she started, and began to read with breathless attention a prominently printed article, headed "A Little Limelight on Sir John Chobham". The colour ebbed away from her face, a look of frightened despair crept into her eyes. Never, in any novel that she had read, had a defenceless young woman been confronted with a situation like this. Sir John, the Hugo of her imagination, was, if anything, rather more depraved and despicable than Robert Bludward. He was mean, evasive, callously indifferent to his country's interests, a cheat, a man who habitually broke his word, and who was responsible, with his associates, for most of the poverty, misery, crime, and national degradation with which the country was afflicted. He was also a candidate for Parliament, it seemed, and as there was only one seat in this particular locality, it was obvious that the success of either Robert or Sir John would mean a check to the ambitions of the other, hence, no doubt, the rivalry and enmity between these otherwise kindred souls. One was seeking to have his enemy done to death, the other was apparently trying to stir up his supporters to an act of "Lynch law". All this in order that there might be an unopposed election, that one or other of the candidates might go into Parliament with honeyed eloquence on his lips and blood on his heart. Were men really so vile?

"I must go back to Webblehinton at once," Alethia informed her astonished hostess at lunch-time; "I have had a telegram. A friend is very seriously ill and I have been sent for."

It was dreadful to have to concoct lies, but it would be more dreadful to have to spend another night under that roof.

Alethia reads novels now with even greater appreciation than before. She has been herself in the world outside Webblehinton, the world where the great dramas of sin and villainy are played unceasingly. She had come unscathed through it, but what might have happened if she had gone unsuspectingly to visit Sir John Chobham and warn him of his danger? What indeed! She had been saved by the fearless outspokenness of the local Press.

Shock Tactics

On a late spring afternoon Ella McCarthy sat on a green-painted chair in Kensington Gardens, staring listlessly at an uninteresting stretch of park landscape, that blossomed suddenly into tropical radiance as an expected figure appeared in the middle distance.

"Hullo, Bertie!" she exclaimed sedately, when the figure arrived at the painted chair that was the nearest neighbour to her own, and dropped into it eagerly, yet with a certain due regard for the set of its trousers; "hasn't it been a perfect spring afternoon?"

The statement was a distinct untruth as far as Ella's own feelings were concerned; until the arrival of Bertie the afternoon had been anything but perfect.

Bertie made a suitable reply, in which a questioning note seemed to hover.

"Thank you ever so much for those lovely hand-kerchiefs," said Ella, answering the unspoken question; "they were just what I've been wanting. There's only one thing spoilt my pleasure in your gift," she added, with a pout.

"What was that?" asked Bertie anxiously, fearful that perhaps he had chosen a size of handkerchief that was not within the correct feminine limit.

"I should have liked to have written and thanked you

for them as soon as I got them," said Ella, and Bertie's sky clouded at once.

"You know what mother is," he protested; "she opens all my letters, and if she found I'd been giving presents to any one there'd have been something to talk about for the next fortnight."

"Surely, at the age of twenty—" began Ella.

"I'm not twenty till September," interrupted Bertie.

"At the age of nineteen years and eight months," persisted Ella, "you might be allowed to keep your correspondence private to yourself."

"I ought to be, but things aren't always what they ought to be. Mother opens every letter that comes into the house, whoever it's for. My sisters and I have made rows about it time and again, but she goes on doing it."

"I'd find some way to stop her if I were in your place," said Ella valiantly, and Bertie felt that the glamour of his anxiously deliberated present had faded away in the disagreeable restriction that hedged round its acknowledgment.

"Is anything the matter?" asked Bertie's friend Clovis when they met that evening at the swimming-bath.

"Why do you ask?" said Bertie.

"When you wear a look of tragic gloom in a swimming-bath," said Clovis, "it's especially noticeable from the fact that you're wearing very little else. Didn't she like the handkerchiefs?"

Bertie explained the situation.

"It is rather galling, you know," he added, "when a girl has a lot of things she wants to write to you and can't send a letter except by some roundabout, underhand way."

"One never realises one's blessings while one enjoys

them," said Clovis; "now I have to spend a considerable amount of ingenuity inventing excuses for not having written to people."

"It's not a joking matter," said Bertie resentfully: "you wouldn't find it funny if your mother opened all your letters."

"The funny thing to me is that you should let her do it."

"I can't stop it. I've argued about it—"

"You haven't used the right kind of argument, I expect. Now, if every time one of your letters was opened you lay on your back on the dining-table during dinner and had a fit, or roused the entire family in the middle of the night to hear you recite one of Blake's 'Poems of Innocence', you would get a far more respectful hearing for future protests. People yield more consideration to a mutilated mealtime or a broken night's rest, than ever they would to a broken heart."

"Oh, dry up," said Bertie crossly, inconsistently splashing Clovis from head to foot as he plunged into the water.

It was a day or two after the conversation in the swimming-bath that a letter addressed to Bertie Heasant slid into the letter-box at his home, and thence into the hands of his mother. Mrs. Heasant was one of those empty-minded individuals to whom other people's affairs are perpetually interesting. The more private they are intended to be the more acute is the interest they arouse. She would have opened this particular letter in any case; the fact that it was marked "private", and diffused a delicate but penetrating aroma merely caused her to open it with headlong haste rather than matter-of-course deliberation. The harvest of sensation that rewarded her was beyond all expectations.

"Bertie, carissimo," it began, "I wonder if you will have the nerve to do it: it will take some nerve, too. Don't forget the jewels. They are a detail, but details interest me.
                              "Yours as ever,
                                        "CLOTILDE.
"Your mother must not know of my existence. If questioned swear you never heard of me."

For years Mrs. Heasant had searched Bertie's correspondence diligently for traces of possible dissipation or youthful entanglements, and at last the suspicions that had stimulated her inquisitorial zeal were justified by this one splendid haul. That any one wearing the exotic name "Clotilde" should write to Bertie under the incriminating announcement "as ever" was sufficiently electrifying, without the astounding allusion to the jewels. Mrs. Heasant could recall novels and dramas wherein jewels played an exciting and commanding rôle, and here, under her own roof, before her very eyes as it were, her own son was carrying on an intrigue in which jewels were merely an interesting detail. Bertie was not due home for another hour, but his sisters were available for the immediate unburdening of a scandal-laden mind.

"Bertie is in the toils of an adventuress," she screamed; "her name is Clotilde," she added, as if she thought they had better know the worst at once. There are occasions when more harm than good is done by shielding young girls from a knowledge of the more deplorable realities of life.

By the time Bertie arrived his mother had discussed every possible and improbable conjecture as to his guilty secret; the girls limited themselves to the opinion that their brother had been weak rather than wicked.

"Who is Clotilde?" was the question that confronted Bertie almost before he had got into the hall. His denial of any knowledge of such a person was met with an outburst of bitter laughter.

"How well you have learned your lesson!" exclaimed Mrs. Heasant. But satire gave way to furious indignation when she realised that Bertie did not intend to throw any further light on her discovery.

"You shan't have any dinner till you've confessed everything," she stormed.

Bertie's reply took the form of hastily collecting material for an impromptu banquet from the larder and locking himself into his bedroom. His mother made frequent visits to the locked door and shouted a succession of interrogations with the persistence of one who thinks that if you ask a question often enough an answer will eventually result. Bertie did nothing to encourage the supposition. An hour had passed in fruitless one-sided palaver when another letter addressed to Bertie and marked "private" made its appearance in the letter-box. Mrs. Heasant pounced on it with the enthusiasm of a cat that has missed its mouse and to whom a second has been unexpectedly vouchsafed. If she hoped for further disclosures assuredly she was not disappointed.

"So you have really done it!" the letter abruptly commenced; "Poor Dagmar. Now she is done for I almost pity her. You did it very well, you wicked boy, the servants all think it was suicide, and there will be no fuss. Better not touch the jewels till after the inquest.

"CLOTILDE."

Anything that Mrs. Heasant had previously done in the way of outcry was easily surpassed as she raced upstairs and beat frantically at her son's door.

"Miserable boy, what have you done to Dagmar?"

"It's Dagmar now, is it?" he snapped; "it will be Geraldine next."

"That it should come to this, after all my efforts to keep you at home of an evening," sobbed Mrs. Heasant; "it's no use you trying to hide things from me; Clotilde's letter betrays everything."

"Does it betray who she is?" asked Bertie. "I've heard so much about her, I should like to know something about her home-life. Seriously, if you go on like this I shall fetch a doctor; I've often enough been preached at about nothing, but I've never had an imaginary harem dragged into the discussion."

"Are these letters imaginary?" screamed Mrs. Heasant. "What about the jewels, and Dagmar, and the theory of suicide?"

No solution of these problems was forthcoming through the bedroom door, but the last post of the evening produced another letter for Bertie, and its contents brought Mrs. Heasant that enlightenment which had already dawned on her son.

"DEAR BERTIE," it ran; "I hope I haven't distracted your brain with the spoof letters I've been sending in the name of a fictitious Clotilde. You told me the other day that the servants, or somebody at your home, tampered with your letters, so I thought I would give any one that opened them something exciting to read. The shock might do them good.

"Yours,

"CLOVIS SANGRAIL."

Mrs. Heasant knew Clovis slightly, and was rather afraid of him. It was not difficult to read between the lines of his successful hoax. In a chastened mood she rapped once more at Bertie's door.

"A letter from Mr. Sangrail. It's all been a stupid hoax. He wrote those other letters. Why, where are you going?"

Bertie had opened the door; he had on his hat and overcoat.

"I'm going for a doctor to come and see if anything's the matter with you. Of course it was all a hoax, but no person in his right mind could have believed all that rubbish about murder and suicide and jewels. You've been making enough noise to bring the house down for the last hour or two."

"But what was I to think of those letters?" whimpered Mrs. Heasant.

"I should have known what to think of them," said Bertie; "if you choose to excite yourself over other people's correspondence it's your own fault. Anyhow, I'm going for a doctor."

It was Bertie's great opportunity, and he knew it. His mother was conscious of the fact that she would look rather ridiculous if the story got about. She was willing to pay hush-money.

"I'll never open your letters again," she promised.

And Clovis has no more devoted slave than Bertie Heasant.

The Seven Cream Jugs

"I suppose we shall never see Wilfred Pigeoncote here now that he has become heir to the baronetcy and to a lot of money," observed Mrs. Peter Pigeoncote regretfully to her husband.

"Well, we can hardly expect to," he replied, "seeing that we always choked him off from coming to see us when he was a prospective nobody. I don't think I've set eyes on him since he was a boy of twelve."

"There was a reason for not wanting to encourage his acquaintanceship," said Mrs. Peter. "With that notorious failing of his he was not the sort of person one wanted in one's house."

"Well, the failing still exists, doesn't it?" said her husband; "or do you suppose a reform of character is entailed along with the estate?"

"Oh, of course, there is still that drawback," admitted the wife, "but one would like to make the acquaintance of the future head of the family, if only out of mere curiosity. Besides, cynicism apart, his being rich *will* make a difference in the way people will look at his failing. When a man is absolutely wealthy, not merely well-to-do, all suspicion of sordid motive naturally disappears; the thing becomes merely a tiresome malady."

Wilfrid Pigeoncote had suddenly become heir to his

uncle, Sir Wilfrid Pigeoncote, on the death of his cousin, Major Wilfrid Pigeoncote, who had succumbed to the after-effects of a polo accident. (A Wilfrid Pigeoncote had covered himself with honours in the course of Marlborough's campaigns, and the name Wilfrid had been a baptismal weakness in the family ever since.) The new heir to the family dignity and estates was a young man of about five-and-twenty, who was known more by reputation than by person to a wide circle of cousins and kinsfolk. And the reputation was an unpleasant one. The numerous other Wilfrids in the family were distinguished one from another chiefly by the names of their residences or professions, as Wilfrid of Hubble-down, and young Wilfrid the Gunner, but this particular scion was known by the ignominious and expressive label of Wilfrid the Snatcher. From his late schooldays onward he had been possessed by an acute and obstinate form of kleptomania; he had the acquisitive instinct of the collector without any of the collector's discrimination. Anything that was smaller and more portable than a sideboard, and above the value of ninepence, had an irresistible attraction for him, provided that it fulfilled the necessary condition of belonging to some one else. On the rare occasions when he was included in a country-house party, it was usual and almost necessary for his host, or some member of the family, to make a friendly inquisition through his baggage on the eve of his departure, to see if he had packed up "by mistake" any one else's property. The search usually produced a large and varied yield.

"This is funny," said Peter Pigeoncote to his wife, some half-hour after their conversation; "here's a telegram from Wilfrid, saying he's passing through here in his motor, and would like to stop and pay us his respects. Can stay for the night if it doesn't inconvenience us. Signed 'Wilfrid Pigeoncote.' Must be the Snatcher; none of the others have a motor. I suppose he's bringing us a present for the silver wedding."

"Good gracious!" said Mrs. Peter, as a thought struck her; "this is rather an awkward time to have a person with his failing in the house. All those silver presents set out in the drawing-room, and others coming by every post; I hardly know what we've got and what are still to come. We can't lock them all up; he's sure to want to see them."

"We must keep a sharp look-out, that's all," said Peter reassuringly.

"But these practised kleptomaniacs are so clever," said his wife, apprehensively, "and it will be so awkward if he suspects that we are watching him."

Awkwardness was indeed the prevailing note that evening when the passing traveller was being entertained. The talk flitted nervously and hurriedly from one impersonal topic to another. The guest had none of the furtive, half-apologetic air that his cousins had rather expected to find; he was polite, well-assured, and, perhaps, just a little inclined to "put on side". His hosts, on the other hand, wore an uneasy manner that might have been the hallmark of conscious depravity. In the drawing-room, after dinner, their nervousness and awkwardness increased.

"Oh, we haven't shown you the silver-wedding presents," said Mrs. Peter, suddenly, as though struck by a brilliant idea for entertaining the guest; "here they all are. Such nice, useful gifts. A few duplicates, of course."

"Seven cream jugs," put in Peter.

"Yes, isn't it annoying," went on Mrs. Peter; "seven of them. We feel that we must live on cream for the rest of our lives. Of course, some of them can be changed."

Wilfrid occupied himself chiefly with such of the gifts as were of antique interest, carrying one or two of them over to the lamp to examine their marks. The anxiety of his hosts at these moments resembled the solicitude of a cat whose newly born kittens are being handed round for inspection.

"Let me see; did you give me back the mustard-pot? This is its place here," piped Mrs. Peter.

"Sorry. I put it down by the claret-jug," said Wilfrid, busy with another object.

"Oh, just let me have the sugar-sifter again," asked Mrs. Peter, dogged determination showing through her nervousness. "I must label it who it comes from before I forget."

Vigilance was not completely crowned with a sense of victory. After they had said "Good-night" to their visitor, Mrs. Peter expressed her conviction that he had taken something.

"I fancy, by his manner, that there was something up," corroborated her husband. "Do you miss anything?"

Mrs. Peter hastily counted the array of gifts.

"I can only make it thirty-four, and I think it should be thirty-five," she announced. "I can't remember if thirty-five includes the Archdeacon's cruet-stand that hasn't arrived yet."

"How on earth are we to know?" said Peter. "The mean pig hasn't brought us a present, and I'm hanged if he shall carry one off."

"Tomorrow, when's he having his bath," said Mrs. Peter excitedly, "he's sure to leave his keys somewhere, and we can go through his portmanteau. It's the only thing to do."

On the morrow an alert watch was kept by the conspirators behind half-closed doors, and when Wilfrid, clad in a gorgeous bath-robe, had made his way to the bath-room, there was a swift and furtive rush by two excited individuals towards the principal guest-chamber. Mrs. Peter kept guard outside, while her husband first made a hurried and successful search for the keys, and then plunged at the portmanteau with the air of a disagreeably conscientious Customs official. The quest was a brief one; a silver cream jug lay embedded in the folds of some zephyr shirts.

"The cunning brute," said Mrs. Peter; "he took a cream jug because there were so many; he thought one wouldn't be missed. Quick, fly down with it and put it back among the others."

Wilfrid was late in coming down to breakfast, and his manner showed plainly that something was amiss.

"It's an unpleasant thing to have to say," he blurted out presently, "but I'm afraid you must have a thief among your servants. Something's been taken out of my portmanteau. It was a little present from my mother and myself for your silver wedding. I should have given it to you last night after dinner, only it happened to be a cream jug, and you seemed annoyed at having so many duplicates, so I felt rather awkward about giving you another. I thought I'd get it changed for something else, and now it's gone."

"Did you say it was from your *mother* and yourself?" asked Mr. and Mrs. Peter almost in unison. The Snatcher had been an orphan these many years.

"Yes, my mother's at Cairo just now, and she wrote to me at Dresden to try and get you something quaint and pretty in the old silver line, and I pitched on this cream jug."

Both the Pigeoncotes had turned deadly pale. The mention of Dresden had thrown a sudden light on the situation. It was Wilfrid the Attaché, a very superior young man, who rarely came within their social horizon, whom they had been entertaining unawares in the supposed character of Wilfrid the Snatcher. Lady Ernestine Pigeoncote, his mother, moved in circles which were entirely beyond their compass or ambitions, and the son would probably one day be an Ambassador. And they had rifled and despoiled his portmanteau! Husband and wife looked blankly and desperately at one another. It was Mrs. Peter who arrived first at an inspiration.

"How dreadful to think there are thieves in the house! We keep the drawing-room locked up at night, of course, but anything might be carried off while we are at breakfast."

She rose and went out hurriedly, as though to assure herself that the drawing-room was not being stripped of its silverware, and returned a moment later, bearing a cream jug in her hands.

"There are eight cream jugs now, instead of seven," she cried; "this one wasn't there before. What a curious trick of memory, Mr. Wilfrid! You must have slipped downstairs with it last night and put it there before we locked up, and forgotten all about having done it in the morning."

"One's mind often plays one little tricks like that," said Mr. Peter, with desperate heartiness. "Only the other day I went into the town to pay a bill, and went in again next day, having clean forgotten that I'd—"

"It is certainly the jug I brought for you," said Wilfrid, looking closely at it; "it was in my portmanteau when I got my bath-robe out this morning, before going to my bath, and it was not there when I unlocked the portmanteau on my return. Some one had taken it while I was away from the room."

The Pigeoncotes had turned paler than ever. Mrs. Peter had a final inspiration.

"Get me my smelling-salts, dear," she said to her husband; "I think they're in the dressing-room."

Peter dashed out of the room with glad relief; he had lived so long during the last few minutes that a golden wedding seemed within measurable distance.

Mrs. Peter turned to her guest with confidential coyness.

"A diplomat like you will know how to treat this as if it hadn't happened. Peter's little weakness; it runs in the family."

"Good Lord! Do you mean to say he's a kleptomaniac, like Cousin Snatcher?"

"Oh, not exactly," said Mrs. Peter, anxious to whitewash her husband a little greyer than she was painting him. "He would never touch anything he found lying about, but he can't resist making a raid on things that are locked up. The doctors have a special name for it. He must have pounced on your portmanteau the moment you went to your bath, and taken the first thing he came across. Of course, he had no motive for taking a cream jug; we've already got *seven*, as you know—not, of course, that we don't value the kind gift you and your mother—Hush, here's Peter coming."

Mrs. Peter broke off in some confusion, and tripped out to meet her husband in the hall.

"It's all right," she whispered to him; "I've explained everything. Don't say anything more about it."

"Brave little woman," said Peter, with a gasp of relief; "I could never have done it."

Diplomatic reticence does not necessarily extend to family affairs. Peter Pigeoncote was never able to understand why Mrs. Consuelo van Bullyon, who stayed with them in the spring, always carried two very obvious jewel-cases with her to the bath-room, explaining them to any one she chanced to meet in the corridor as her manicure and face-massage set.

The Occasional Garden

"Don't talk to me about town gardens," said Elinor
Rapsley; "which means, of course, that I want you to
listen to me for an hour or so while I talk about nothing
else. 'What a nice-sized garden you've got,' people said
to us when we first moved here. What I suppose they
meant to say was what a nice-sized site for a garden
we'd got. As a matter of fact, the size is all against it;
it's too large to be ignored altogether and treated as a
yard, and it's too small to keep giraffes in. You see, if we
could keep giraffes or reindeer or some other species of
browsing animal there we could explain the general
absence of vegetation by a reference to the fauna of the
garden: 'You can't have wapiti *and* Darwin tulips, you
know, so we didn't put down any bulbs last year.' As it is,
we haven't got the wapiti, and the Darwin tulips haven't
survived the fact that most of the cats of the
neighbourhood hold a parliament in the centre of
the tulip bed; that rather forlorn looking strip that we
intended to be a border of alternating geranium and
spiræa has been utilised by the cat-parliament as a
division lobby. Snap divisions seem to have been rather
frequent of late, far more frequent than the geranium
blooms are likely to be. I shouldn't object so much to
ordinary cats, but I do complain of having a congress of

Saki

vegetarian cats in my garden; they must be vegetarians, my dear, because, whatever ravages they may commit among the sweet-pea seedlings, they never seem to touch the sparrows; there are always just as many adult sparrows in the garden on Saturday as there were on Monday, not to mention newly fledged additions. There seems to have been an irreconcilable difference of opinion between sparrows and Providence since the beginning of time as to whether a crocus looks best standing upright with its roots in the earth or in a recumbent posture with its stem neatly severed; the sparrows always have the last word in the matter, at least in our garden they do. I fancy that Providence must have originally intended to bring in an amending Act, or whatever it's called, providing either for a less destructive sparrow or a more indestructible crocus. The one consoling point about our garden is that it's not visible from the drawing-room or the smoking-room, so unless people are dining or lunching with us they can't spy out the nakedness of the land. That is why I am so furious with Gwenda Pottingdon, who has practically forced herself on me for lunch on Wednesday next; she heard me offer the Paulcote girl lunch if she was up shopping on that day, and, of course, she asked if she might come too. She is only coming to gloat over my bedraggled and flowerless borders and to sing the praises of her own detestably over-cultivated garden. I'm sick of being told that it's the envy of the neighbourhood; it's like everything else that belongs to her—her car, her dinner-parties, even her headaches, they are all superlative; no one else ever had anything like them. When her eldest child was confirmed it was

276

such a sensational event, according to her account of it, that one almost expected questions to be asked about it in the House of Commons, and now she's coming on purpose to stare at my few miserable pansies and the gaps in my sweet-pea border, and to give me a glowing, full-length description of the rare and sumptuous blooms in her rose-garden."

"My dear Elinor," said the Baroness, "you would save yourself all this heart-burning and a lot of gardner's bills, not to mention sparrow anxieties, simply by paying an annual subscription to the O.O.S.A."

"Never heard of it," said Elinor; "what is it?"

"The Occasional-Oasis Supply Association," said the Baroness; "it exists to meet cases exactly like yours, cases of backyards that are of no practical use for gardening purposes, but are required to blossom into decorative scenic backgrounds at stated intervals, when a luncheon or dinner-party is contemplated. Supposing, for instance, you have people coming to lunch at one-thirty; you just ring up the Association at about ten o'clock the same morning, and say 'Lunch garden'. That is all the trouble you have to take. By twelve forty-five your yard is carpeted with a strip of velvety turf, with a hedge of lilac or red may, or whatever happens to be in season, as a background, one or two cherry trees in blossom, and clumps of heavily flowered rhododendrons filling in the odd corners; in the foreground you have a blaze of carnations or Shirley poppies, or tiger lilies in full bloom. As soon as the lunch is over and your guests have departed the garden departs also, and all the cats in Christendom can sit in council in your yard without causing you a moment's anxiety. If you have a bishop or an antiquary or something of that sort coming to lunch you just mention the fact when you are ordering the garden, and you get an old-world pleasaunce, with clipped yew hedges and a sun-dial and hollyhocks, and perhaps a mulberry tree, and borders of sweet-williams and Canterbury bells, and an old-fashioned beehive or two tucked away in a corner. Those are the ordinary lines of supply that the Oasis Association undertakes, but by paying a few guineas a year extra you are entitled to its emergency E.O.N. service."

"What on earth is an E.O.N. service?"

"It's just a conventional signal to indicate special cases like the incursion of Gwenda Pottingdon. It means you've got some one coming to lunch or dinner whose garden is alleged to be 'the envy of the neighbourhood'."

"Yes," exclaimed Elinor, with some excitement, "and what happens then?"

"Something that sounds like a miracle out of the Arabian Nights. Your backyard becomes voluptuous with pomegranate and almond trees, lemon groves, and hedges of flowering cactus, dazzling banks of azaleas, marble-basined fountains, in which chestnut-and-white pond-herons step daintly amid exotic water-lilies, while golden pheasants strut about on alabaster terraces. The whole effect rather suggests the idea that Providence and Norman Wilkinson have dropped mutual jealousies and collaborated to produce a background for an open-air Russian Ballet; in point of fact, it is merely the background to your luncheon party. If there is any kick left in Gwenda Pottingdon, or whoever your E.O.N. guest of the moment may be, just mention carelessly that your climbing putella is the only one in England, since the one at Chatsworth died last winter. There isn't such a thing as a climbing putella, but Gwenda Pottingdon and her kind don't usually know one flower from another without prompting."

"Quick," said Elinor, "the address of the Association."

Gwenda Pottingdon did not enjoy her lunch. It was a simple yet elegant meal, excellently cooked and daintily served, but the piquant sauce of her own conversation was notably lacking. She had prepared a long succession of eulogistic comments on the wonders of her town garden, with its unrivalled effects of horticultural magnificence, and, behold, her theme was shut in on every side by the luxuriant hedge of Siberian berberis that formed a glowing background to Elinor's bewildering fragment of fairyland. The pomegranate and lemon trees, the terraced fountain, where golden carp slithered and wriggled amid the roots of gorgeous-hued irises, the banked masses of exotic blooms, the pagoda-like enclosure, where Japanese sand-badgers disported themselves, all these contributed to take away Gwenda's appetite and moderate her desire to talk about gardening matters.

"I can't say I admire the climbing putella," she observed shortly, "and anyway it's not the only one of its kind in England; I happen to know of one in Hampshire. How gardening is going out of fashion. I suppose people haven't the time for it nowadays."

Altogether it was quite one of Elinor's most successful luncheon parties.

It was distinctly an unforeseen catastrophe that Gwenda should have burst in on the household four days later at lunch-time and made her way unbidden into the dining-room.

"I thought I must tell you that my Elaine has had a water-colour sketch accepted by the Latent Talent Art Guild; it's to be exhibited at their summer exhibition at the Hackney Gallery. It will be the sensation of the moment in the art world—Hullo, what on earth has happened to your garden? It's not there!"

"Suffragettes," said Elinor promptly; "didn't you hear about it? They broke in and made hay of the whole thing in about ten minutes. I was so heartbroken at the havoc that I had the whole place cleared out; I shall have it laid out again on rather more elaborate lines."

"That," she said to the Baroness afterwards, "is what I call having an emergency brain."

The Sheep

The enemy had declared "no trumps". Rupert played out his ace and king of clubs and cleared the adversary of that suit; then the Sheep, whom the Fates had inflicted on him for a partner, took the third round with the queen of clubs, and, having no other club to lead back, opened another suit. The enemy won the remainder of the tricks—and the rubber.

"I had four more clubs to play; we only wanted the odd trick to win the rubber," said Rupert.

"But I hadn't another club to lead you,"exclaimed the Sheep, with his ready, defensive smile.

"It didn't occur to you to throw your queen away on my king and leave me with the command of the suit," said Rupert, with polite bitterness.

"I suppose I ought to have—I wasn't certain what to do. I'm awfully sorry," said the Sheep.

Being awfully and uselessly sorry formed a large part of his occupation in life. If a similar situation had arisen in a subsequent hand he would have blundered just as certainly, and he would have been just as irritatingly apologetic.

Rupert stared gloomily across at him as he sat smiling and fumbling with his cards. Many men who have good brains for business do not possess the rudiments of a card-brain, and Rupert would not have judged and condemned his prospective brother-in-law on the evidence of his bridge play alone. The tragic part of it was that he smiled and fumbled through life just as fatuously and apologetically as he did at the card-table. And behind the defensive smile and the well-worn expressions of regret there shone a scarcely believable but quite obvious self-satisfaction. Every sheep of the pasture probably imagines that in an emergency it could become terrible as an army with banners—one has only to watch how they stamp their feet and stiffen their necks when a minor object of suspicion comes into view and behaves meekly. And probably the majority of human sheep see themselves in imagination taking great parts in the world's more impressive dramas, forming swift, unerring decisions in moments of crisis, cowing mutinies, allaying panics, brave, strong, simple, but, in spite of their natural modesty, always slightly spectacular.

"Why in the name of all that is unnecessary and perverse should Kathleen choose this man for her future husband?" was the question that Rupert asked himself ruefully. There was young Malcolm Athling, as nice-looking, decent, level-headed a fellow as any one could wish to meet, obviously her very devoted admirer, and yet she must throw herself away on this pale-eyed, weak-mouthed embodiment of self-approving ineptitude. If it had been merely Kathleen's own affair Rupert would have shrugged his shoulders and philosophically hoped that she might make the best of an undeniably bad bargain. But Rupert had no heir; his own boy lay underground somewhere on the Indian frontier, in goodly company. And the property would pass in due course to Kathleen and Kathleen's husband. The Sheep would live there in the beloved old home, rearing up other little Sheep, fatuous and rabbit-faced and self-satisfied like himself, to dwell in the land and possess it. It was not a soothing prospect.

Towards dusk on the afternoon following the bridge experience Rupert and the Sheep made their way homeward after a day's mixed shooting. The Sheep's cartridge bag was nearly empty, but his game bag showed no signs of overcrowding. The birds he had shot at had seemed for the most part as impervious to death or damage as the hero of a melodrama. And for each failure to drop his bird he had some explanation or apology ready on his lips. Now he was striding along in front of his host, chattering happily over his shoulder, but obviously on the look-out for some belated rabbit or wood-pigeon that might haply be secured as an eleventh-hour addition to his bag. As they passed the edge of a small copse a large bird rose from the ground and flew slowly towards the trees, offering an easy shot to the oncoming sportsmen. The Sheep banged forth with both barrels, and gave an exultant cry.

"Horray! I've shot a thundering big hawk!"

"To be exact, you've shot a honey-buzzard. That is the hen bird of one of the few pairs of honey-buzzards breeding in the United Kingdom. We've kept them under the strictest preservation for the last four years; every game-keeper and village gun loafer for twenty miles round has been warned and bribed and threatened to respect their sanctity, and egg-snatching agents have been carefully guarded against during the breeding season. Hundreds of lovers of rare birds have delighted in seeing their snap-shotted portraits in *Country Life*, and now you've reduced the hen bird to a lump of broken feathers."

Rupert spoke quietly and evenly, but for a moment or two a gleam of positive hatred shone in his eyes.

"I say, I'm so sorry," said the Sheep, with his apologetic smile. "Of course I remember hearing about the buzzards, but somehow I didn't connect this bird with them. And it was such an easy shot—"

"Yes," said Rupert; "that was the trouble."

Kathleen found him in the gun-room smoothing out the feathers of the dead bird. She had already been told of the catastrophe.

"What a horrid misfortune," she said sympathetically.

"It was my dear Robbie who first discovered them, the last time he was home on leave. Don't you remember how excited he was about them? Let's go and have some tea."

Both bridge and shooting were given a rest for the next two or three weeks. Death, who enters into no compacts with party whips, had forced a Parliamentary vacancy on the neighbourhood at the least convenient season, and the local partisans on either side found themselves immersed in the discomforts of a midwinter election. Rupert took his politics seriously and keenly. He belonged to that type of strangely but rather happily constituted individuals which these islands seem to produce in a fair plenty; men and women who for no personal profit or gain go forth from their comfortable firesides or club card-rooms to hunt to and fro in the mud and rain and wind for the capture or tracking of a stray vote here and there on their party's behalf—not because they think they ought to, but because they want to. And his energies were welcome enough on this occasion, for the seat was a closely disputed possession, and its loss or retention would count for much in the present position of the Parliamentary game. With Kathleen to help him, he had worked his corner of the constituency with tireless, well-directed zeal, taking his share of the dull routine work as well as of the livelier episodes. The talking part of the campaign wound up on the eve of the poll with a meeting in a centre where more undecided votes were supposed to be concentrated than anywhere else in the division. A good final meeting here would mean everything. And the speakers, local and imported, left nothing undone to improve the occasion. Rupert was down for the unimportant task of moving the complimentary vote to the chairman which should close the proceedings.

"I'm so hoarse," he protested, when the moment arrived; "I don't believe I can make my voice heard beyond the platform."

"Let me do it," said the Sheep; "I'm rather good at that sort of thing."

The chairman was popular with all parties, and the Sheep's opening words of complimentary recognition received a round of applause. The orator smiled expansively on his listeners and seized the opportunity to add a few words of political wisdom on his own account. People looked at the clock or began to grope for umbrellas and discarded neck-wraps. Then, in the midst of a string of meaningless platitudes, the Sheep delivered himself of one of those blundering remarks which travel from one end of a constituency to the other in half an hour, and are seized on by the other side as being more potent on their behalf than a ton of election literature. There was a general shuffling and muttering across the length and breadth of the hall, and a few hisses made themselves heard. The Sheep tried to whittle down his remark, and the chairman unhesitatingly threw him over in his speech of thanks, but the damage was done.

"I'm afraid I lost touch with the audience rather over that remark," said the Sheep afterwards, with his apologetic smile abnormally developed.

"You lost us the election," said the chairman, and he proved a true prophet.

A month or so of winter sport seemed a desirable pick-me-up after the strenuous work and crowning discomfiture of the election. Rupert and Kathleen hied them away to a small Alpine resort that was just coming into prominence, and thither the Sheep followed them in due course, in his rôle of husband-elect. The wedding had been fixed for the end of March.

It was a winter of early and unseasonable thaws, and the far end of the local lake, at a spot where swift currents flowed into it, was decorated with notices, written in three languages, warning skaters not to venture over certain unsafe patches. The folly of approaching too near these danger spots seemed to have a natural fascination for the Sheep.

"I don't see what possible danger there can be," he protested, with his inevitable smile, when Rupert beckoned him away from the proscribed area; "the milk that I put out on my window-sill last night was frozen an inch deep."

"It hadn't got a strong current flowing through it," said Rupert; "in any case, there is not much sense in hovering round a doubtful piece of ice when there are acres of good ice to skate over. The secretary of the ice-committee has warned you once already."

A few minutes later Rupert heard a loud squeal of fear, and saw a dark spot blotting the smoothness of the lake's frozen surface. The Sheep was struggling helplessly in an ice-hole of his own making. Rupert gave one loud curse, and then dashed full tilt for the shore; outside a low stable building on the lake's edge he remembered having seen a ladder. If he could slide it across the ice-hole before the Sheep went under the rescue would be comparatively simple work. Other skaters were dashing up from a distance, and, with the ladder's help, they could get him out of his death-trap without having to trust themselves on the margin of rotten ice. Rupert sprang on to the surface of lumpy, frozen snow, and staggered to where the ladder lay. He had already lifted it when the rattle of a chain and a furious outburst of growls burst on his hearing, and he was dashed to the ground by a mass of white and tawny fur. A sturdy young yard-dog, frantic with the pleasure of performing his first piece of actice guardian service, was ramping and snarling over him, rendering the task of regaining his feet or securing the ladder a matter of considerable difficulty. When he had at last succeeded in both efforts he was just by a hair's-breadth too late to be of any use. The Sheep had definitely disappeared under the ice-rift.

Kathleen Athling and her husband stay the greater

part of the year with Rupert, and a small Robbie stands in some danger of being idolised by a devoted uncle. But for twelve months of the year Rupert's most inseparable and valued companion is a sturdy tawny and white yard-dog.

Hyacinth

"The new fashion of introducing the candidate's children into an election contest is a pretty one," said Mrs. Panstreppon; "it takes away something from the acerbity of party warfare, and it makes an interesting experience for children to look back on in after years. Still, if you will listen to my advice, Matilda, you will not take Hyacinth with you down to Luffbridge on election day."

"Not take Hyacinth!" exclaimed his mother; "but why not? Jutterly is bringing his three children, and they are going to drive a pair of Nubian donkeys about the town, to emphasise the fact that their father has been appointed Colonial Secretary. We are making the demand for a strong Navy a special feature in *our* campaign, and it will be particularly appropriate to have Hyacinth dressed in his sailor suit. He'll look heavenly."

"The question is, not how he'll look, but how he'll behave. He's a delightful child, of course, but there is a strain of unbridled pugnacity in him that breaks out at times in a really alarming fashion. You may have forgotten the affair of the little Gaffin children; I haven't."

"I was in India at the time, and I've only a vague recollection of what happened; he was very naughty, I know."

"He was in his goat-carriage, and met the Gaffins in their perambulator, and he drove the goat full tilt at them and sent the perambulator spinning. Little Jacky Gaffin was pinned down under the wreckage, and while the nurse had her hands full with the goat Hyacinth was laying into Jacky's legs with his belt like a small fury".

"I'm not defending him," said Matilda, "but they must have done something to annoy him."

"Nothing intentionally, but some one had unfortunately told him that they were half French—their mother was a Duboc, you know—and he had been having a history lesson that morning, and had just heard of the final loss of Calais by the English, and was furious about it. He said he'd teach the little toads to go snatching towns from us, but we didn't know at the time that he was referring to the Gaffins. I told him afterwards that all bad feeling between the two nations had died out long ago, and that anyhow the Gaffins were only half French, and he said that it was only the French half of Jacky that he had been hitting; the rest had been buried under the perambulator. If the loss of Calais unloosed such fury in him, I tremble to think what the possible loss of the election might entail."

"All that happened when he was eight; he's older now and knows better."

"Children with Hyacinth's temperament don't know better as they grow older; they merely know more."

"Nonsense. He will enjoy the fun of the election, and in any case he'll be tired out by the time the poll is declared, and the new sailor-suit that I've had made for him is just in the right shade of blue for our election colours, and it will exactly match the blue of his eyes.

He will be a perfectly charming note of colour."

"There is such a thing as letting one's aesthetic sense override one's moral sense," said Mrs. Panstreppon. "I believe you would have condoned the South Sea Bubble and the persecution of the Albigenses if they had been carried out in effective colour schemes. However, if anything unfortunate should happen down at Luffbridge, don't say it wasn't foreseen by one member of the family."

The election was keenly but decorously contested. The newly appointed Colonial Secretary was personally popular, while the Government to which he adhered was distinctly unpopular, and there was some expectancy that the majority of four hundred, obtained at the last election, would be altogether wiped out. Both sides were hopeful, but neither could feel confident. The children were a great success; the little Jutterlys drove their chubby donkeys solemnly up and down the main streets, displaying posters which advocated the claims of their father on the broad general grounds that he was their father, while as for Hyacinth, his conduct might have served as a model for any seraph-child that had strayed unwittingly on to the scene of an electoral contest. Of his own accord, and under the delighted eyes of half a dozen camera operators, he had gone up to the Jutterly children and presented them with a packet of butterscotch; "we needn't be enemies because we're wearing the opposite colours," he said with engaging friendliness, and the occupants of the donkey-cart accepted his offering with polite solemnity. The grown-up members of both political camps were delighted at the incident—with the exception of Mrs.

Panstreppon, who shuddered.

"Never was Clytemnestra's kiss sweeter than on the night she slew me," she quoted, but made the quotation to herself.

The last hour of the poll was a period of unremitting labour for both parties; it was generally estimated that not more than a dozen votes separated the candidates, and every effort was made to bring up obstinately wavering electors. It was with a feeling of relaxation and relief that every one heard the clocks strike the hour for the close of the poll. Exclamations broke out from the tired workers, and corks flew out from bottles.

"Well, if we haven't won; we've done our level best."
"It has been a clean straight fight, with no rancour."
"The children were quite a charming feature, weren't they?"

The children? It suddenly occurred to everybody that they had seen nothing of the children for the last hour. What had become of the three little Jutterlys and their donkey-cart, and, for the matter of that, what had become of Hyacinth. Hurried, anxious embassies went backwards and forwards between the respective party headquarters and the various committee-rooms, but there was blank ignorance everywhere as to the where-abouts of the children. Every one had been too busy in the closing moments of the poll to bestow a thought on them. Then there came a telephone call at the Unionist Women's Committee-rooms, and the voice of Hyacinth was heard demanding when the poll would be declared.

"Where are you, and where are the Jutterly children?" asked his mother.

"I've just finished having high-tea at a pastry-

292

cook's," came the answer; "and they let me telephone. I've had a poached egg and a sausage roll and four meringues."

"You'll be ill. Are the little Jutterlys with you?"

"Rather not. They're in a pigsty."

"A pigsty? Why? What pigsty?"

"Near the Crawleigh Road. I met them driving about a back road, and told them they were to have tea with me, and put their donkeys in a yard that I knew of. Then I took them to see an old sow that had got ten little pigs. I got the sow into the outer sty by giving her bits of bread, while the Jutterlys went in to look at the litter, then I bolted the door and left them there."

"You wicked boy, do you mean to say you've left those poor children there alone in the pigsty?"

"They're not alone, they've got ten little pigs in with them; they're jolly well crowded. They were pretty mad at being shut in, but not half as mad as the old sow is at being shut out from her young ones. If she gets in while they're there she'll bite them into mincemeat. I can get them out by letting a short ladder down through the top window, and that's what I'm going to do *if we win*. If their blighted father gets in, I'm just going to open the door for the sow, and let her do what she dashed well likes to them. That's why I want to know when the poll will be declared."

Here the narrator rang off. A wild stampede and a frantic sending-off of messengers took place at the other end of the telephone. Nearly all the workers on either side had disappeared to their various club-rooms and public-house bars to await the declaration of the poll, but enough local information could be secured to

293

determine the scene of Hyacinth's exploit. Mr. John Ball had a stable yard down near the Crawleigh Road, up a short lane, and his sow was known to have a litter of ten young ones. Thither went in headlong haste both the candidates, Hyacinth's mother, his aunt (Mrs. Panstreppon), and two or three hurriedly summoned friends. The two Nubian donkeys, contentedly munching at bundles of hay, met their gaze as they entered the yard. The hoarse savage grunting of an enraged animal and the shriller note of thirteen young voices, three of them human, guided them to the sty, in the outer yard of which a huge Yorkshire sow kept up a ceaseless raging patrol before a closed door. Reclining on the broad ledge of an open window, from which point of vantage he could reach down and shoot the bolt of the door, was Hyacinth, his blue sailor-suit somewhat the worse of wear, and his angel smile exchanged for a look of demoniacal determination.

"If any of you come a step nearer," he shouted, "the sow will be inside in half a jiffy."

A storm of threatening, arguing, entreating expostulation broke from the baffled rescue party, but it made no more impression on Hyacinth than the squealing tempest that raged within the sty.

"If Jutterly heads the poll I'm going to let the sow in. I'll teach the blighters to win elections from us."

"He means it," said Mrs. Panstreppon; "I feared the worst when I saw that butterscotch incident."

"It's all right, my little man," said Jutterly, with the duplicity to which even a Colonial Secretary can sometimes stoop, "your father has been elected by a large majority."

"Liar!" retorted Hyacinth, with the directness of speech that is not merely excusable, but almost obligatory, in the political profession; "the votes aren't counted yet. You won't gammon me as to the result, either. A boy that I've palled with is going to fire a gun when the poll is declared; two shots if we've won, one shot if we haven't."

The situation began to look critical. "Drug the sow," whispered Hyacinth's father.

Some one went off in the motor to the nearest chemist's shop and returned presently with two large pieces of bread, liberally dosed with narcotic. The bread was thrown deftly and unostentatiously into the sty, but Hyacinth saw through the manœuvre. He set up a piercing imitation of a small pig in Purgatory, and the infuriated mother ramped round and round the sty; the pieces of bread were trampled into slush.

At any moment now the poll might be declared. Jutterly flew back to the Town Hall, where the votes were being counted. His agent met him with a smile of hope.

"You're eleven ahead at present, and only about eighty more to be counted; you're just going to squeak through."

"I mustn't squeak through," exclaimed Jutterly, hoarsely. "You must object to every doubtful vote on our side that can possibly be disallowed. I must *not* have the majority."

Then was seen the unprecedented sight of a party agent challenging the votes on his own side with a captiousness that his opponents would have hesitated to display. One or two votes that would have certainly passed muster under ordinary circumstances were disallowed, but even so Jutterly was six ahead with only thirty more to be counted.

To the watchers by the sty the moments seemed intolerable. As a last resort some one had been sent for a gun with which to shoot the sow, though Hyacinth would probably draw the bolt the moment such a weapon was brought into the yard. Nearly all the men were away from their homes, however, on election night, and the messenger had evidently gone far afield in his search. It must be a matter of minutes now to the declaration of the poll.

A sudden roar of shouting and cheering was heard from the direction of the Town Hall. Hyacinth's father clutched a pitchfork and prepared to dash into the sty in the forlorn hope of being in time.

A shot rang out in the evening air. Hyacinth stooped down from his perch and put his finger on the bolt. The sow pressed furiously against the door.

"Bang!" came another shot.

Hyacinth wriggled back, and sent a short ladder down through the window of the inner sty.

"Now you can come up, you unclean little blighters," he sang out; "my daddy's got in, not yours. Hurry up, I can't keep the sow waiting much longer. And don't you jolly well come butting into any election again where I'm on the job."

In the reaction that set in after the deliverance furious recriminations were indulged in by the lately opposed candidates, their women folk, agents, and party helpers. A recount was demanded, but failed to establish the fact that the Colonial Secretary had obtained a majority. Altogether the election left a legacy of soreness behind it, apart from any that was experienced by Hyacinth in person.

"It is the last time I shall let him go to an election," exclaimed his mother.

"There I think you are going to extremes," said Mrs. Panstreppon; "if there should be a general election in Mexico I think you might safely let him go there, but I doubt whether our English politics are suited to the rough and tumble of an angel-child."